IDEAL HIGH

IDEAL HIGH

VALERIE IPSON

RIVERSIDE PARK PRESS

Ideal High

Riverside Park Press
RiversideParkPress.com
Email: riversideparkpress@msn.com

Cover design by Niles Giberson 2015
www.nilesdesign.co

Library of Congress Control Number 2015900871

ISBN 978-0-9864246-1-8

1. High School—Fiction. 2. Bullying—Fiction. 3. Texas Panhandle—Fiction.

Printed in the United States of America
First Printing February 2015

for

(and because of)

Lance

1

Whose idea is it to broadcast the super-size faces of those who died to the far reaches of the school's auditorium? Everybody knows they're gone. Why emphasize the obvious even for the sake of a memorial? And why no rain on this joyless day? Never a good Texas thunderstorm when you need one.

I force a glance at the pull-down screen behind me, but immediately turn to focus on the line where the ceiling meets the wall at the back of the room. I can't bear to look into the crowd, but I can't look at the screen either. A giant reminder that I will never see those faces again. Weeks of grief have left me numb, but I should have worn my hair down to give me something to hide behind. Just in case.

Light pours in through the ribbon of windows high along the back wall. It crisscrosses the podium, making me squint at the sheet of paper in front of me.

It doesn't matter. I know the list by heart.

I blink through the glare and lean in to the microphone, not sure how loud I need to be. “Ashley Bannister.”

My voice echoes across the vast room. Plenty loud.

All eyes rivet on the screen and a kid from Drama Club tugs the rope of the school bell slowly and deliberately for maximum effect. It must have taken practice to get a perfect *mournful* clang.

The audience’s collective gaze swings to my right. To Chelsea standing at a matching podium, staring at her own list. She’s leaning heavy on her crutches, and on the podium, too. She needs both to keep her vertical, apparently. I’m just glad I don’t have to share the same half of the stage with her. As always, I need my distance. That hasn’t changed.

“Weston James Brown.” Chelsea’s lips tighten into a thin line. I’m amazed she gets the name out. The bell sounds again, even more slowly than the first time, and a chorus of sniffles and muffled sobs grows slightly louder.

I measure my breathing and tap my fingers along the edge of the sheet of paper in front of me. I have to keep my hands busy, distracted. Maybe if I keep moving I won’t think too hard about the next name.

I switch to rubbing my palms up and down the

sides of my pants. I just can't look at Kayla's parents who sit with my mom and dad in the front row. I pause too long and the principal clears his throat behind me. Very cliché, Mr. Myers. Doesn't he get that this is beyond difficult?

"Kayla … Marie … Carter." I speak her name to the back wall then take up tapping on the podium again. But not so loud anyone can hear. So much for avoiding the faces on the screen. All that loops through my brain is Kayla's wide smile.

Quit worrying, Taryn. Blake's not getting back with Chelsea, Kayla had said that night after the party. *I'll go find him for you and you'll see I'm right.* Then she walked right back into the old Gin Co. building.

Why was I forced to do this? I'm not the one who should be speaking the names of the dead in front of all these people. The list reads like the school's Who's Who, and I have no business pretending I'm one of them.

Except for him. How many more names until his? I'd scanned both versions as soon as they were held out to us, snatching the one with his name among those highlighted. Chelsea has no right to it, to him. Not like I do. At least that's what I tell myself.

The light flickers from behind me, so I know

they've moved on to the next abnormous face. A face that should be in the yearbook, not on a screen at a memorial.

A moan rises from the second row, competing with the plaintive tones of the bell. *Plaintive?* Where'd that come from? Now I'm conjuring up junior year Vocab?

One of Chelsea's crutches bangs against her podium. I can't help shooting her a sideways glance. She's still hunched forward. Definitely struggling and the service is just getting started.

Thankfully, I don't have to maneuver crutches and the names in front of me. Still, I will it to be over. My knotted stomach begs for it, and the fetal-position imprint on my bed is only growing colder. Who knows how long Principal Myers will feel obligated to address the assembled after our part is done?

Chelsea finally speaks, but the name comes out in a hiccupped sob. The noise of a bump, then a scrape carry through the sound system when she adjusts her crutches again.

"Keisha Lambert." I blurt it out when it's my turn, afraid to get stuck on a name again. I shut my eyes and try to erase the image that the crowd views behind me. Her exotic-for-small-town, multi-colored cornrows and pierced eyebrow, her excitement at being named cheerleader last May.

Chelsea reads the next name, verbally struggling yet again. It's understandable. She and Becca Martin were closer than sisters.

My throat tightens when I move in closer to the mic, but I'm determined not to lose it like Chelsea. Fixating on the list, I draw in a breath and the amplification of it hits the back wall. I cover my mouth, but it doesn't hide my embarrassment. The faces of the crowd blur, and all I can see is Blake's, creased with alarm as flames leap out of the building behind him.

Don't turn to look at the screen. Say his name, but don't look at his face. I hesitate, wanting — needing to. Wishing I could ask him the questions that plague me. They all start with "Why?"

Chelsea's crutches bump and scrape again, sending javelins of adrenaline into the pit of my stomach. I drop both hands onto the podium in front of me. I suddenly need something to hang onto.

Just say it. Say his name loud and strong. He deserves that. My lips brush the microphone and I taste metal.

"Blake Austin Montgomery."

His name erupts from my mouth and startles the crowd. The hushed crying and sniffling silences for a moment as if proper tribute to the late student body president mandates it.

Ignoring the looks from the audience, I clench the neatly-typed names on the paper into a fist. Relief surges through me now that my part of the program is over.

But it isn't over, not really. The memorial is only the beginning of what was supposed to be the perfect senior year.

Blake, the object of my years-long crush, and I were a couple. Sort of.

We'd been elected student body officers — president and vice-president. We spent the entire last month of school sitting in homeroom eating doughnuts on the sly, discussing senior year. True, Blake had done most of the talking and me a lot of nodding, but he intended for us to be a couple, right? I was his date to Junior Prom. That has to mean something.

I head to my seat on the stage, avoiding Chelsea's eyes as the too-tanned blonde hobbles over to drop into the chair next to me. The principal takes my place at the podium on the left.

"I want to thank these ladies for volunteering for this assignment." He nods in our general direction, before addressing the audience. "As you know, Taryn Young will step into the position of student body president and Chelsea Manor as head of the cheerleading squad."

Volunteered? Yeah, right. I stare at my shoes, afraid to look anyone in the eyes. I'm on stage by default. I'm the only one of the newly-elected class officers to survive the fire. But more than that I am a fraud. An abnormous fraud. An enormous abnormal fraud.

I would have never run for vice president if Blake hadn't talked me into it. The position full-out scared me, but how could I turn him down? Ever since that day in homeroom when he first noticed the doughnut glaze on my shirt sleeves, I couldn't tell the difference between dream and reality anymore. They were the same. Now I wish I could erase the nightmare, or better yet, rewind it all so the night of the Ideal Gin Co. fire never happened.

I squirm in my seat, trying to get comfortable as Mr. Myers' words buzz through the sound system. No rewinds. No do-overs. Now I sit with the only other survivor of the fire in front of an auditorium full of people with questions. Why Taryn Young, they must be thinking? Why not my son or daughter, my sister or brother? No, just Taryn and Chelsea. A cruel reminder of those who hadn't made it out alive.

Things like this don't happen at my school. Not in a town called Ideal, Texas.

I half-listen as the principal begins his concluding remarks. “The first day of class is one week from today and counselors will be available. Line up outside Ms. McKinney’s door, no appointments needed. Our goal is to get things back to normal as quickly as possible. Let’s not forget,” he stresses, “here at Ideal High School we have a long-standing tradition of unity, pride, and respect. This will carry us through.”

I just want to crawl back into bed where only my pillow hears me scream.

“What about my brother?” A masculine voice coming from the side of the stage jars me. From the shadowed steps, the voice addresses the principal again. “You didn’t call out his name. Isn’t he good enough for your program?”

A figure steps into the stage lights. He wears faded jeans and a gray plaid shirt with sleeves rolled up and shirt tails hanging. The thud of cowboy boots punctuates his step as he edges closer to the podium opposite the principal. He’s about my age, and I can’t help noticing the square confidence of his shoulders, despite the pain that ruts his brow.

“My brother died in the fire, too.”

“Who’s that?” hisses Chelsea. She doubles over like she’s in pain, but maybe she’s just trying to get a better look. The same question seems to vibrate across the auditorium.

I fix my eyes on the intruder. I can't wrap my brain around his claim. I know everyone who was at Ritter's Crossing that night where the crumbling old cotton gin had stood for a hundred years before the fire destroyed it.

Mr. Myers takes a step toward the young man. "May I help you after the service? We're almost finished here."

"You can help me. You can have one of these pretty girls with their expensive clothes and neon-white teeth stand at the microphone and shout out Tim's name." The stranger's voice breaks, but he continues, "He's important, too, even though no one knows his name."

"Son, please," Mr. Myers begins again. "Let's discuss this afterwards in my office. I'm sure we can clear up any misunderstanding."

I sense movement among the faculty members sitting on the stage around me, but I don't take my eyes off the stranger. Mr. Myers seems unruffled, but my mood moves quickly from confusion to irritation. Who is this guy? Who's his brother?

"Let me do it. Then I'll leave y'all alone." He reaches the podium where Chelsea stood moments before. The mic's movement grates through the sound system when he pulls it to him, and I slide to the edge of my seat. I have to admit, now he's really got my attention.

"He was my younger brother. My only brother." The guy turns away from the mic, momentarily pressing his left thumb and index finger to his eyes. Mr. Myers motions for the others to hold back as the young man continues. "Sure he was new, an easy target for bullies. But he was a student here."

His words are half-whispers now where before he had been practically shouting. "Can't you say his name? Can't you give him even that much?"

The guy takes a deep breath. His next words echo across the room, calm and clear. "Timothy Wade Jenks."

He turns, steps straight to the bell, and grabs the rope. Yanking it, he sends a single deafening bong reverberating across the room. He pauses, head bowed, then disappears down the same steps from which he came, leaving behind a brief, bewildered silence.

As the auditorium door closes behind him, the room erupts into chaos.

2

The principal reads my mind, I guess, because he ends the memorial service, his voice barely audible over the din. The crowd is past listening to him unless he somehow has an explanation for what happened on stage. I'm just relieved not to have to listen to any more of his nonsense about unity and respect. I know what matters at Ideal High and it isn't A-plus citizenship.

Chelsea's ashen face matches her posture as she droops into the molded plastic chair, but I barely give her a passing glance. One more funeral to attend, then avoiding Chelsea will be pain-free again. I drop the list on a chair and bolt to the stairs. As much as that is possible in heels anyway. Thankfully, the buzz of the crowd will allow me to leave unnoticed.

Except for my parents. They wait at the bottom of the stairs with Kayla's mom and dad. Mom plucks me off the last step.

"You okay, honey?" She hugs me a little too tight. She's been doing that a lot lately.

Dad takes his turn. "See, you survived after all."

I grimace into his shoulder. How can he use the word "survived" around the Carters? I have no choice but to hug Kayla's parents, and hope no one else is joining the assembly line. I wish for the thousandth time things were different. Why Kayla and not me?

The hugs end, but not the awkwardness. No one seems to know what to say. I certainly don't.

Finally, Mrs. Carter makes an attempt by taking my hands in hers. "Thank you, Taryn. I know that was not an easy thing to do."

Please, stop. I feel guilty enough.

Fortunately, Dad quietly takes control of the conversation and I get away with just a nod to Kayla's mom. "So what about that boy coming on stage like that?"

"Who interrupts a memorial?" Mr. Carter responds to my dad's question. "If something happened to his brother there are better ways to handle it."

Mom puts an arm back around my shoulder. "Do you know him or his brother, Taryn?"

I grip my purse and try to swallow past what

feels like sandpaper lining my throat. I don't have the energy for this or any conversation. "I don't know, Mom, but I have to go. I'll be home soon, though." I make a beeline to the exit, the noises of the crowd only adding to the ache that pulses in my head.

I push through the back entrance into the main offices, stopping short when memories assault me. The last time I stood here was May. The last day of school. The last time things felt right in my life.

The hallway smells of fresh paint, so no surprise there's a new patch in the wall opposite the principal's office. Zeke Miller, a senior last year, put his fist through it, unhappy about his suspension for fighting. It had been the talk of the school till prom theme was announced and tickets went on sale. Priorities. Normally I'd say that with major eye rolling, but once Blake asked me to go with him that's pretty much all I thought about, too.

Zeke would have tackled that guy for interrupting the memorial if he'd been there. Thinking of the incident and the intruder's accusation forces a shudder across my shoulders. Someone named Tim is dead. But he was not in the fire. The guy doesn't know what he's talking about. The sound of footsteps coming from the school's main foyer reminds me of the echo of the stranger's boots hitting the stage and I shudder again. The guy's feelings seemed real, right at the surface. Like a brother's would be.

I really can't think about it. I have to find the student council advisor, Mrs. Ames, and tell her I won't be student body president. Even if the bylaws require it, there's no way I'm taking Blake's position. And I won't stay on as vice president, either. He'd been the one with all the ideas. I didn't think things at school could change for the better. That was all Blake.

"Hey, sweetie! How are you doing?" Phyllis is already at her desk in the attendance office. "Let me give you some Miss Phyllis-lovin'."

Phyllis mothers all the students, but she's always been extra-nice to me because of what happened on my first day as a sophomore at Ideal High. It was no big deal, but I came into the office to turn in a lost cell phone and found her in tears. I sat for nearly fifteen minutes listening to her lament the fact that her son was growing up too fast because he had started the fourth grade. She had to write me a pass to second hour.

When I reach the secretary's desk, her big arms wrap around me, folding me in a Texas-size squeeze. "You lost weight. Now stop that." Her hug makes it impossible to breathe, much less comment.

"I need to find Mrs. Ames," I manage to say when she lets me go.

"Don't know if teachers are staying 'round today. Did you check her room?"

"Uh —" I freeze. An old copy of the *Lubbock Avalanche-Journal* sits on the counter. The extra-bold headline leaps from the page: 7 STUDENTS DECLARED DEAD IN IDEAL FIRE. I cringe at the ill-placed town name, but there is another reason I find the headline jarring. I have vigilantly avoided all news of the fire. I don't need anyone reminding me what happened that night.

"Oh, baby, I'm so sorry." Phyllis swoops over to slide the paper into the trash can. "Don't know why that's still sittin' here. I guess no one dared touch it when it came the beginning of June." She sinks back in her seat and dabs at her eyes with a limp tissue. She pulls a fresh one from a box perched on her desk and waves it at me. "Now sit right down, tell me how you're doin'."

I drop into an empty chair. "I'm okay."

"No, you're not okay, sweetie, you're not." She sniffles into her tissue before grabbing another one. "It's horrible, just horrible."

I brace myself. Even after weeks of hiding in my room alone with my thoughts, I'm not prepared to discuss the tragedy with anyone besides the police. Of course, I had no choice about that.

"It's your senior year. Don't know how you're going to get through it." Phyllis closes her eyes and rocks back and forth slowly. Then the moaning starts. Any moment I think she's either going to break into gospel song or fall to her knees to pray. Then she takes up talking again about dreadful senior years.

I nod whenever she pauses to take a breath, but a tightening across my chest eventually forces me out of the seat. "I should go find Mrs. Ames. Are you going to be okay, Phyllis?"

That makes her moan again, only louder.

I slip back the way I came. As I pass the principal's office again, the door swings open to reveal a guy wearing faded jeans, gray plaid shirt, and scuffed cowboy boots. The one from the memorial. He brushes past, his steely eyes drilling through me as he makes a hurried exit.

Mr. Myers appears at my side. "Excuse me, Miss Young. Sorry you had to witness such a rude display." Is he talking about just now, the memorial, or both?

"He's got problems," I can't help muttering.

"He'll be fine." Mr. Myers shakes his head implying the opposite is true.

"So, what he said . . . another student died in

the fire?" But I know it isn't possible.

"It's not your concern, Miss Young. You've got more important tasks ahead of you as student body president." He clears his throat. "Moving forward we'll definitely want your input on the design for a permanent memorial marker." Before I can reply he returns to his office and shuts the door.

Input for a memorial marker? That's how he views the student body president's role? What about a bullied kid that no one cared about? Any half-decent student council member could help fix that. I look down the hall in the direction the guy took and then I'm just upset again.

How dare he march on stage and stir things up. I'd say a few choice things to him if given a real chance. Gritting my teeth I search for the words: *Sorry something happened to your brother, but what gives you the right to intrude on our tragedy? I know who was there. Ashley, Weston, Kayla, Vaughn, Keisha, Becca, Blake.*

It's sickening — they've been reduced to alphabetical-order-by-last-name because of that stupid list I had to read at the memorial.

I don't know what happened to his brother, but I don't need another reason to revisit the night of the fire, the after-party gone wrong. I don't need the drama. Especially from the rage that simmers behind those blue eyes. Were they blue?

I run my palm along the poor patch job done on Zeke's hole-in-the-wall. Strange Mr. Myers didn't insist it be perfectly glossed over, as if it had never happened. At the time it probably pained him to have to suspend the popular athlete, but at least it had been way past football season. Zeke didn't have to sit out any games.

I pick at an off-white glob of paint sticking out around the edge of the hole-repair. I didn't see Zeke at the memorial. He hadn't come to any of the funerals, either, though he was pretty tight with those who died.

The fresh paint fumes smother me, forcing me toward the exit. They remind me not of the newness of being back to school, but of the past the paint tries to cover. Ideal High isn't a perfect school — a target for bullies the guy said about his brother's experience. But because of Blake I had hope. At least a sliver.

Taryn and Blake. Blake and Taryn. Do our names even belong in the same breath? I push the door open and mentally push thoughts of Blake away. I want to find Mrs. Ames, tell her my decision, and then put some distance between me and the school. At least until I'm required to start class next week. After that it's the bare minimum —

get by and get my senior year over with.

Wind gusts accompany my entry into the 200 Building, which houses all the language and history classes. I duck into the nearest bathroom. I only want to throw some water on my face, but the sink area is clogged with girls.

Go home, people. I need an empty bathroom.

"I cried my eyes out," a redhead murmurs to her closest mirror-mate. I know them, but only in the way I know everyone at Ideal High, just kind of.

"My mascara's history. Can I borrow some?" The redhead pushes a makeup bag toward her friend.

I inch my way forward to grab a paper towel, then hold it out toward the closest faucet. "Excuse me, can I get this wet?"

After noticing my reflection in the mirror one of them flips the water on and they both offer matching sympathetic smiles.

"Thanks." I wring the dripping paper towel and press it to my face, its cool wetness spreading across my forehead and cheeks. I step back to allow a few girls to glide around me. More sympathetic looks.

A chunky girl that lives in my neighborhood emerges from a bathroom stall at the end of the row. "Can you believe that guy that came on stage?" She speaks to her friend at the sink, but her voice carries. “I was freaking out thinking he was going to pull out a gun.”

Adrenaline shoots up my spine. I’d been so shaken by the intruder’s question I hadn’t considered the possibility.

The girl worms her way in close to the mirror to apply multiple layers of lip gloss, then passes the glittery tube to the girl behind her.

“I know. And who was he talking about?” Her friend drops the lip gloss into her cavernous bag. “Not that I was best friends with anybody who died. I mean some of them were in my classes last year, but, you know, ‘ideal to your face, but watch your back.’” She adjusts her rhinestone-studded hair clip, then her jean skirt, turning to view it from the backside.

I flinch at the way she mentions those who died. A vocabulary word comes to mind. *Flippant*. I never was a fan of the “ideal to your face” phrase anyway. Pathetic way to describe a high school.

“It was that sophomore, the skinny one that was, you know, slow. He was in some of my sister’s classes. He transferred here from Lubbock, like, in March.” The chunky girl purses her lips, checking her lip gloss again before she’s back on the other topic. “Remember the week of cheer tryouts when

Ashley Bannister and Keisha Lambert actually talked to us in Geometry?" She fiddles with an earring. "Where'd you get that skirt, Coleman's?"

"Duh, you were with me," the girl with the hair clip replies. "Do you remember when Becca Martin loaned me a pen in homeroom right before time to vote for student body officers? I borrowed her pen, then didn't even vote for her." The pair laughs as they head to the door. "So he died? Double weird."

I turn away, pretending the paper towel and my dark bangs are enough to shield my face. I don't want to be noticed.

They continue their conversation, oblivious to everyone around them. "He was the one Zeke Miller pushed around."

"That guy? There's no way a doof like that would be hanging out with the cheerleaders at the Gin Co. building. Hey, have you ever seen Chelsea Manor looking so hideous?" The door swings shut behind them.

Of course, Zeke's suspension. I remember the boy that was involved. Once in the cafeteria, actually more than once, J.T., Paco, and a few other jocks dumped their lunch trays in front of him when he was eating. They'd leave him to clean it up by himself. It turned into a defining moment for me, because about the third time they did it, Blake stepped in and started gathering up the trays. It was then I knew I wanted to be on Blake's side of whatever he planned for Ideal High.

So that's the brother the guy was talking about? I shake the thought from my brain, wondering instead at the off-handed mention of those who died. Why are they mocking the cheerleaders like that? I look up to several pairs of wide eyes staring at me. The bathroom is still full, all honed in to the two girls' conversation.

The redhead catches my eye in the mirror. "Don't listen to them, they're lame. It's awful what happened to Blake Montgomery and the cheerleaders." I drop eye contact, but she's not done. "And you and Chelsea looked great up there. I mean, who would look their best when they had to, you know, do that."

I toss the paper towel in the trashcan and duck out the door. Being around people. That's my first mistake.

Mere steps beyond the bathroom, memories of homeroom assault me. Where I worshipped Blake from afar since day one at Ideal as a sophomore. That was back when I referred to him by his full name, like the redhead in the bathroom. Like he was some kind of celebrity. That lasted till halfway through junior year, when either our teacher had a bad day or the stars aligned, because we were forced to sit alphabetically. Blake moved to the row right next to mine. Soon he was breaking up with Chelsea and noticing the doughnut glaze sweetly-stuck to the ends of my jacket sleeves from my morning shifts at Donut King. I helped my older sister out during the coffee rush every morning and hated it, but I quit complaining the day Blake talked to me.

I force myself to keep walking past homeroom and try to focus on happy memories of Blake. His surprised smile when I pulled out his favorite cinnamon-sugar doughnut twist from my backpack. His light brown hair curled up at the ends because it was still wet from his morning shower. The way he talked about making Ideal High better. Unfortunately, the pictures in my head never last. They always end with the fire.

I peek into Room 212, but it's empty. Two desks are pulled close together, just like me and Blake used to do when we'd meet in Mrs. Ames' room after we'd been elected to student council.

"Tare!" J.T. Webb pulls me into a suffocating hug. There's a reason he plays lineman for the Bulldog football team. "I haven't seen you since the last funeral." He paws my back. "Hey, you looked nice up there today."

“Thanks,” I mumble into his broad chest. I always felt a little on the fringe of the popular crowd, dragged to parties and dances because Kayla was so nice and our parents best friends — until Blake and student elections rocketed me to the head of the class. Now I’m unsure of my status.

J.T. lets me go. “I’m thinking of running for class officer. What do you say to that, Prez?”

“I haven’t heard anything about new elections.” I really need to talk to Mrs. Ames.

“Maybe I’ll be secretary/treasurer, like Kayla.” He pounds a fist on the left side of his chest. A few of his football buddies yell from the end of the hall.

“There’s my ride. See ya’.” He jogs toward the exit. “Hey, you’ll vote for me, right, Taryn?” he calls back.

“Sure, J.T.” But the door has already slammed behind him.

I’ve been here way too long. Talking to Mrs. Ames will have to wait.

I’m almost to the door when she appears from around a corner. “Taryn, I’ve been looking for you. Do you have a minute to talk about student council?”

Sandpaper lines my throat again. I don’t know if I can get the words out, so I stall. “It feels so strange being at school. Everything’s different and everything's the same. It's messed up."

"I know. I'm so sorry for what you've been through." She pats my arm. The patting, the hugging, it has to stop. "Have you talked to one of the grief counselors?"

I shake my head. The sandpaper morphs into gravel and then just one big lump. I swallow it and look her straight in the eye. "Mrs. Ames, I'm sorry. I can't be president."

She leads me to her classroom door. "Can we talk about this? I know how you looked forward to it, Taryn." She folds her arms across her ample figure and places a hand at her throat.

"Looked forward to vice president," I correct her. "But not —" I look at the floor. "Not like this." Not without Blake to stand behind. Let someone else figure out how to make something of this year.

Mrs. Ames doesn't say anything until I look at her again. "So is this your official resignation?"

"Nina, do you have a minute?" Ms. Hightower, an American History teacher from two rooms down approaches us. Besides teaching American History, she is also the advisor to the cheer squad, and despite the fact that she was a cheerleader at Ideal High about a hundred years ago, she tries to keep up the image. She's not fooling anyone.

She gives me a nod of her bleached-blonde

head. "Good to see you, Taryn. Actually, this might interest you." She pats my arm, but the intention seems different than when Mrs. Ames did it. "I want to talk about coordinating cheerleading tryouts and new student council elections."

Mrs. Ames narrows her eyes. She's clearly not happy Ms. Hightower is bringing it up in front of me. "Julia, can you give us a minute?"

Ms. Hightower takes a step back, her fingers playing casually with the chains dangling down the front of her snug silk blouse. "Oh, I didn't mean to interrupt."

Mrs. Ames pulls me aside. "Our highest priority is to get everything back to normal as quickly as possible. The principal and the entire faculty agree completely on this, but please, take some time to think about your decision." She is back to her usual stance, arms crossed, hand at her throat. "It may not feel like it right now, but you can rise above this. Let's talk again, okay?"

I manage a weak smile and nod before turning toward the exit, leaving the teachers to their discussion. I reach the end of the hall and with all of my might shove the heavy door against the West Texas wind.

A gang of skaters, dressed in skinny jeans and graffiti-printed T-shirts, hover on the sidewalk with their long boards, near my parked car. I skirt around them and unlock my door, but I can't ignore the concrete bench with its base in the shape of fat stone letters, I-H-S, the school's initials. Blake gave me a last-minute pep talk there the morning of election-day speeches. I press my lips together and squeeze my eyes shut.

Immediately, a bitter scene replaces the sweet one — images of a makeshift memorial that started at the bench once news of the fire spread. Flowers, posters, balloons, and candles flicker in my mind's eye, reminding me of a tragedy I will never be free from. I get into my car and pull the door shut.

Normal. Is that even possible?

3

It's the smoke, always the smoke. It's paralyzing. No, it's the bodies. I can't move because with every step there's a thick mound underfoot. The mounds turn into bodies. Every time.

And every time, I am stuck in this field with no way out.

I fight to blink away the nightmare, wondering the same thing as always. If I can't wake up from a dream is it considered reality?

The smoke that billows around me in unearthly shapes gives way to the safety of my room with its raspberry-pink walls, white wicker furniture, and zebra-striped bean bag chair. My magnet board still overflows with pics of Blake and junior year carefree-ness.

Life before.

Before the party.

Before night games at the Ideal Gin Co. building.

Before the fire.

Before the death of everything.

I focus on the stuffed toy bulldog, sporting Ideal High School royal blue and red, that presides from the top of my bookshelf, and then Mom's face.

No more field. Thank goodness.

"We leave for Kayla's funeral in a half hour." Mom strokes my hair like I'm a four-year-old with a fever.

"I can't do another one, Mom." I pull my black and white paisley comforter over my head.

Mom pulls it back down. "It's Kayla's. Of course you can do it."

Kayla's remains were among the last to be released after the investigation and today she will be laid to rest at Ideal City Cemetery where all the other victims are buried. Six funerals consumed the last half of the summer and I don't think I can choke down one more, especially because it is Kayla's.

"I can't take her mom looking at me. When I see her, she just stares at me with this awful look on her face like it's my fault."

"That is not true and you know it. Besides it's no one's fault. It was an accident, Taryn." Mom sighs. Her excessive sighing ranks right up there with the hugging too much. "You're going to the funeral. You'll be supportive, then it'll be over."

"It will never be over, Mom. You're still going

to be friends with the Carters. They're still going to live two doors down. She's always going to look at me that way."

"We'll discuss this later. Please, just get ready. I want to be early."

I roll onto my side to face her. "Mom, I can't. Not Kayla's."

Her face goes soft and she strokes my hair again. "I know how hard this is, but we have to for Carters."

Just one more.

I sit up and swing my feet to the floor, then snatch up my fuzzy pink robe from the end of the bed. I hug it close all the way to the bathroom.

For Kayla.

Once in the shower, the water massages my shoulders, its pulse forcing the release of too-near-the-surface emotion. I turn toward the spray and let it drown my tears. My body numbs to the heat, but thoughts of Kayla sting. And Blake. Always doing the good-guy thing. He had to help the rest instead of saving himself.

I lean against the wall, as the water beats on me. I am sick to death of death. So tired of being the one who lived.

I stare out the window as we reach Lubbock

city limits. In the thirty-minute drive from Ideal, we pass nothing but cotton fields it seems, prompting Dad's annoyingly-familiar observations about each cotton producer. Maybe he thinks he can make us forget the reason for the trip.

Mom studies her phone. "Turn right at the light, Jim."

"How long's this going to last, Mom?" My brother, Caleb, pulls at his navy blue-striped tie. "I don't know how long I can stand this thing." Thirteen years old and probably his first time wearing a tie. Kayla's is the only one Mom insisted he attend, but we don't go to funerals much. Until now.

"Me, neither." Dad adjusts his own tie.

The parking lot is filling fast as we pull into a spot on the north side of the church. I check my pocket mirror like for the tenth time since leaving home. Unfortunately, even the best cover up can't disguise grief.

My family waits while I drop the mirror into my purse and step out of the car. Straightening my skirt, I scour the lot for familiar faces I'll want to avoid. Somehow last May I thought I was ready to take on the school as student body vice-president and now there's not a pile of comforters high enough for me to cower under.

"Those guys aren't wearing ties," Caleb whines. He points to the sidewalk where I recognize several boys from school. "Some are even wearing jeans." He frowns at his dark blue slacks and shiny new dress shoes bought for the occasion.

"You'll be fine," Mom says. She steers him in the direction of the front doors. I look up at the stark white steeple adorning the roof, wondering if I will.

"You okay, honey?" Mom puts an arm around my shoulder.

She doesn't expect an answer, but I nod anyway, bracing myself for the emotional onslaught that will begin once we enter the church. Turns out I'm wrong. We're met only by quiet organ music and hushed voices. Maybe I can get through this.

"Carters invited us to the Family Prayer. Would you like to come?" Mom raises her eyebrows at me like she's hoping I'll say yes, but I'm grateful she gives me a choice.

"No. We'll just find some seats and wait for Tracy." My older sister is meeting us.

"Okay, we'll be right back. Caleb, stay with Taryn."

The chapel is nearly full except for reserved seating near the front. An elderly man wearing a white usher badge directs us to seats halfway back on the right. Behind us another opens up an accordion-style wall to reveal rows of chairs extending out onto what appears to be a basketball court. Half the Ideal High football team already fills the first few rows.

"Taryn!" J.T. calls in a loud whisper. He stands up and waves his arms.

Travis Patterson, Ideal's quarterback, joins J.T.'s plea, "Taryn, c'mon!"

People glance my direction. Great.

"Save our seats, Caleb." I move to the back just as a group of girls from school enters the side door. The only time I've seen any of them this summer is at the funerals. Even then I'd kept to myself. Jen Foster waves, forcing me to wave back. I wish I'd stayed in my seat.

"Y'all sit with us. We'll make room," says a football player at the end. A couple of girls squeeze in next to him. Jen makes a show of stepping across several guys on the next row till she gets to J.T., then slides in next to him.

Behind them Travis moves over and motions to me. "Right here."

"I can't. I'm sitting with my parents."

"They won't care, c'mon." He points at the empty folding chair beside him.

I shake my head. "They're saving my spot."

All eyes are drawn to the door when the five

impeccably-dressed, blonde-headed members of the Manor family enter the chapel like royalty. Chelsea, now without crutches, is supported on both sides by her parents, while her two younger sisters follow behind like shadows.

Who even cares? It's a Mormon church in the middle of Lubbock. I turn back to my classmates, hoping Chelsea won't notice us. Unfortunately, the instantaneous half-whispered chorus of "Chel-SEA" from the three rows of jocks makes that an immediate impossibility.

Mr. and Mrs. Manor and their younger daughters take their seats while Chelsea, looking model-like even while hobbling on a walking cast, heads toward us. Wearing a deep purple blouse and dark slacks, she looks more her self-possessed self than she did on Monday.

"Hi, Taryn."

"Chelsea." It's a funeral. I guess I have to be polite.

She moves in close and keeps her voice low. "So you don't want to be president? You're just going to bail on the school?" Her perfectly-plucked eyebrows raise an inch.

So much for being nice.

I don't want to talk about this here. And I definitely don't want to talk about it with her.

"I guess the president should be someone who cares about Ideal High." She's not going to drop it.

I whisper back. "Why do you think I ran for vice president in the first place?"

"We know the answer to that. And it's also the only reason you won."

My mind reels. Is Chelsea really bringing up Blake right now?

"Maybe I should run. That was the original plan all along."

Thankfully, Chelsea doesn't expect a response. Because I'm speechless.

She turns away from me and brings up a new topic. "I hope y'all are trying out for cheerleader."

I steal a glance at my brother, longing to be back in that pew.

J.T. glares at Chelsea. "Cool it! It's Kayla's funeral. Talk about this stuff later." All these funerals have put everyone on edge.

I look across the wood floor, not surprised at the number of people filling the seats. I spot the principal huddling with the head football coach while their wives chat with Ms. Hightower. Mrs. Ames waves from a few rows behind them. She called the day before, but it was late when I crawled out of bed to warm up the dinner I missed. Too late to call back and hear another plea not to resign from student council. To think about it some more. As if I even let my mind go there.

The talk of new elections and cheerleader tryouts is overwhelming. Senior year is going to happen whether I'm involved or not. But please not Chelsea as student body president.

"I've got a spot for you right here, Chelsea." J.T. knocks his sidekick, Paco, in the shoulder, forcing a chain reaction till the person at the end of the row moves over a seat.

"I'm sitting with my family." But Chelsea doesn't move. Instead she fixates on what is taking place in the foyer. I follow her gaze to glimpse Kayla's casket positioned at the door of the chapel.

Turning slightly, we lock eyes for a split second, then head to our pews. I slide in next to Tracy and the rest of my family, in time to stand as the casket, adorned with white roses tied with Ideal High blue and red ribbons, is wheeled into the room and down the aisle.

4

After the service I join my friends on the lawn out front. We're quiet as we hold onto each other and exchange glances. Even the oppressive heat isn't enough to hurry us to air-conditioned cars.

I'm a part of the informal group hug, but feel miles away, detached from everything familiar. I try to imagine a senior year without Blake sitting in the seat next to me in homeroom. A year without Kayla to tag along with.

It will never be okay.

I search the faces of Jen, Travis, and J.T. Will things be different because of what happened? Will everyone be nicer to each other because we don't know if tomorrow will be our last?

J.T. squeezes my shoulder a little too hard, and I'm glad to pull away from him as the group disassembles. As if on cue, Chelsea emerges from the parking lot with a bouquet of blue and red balloons bobbing above her. Kayla's family, and nearly everyone else pouring out of the church, congregates on the lawn to witness the display.

"B'loon." Kayla's little sister's cry pierces me.

Ignoring the somber gaze of the entire Carter family, I reach for a blue one. Jen grabs the string alongside me. We have to pair up because there's only seven balloons.

Only seven. What a messed up thought. Seven is seven too many.

Everyone's hanging onto a balloon, but we just stand there. We must look silly, a bunch of awkward high-schoolers in a circle, staring at the ground, like we can't figure out what to do next. I guess no one wants to be the first to let go. Finally, Jen nudges me slightly with her elbow. When I ignore her she gives me a raised-eyebrow look. I think she's saying, "You first," so I silently say my goodbyes.

Goodbye, Keisha Lambert and Ashley Bannister.

Goodbye Kayla Carter.

Goodbye Blake Montgomery.

Goodbye my life.

Jen and I release our balloon and the rest follow in near unison. Shielding our eyes from the sun, we hold our faces to the sky to watch the four reds and three blues ascend higher and higher. There's no unruly wind propelling them in all directions, so the ascent is almost deliberate, majestic. We're patient, and wait until the last tiny balloon dot disappears.

One moment it's there and then it's just gone. I keep staring at the last spot I saw it, but it never comes back into view.

Finally, mourners head toward their vehicles and the parking lot empties. My parents speak to Mr. and Mrs. Carter in hushed tones, then wait on the curb. Stone-faced, I hug each one in our circle and we pass mumbles of "See you on Monday" back and forth.

I secretly pray Monday will never come.

When I turn from the last embrace I am face to face with Chelsea. Swollen eyes confirm she cried off her designer makeup during the funeral. I move out of her path, but her furtive glance stops me.

"What did you tell the police?" Her accusatory tone instantly rankles, but even more than that, an underlying note of urgency confuses me.

"What are you talking about?"

"The fire, Taryn." Her tone hop-skips from accusatory to guarded.

"I told them what I saw."

"What'd you see?"

"You really want to talk about this here."

She ignores my comment. "And what do you know about that guy at the memorial?"

"I don't know, what do you know?" I flip the question back to her.

"This is not a joke, Taryn."

"I'm being serious. Was Tim whatever-his-name-was at Ritter's Crossing that night or not? You tell me."

Others in the group move in closer, so Chelsea drops the third degree. "We'll talk later."

It almost sounds like a threat. But what else can I expect from Chelsea Manor.

The mini-crowd enveloping her gives me the opportunity to head to the safety of my dad's arm. Caleb's already waiting at the car. Mom and Tracy are talking next to Tracy's brand new minivan, Mom, as always, with her hand on my sister's pregnant-with-twins belly.

Ahead of us a beat-up station wagon rumbles to the curb. A guy with a cigarette hanging out of his mouth puts his head out the open car window. "You seen my sister?" he says to no one in particular.

I press closer to my dad's side. Jen Foster slides in next to me. "Taryn, we haven't talked in forever."

I let her pull me away, though I really want to be heading to the car with Dad.

Jen elbows me in the side. "Why'd she come?"

Jackie Weir, from our high school, hurries down the sidewalk. Her face is beet red, either from the heat or embarrassment, I'm not sure. Certainly everyone can see and hear the car that looks like it's headed for the junkyard instead of the road back to Ideal, and Jackie's brother hanging out of it.

Jackie pulls at the denim hat that is a permanent part of her wardrobe, at least for as long as I can remember anyway. She is the only one at school with permission to wear a hat in class. It's for medical reasons. Some of the students refer to her as "Tacky" but mostly everyone makes sure they ignore her. She never says a word, just pulls her hat tighter and hunches forward in an effort to hide her embarrassment and her thinning white-blond hair.

"Look who it is," Jen says too-loudly. She lets her huge purse slide to the ground in Jackie's path and then pulls it away just as she approaches. The swinging bag forces her to misstep.

I instinctively reach out to steady her, then glare at Jen in disbelief. At a funeral? Really?

"Careful. Watch where you're going." Jen's pretended concern is painful to witness. "I mean, really, Tacky."

The term crawls on my skin. I want to apologize because Jen never will.

"Are you okay?" They're the only words I can get out.

Jackie's pale gray eyes peer briefly into mine, but whatever I see there is interrupted.

"Get in the car," her brother demands, flicking his cigarette butt to the asphalt. Pulling at her hat, Jackie circles the vehicle and ducks into the passenger side.

I watch the car U-turn around the parking lot and chug away, barely noticing that Jen disappears from beside me. I'm still thinking about Jackie.

Does she go home everyday and her mom asks, "How was school today?" And does she answer, "Oh, fine." "Are you making friends?" "Yeah, sure, Mom." At least the boy who died had a brother who cared.

Where did that come from? Just because he's impatient with his sister doesn't make him a bad brother. What I should be thinking is how sad it is that this is the first time I've ever spoken to Jackie Weir.

Cotton fields stream by in reverse as our car drifts back up I-27 toward Ideal, the tone more subdued than before. Not once does my father mention a single cotton producer. Everyone else is quiet, too, and it's fine by me. I recline in the seat, realizing I attended seven funerals this summer. Seven more than I've attended in my entire life.

"That was a nice service." Mom breaks the silence. "Nice sermons. Nice music."

I should let her comment drop, but I don't. "There's nothing nice about a funeral, nothing nice about any of this."

Mom doesn't reply, unless you count noticeably sighing.

I soften my tone. "I guess it was okay." I detest funerals, but none of this is my family's fault.

There was the one speaker who said something interesting. He spoke after Kayla's older sister read the Life Sketch. After quoting several Bible verses, he said something like, *Sorrows, disappointments, and even tragedies are events in life, they are not life itself.* Something like that.

He went on to say they shouldn't become . . . what was it? I try to focus. *They should not become the center of everything you do.*

Yeah, right. I close my eyes, wondering if there really will come a time when me, or the school, or the town is not defined by the tragic event of last June. The *Ideal Fire* the newspaper called it.

Slow-motion memories, some recent, some less so, drift past my mind's eye . . . *Blake yells at me to stay in the car, and a white casket is wheeled down the aisle.*

Now I don't know if I'm dreaming or awake, but the replay continues . . . *the sound of cowboy boots strikes the stage floor and the school bell clangs through a fog. Jackie Weir hunches forward, pulling at her hat. Me and Chelsea giggle and shush ourselves — the last two awake at our first junior high sleepover, and her strange question, "What did you tell police?"*

Dad pulls into the gas station on the outskirts of Ideal, jarring me into consciousness. I stretch and rub my eyes, trying to get my bearings.

"I'm going to fill up here. Stan's always got a better price than anyone in town." Dad says it like there are so many other stations to choose from. There are two "in town." That's it.

"Anybody want anything?" He always asks the same question, but he never waits for an answer.

I want to get some air, so I climb out after him. Stupid one-hundred-degree temperature. It almost forces me back into the air-conditioned van, but I nudge the car door shut anyway. With the engine off, it will be as offensive inside as it is out.

I step gingerly to the edge of the asphalt parking lot. I'm so over my black strappy heels. If there was anything but burning pavement I'd toss them in the car and go barefoot. Blacktop changes to gravel, slowing me even more. I stop where the fields begin and gaze across them, north towards the city.

Stan's station sits at the very outskirts, still

miles from any homes or businesses. Ideal's not much to look at, just a little nothing spot in the Texas Panhandle. For anything really important we have to go into Lubbock.

I study the horizon till I find the high school's flagpole at the city's edge. Focusing on it, I exhale, trying to empty my head of the entire day's events. I purposely avoid looking at the road that leads west from Stan's. The road to Ritter's Crossing.

The annoying growl of an engine behind me interrupts the air's weighty stillness. A white pickup squeals to a stop dangerously close to the side of the convenience store. It spews gravel in its wake and I flinch when a few specks sting my calves.

"Hey, watch it!" I protest, bending down to swipe at the back of my newly-pock-marked legs. I twist around to get a view of my calves, thinking of Jackie and the noisy vehicle she was driven away in.

The driver's side door slams shut and the crunch of footsteps on gravel carries from around the bed of the pickup. The footsteps stop a few feet away and a pair of worn cowboy boots comes into view. I lift my gaze to take in steel blue eyes that immediately rip right through me. It figures.

"It's you." My jaw tightens after I say it. In a split second I'm back on stage reliving the memorial-assembly nightmare.

"What do you mean, 'it's me?'" he counters.

My family pulls up behind the pickup and Dad taps lightly on the horn.

"I mean . . . it's you!" I don't scrimp on tone. "You're the one who interrupted the memorial. Then you ran me over outside the principal's office. Now you're spraying rocks at me. What's your problem?"

"You're the girl that read the names at the —" He stops. "I think you're part of my problem."

"Look, I don't know what happened to your brother, but he wasn't at Ritter's Crossing that night."

"Like you would even care enough to want to know the truth." He jams his keys into his pocket. "Your ride's waiting."

Fuming, I march toward the car, then slam the door shut behind me.

Mom turns in her seat. "Are you okay, honey? Who was that?"

I pull at the straps of my shoes and slide them off. Pointing my toes and stretching my legs as far as I can, I settle back into the seat.

"Just some jerk," I reply.

5

"Phone's ringing." Caleb states the obvious before tearing up the stairs to his room.

I'm as anxious as he is to get out of funeral clothes, but I missed breakfast this morning, so I head to the kitchen instead. Mom asked me to help set up lunch for the Carters when they return from the cemetery, but I told her no. I'm not ready to be in Kayla's house again. To see everything in place like it always is, when I know something is terribly out of place.

Something to eat and a nap. It still seems the only answer. Can't I just sleep away my senior year? Forget about Chelsea's questions and seven caskets? Forget about bullies like Jen and the rest who think they're so much better than anybody else? And forget about guys with deep blue eyes and incredibly bad attitudes. I don't even know his name.

"What's up?" Dad says into the phone.

I grab a glass from the cupboard and fill it with water before opening the fridge.

"Taryn, it's your sister." He holds out the

phone. I take it, but leave the fridge door open.

"You're not answering your cell phone," Tracy says.

"I haven't turned it back on yet." I stare into the fridge. *Sorry, conversations are not on my list right now* is what I want to say.

"Taryn, I have a question. It didn't really seem right to ask you this at Kayla's . . . you know, but I need your help again."

"Again?"

"At Donut King. You helped me through my morning sickness, but now I'm getting so big. My ankles are swollen. My legs cramp up all the time. Taryn, I need you. In the morning like before."

This is an appropriate question for an hour after Kayla's *you know*? She's kidding, right? And FYI to the world, I can never step foot in Donut King again. Not as long as on the far right, top shelf there's a tray full of cinnamon-sugar doughnut twists. Not as long as there's glaze and sprinkles to get caught on my sleeves.

But I think she wants an answer.

"Tracy, I get that you're pregnant with twins, but I'm going to have to pass."

"Pass? There's no pass. You're my sister."

"Exactly. So you, more than anyone, should understand." I mumble something to end the conversation before hanging up.

Dad comes out of the pantry. "Things okay, Taryn?"

"Do you really want an answer to that?" The phone rings again, but I don't even look at it. I told her no.

Dad checks caller ID before answering. "Hello, Mel." Long pause. "Yes, she's here."

I duck my head into the fridge, not sure who I'm more annoyed with at this point. Mel, because he's calling again, or Dad, for assuming I will talk to him . . . again. He's the small-town, on-a-first-name-basis cop assigned to investigate the Ideal Gin Co. building fire, but I thought it was case-closed.

"No, I hadn't heard," Dad says into the phone. He paces a bit before sinking into a kitchen chair. He doesn't say anything, just grunts now and then. It's unnerving, but I ignore him. He and Mel can talk. I'll grab food and be gone.

I poke around till I find cheese and grapes. After adding a handful of crackers to the mix I tiptoe out of the kitchen to the stairs.

I plant my foot on the first step when Dad's voice stops me. "Taryn? Mel wants to talk to you."

Will whining work? "Dad … no."

"He said it will only take a second."

"I've heard that before." I drop down on the

step, cradling my lunch in one hand, and holding out the other with as much drama as I can muster. "Give it to me."

"Will you be okay?" Dad asks before handing me the phone. "I want to run over to Carter's to talk to Mom."

"I won't not be okay." I take the phone, but can't decide if I'm ready to answer it yet. The front door shuts and my dad's gone. I toy briefly with the thought of avoiding Mel altogether with a well-placed press of a button. Something's going on — Dad's tone told me that. But I'm done. I played my part at the memorial. I attended all the funerals. Why can't it be over?

"Hello . . . Miss Karen?" Mel's voice comes from the phone. He always calls me Karen, the concept of new or unusual name variations apparently escapes him and I have given up on correcting.

Get it over with. "Yeah, I'm here."

Mel doesn't mention the conversation with my dad. Instead, just as I assumed, he wants to rehash what happened the night of the fire.

"It's more important than ever to get the full story," Mel says. "You may have to testify. Whoops, I shouldn't have said that."

I ignore his comment because I know Dad will

tell me everything.

"So you saw what happened at the memorial on Monday, Karen. You heard what that boy said. You're sure you didn't see anyone else at Ritter's Crossing?"

"I'm sorry, no."

"It could be the typical bullied kid out for revenge, you know? He sees a bunch of popular kids from school hanging out at the old gin, they're easy targets. No one would be suspicious of a hundred-year-old building going up in flames."

"Revenge? What?" This theory's new to me. Of course, so is the idea that maybe someone else was there.

"Just thinking out loud. The brother says Tim tried to call him that night. He thinks he was in trouble."

"So you're telling me this Tim-guy was there. His body was found in the fire?"

"I'm saying too much, sorry. Just tell me again what you saw."

I juggle the grapes a bit in my palm, but lose a few. Then my crackers begin to slide. I know Mel has this stuff in his notes.

"Miss Karen? Are you still there?"

I give up and replay the narrative — the quick version of what I saw that night. I recite the facts,

I'm not going to get emotional this time.

I left the party with Blake. He got a text about playing night games at the old gin. We went to Ritter's Crossing — we didn't really have a choice because of the road construction on 27. The detour took us right through there. Blake told me to wait in the car, but when he didn't come back, I decided to go looking for him. I had barely entered the building when I heard the first explosion.

I take a deep breath. Do I have to state again, for the record, that Blake dragged me out of the building and yelled at me to get to the car and call 9-1-1 before he disappeared into the dark?

"What about Miss Chelsea? When did you see her?"

"After the explosion when I got back to the car." He has all this in his notes, I swear.

"Just terrible, but there's no way those kids could have known there was old fertilizer stored in the gin. Someone plays with matches and, well, you've got yourself a tragedy, that's what you've got." Mel pauses, but not long enough for me to stop him. "Just thinking out loud here —" he begins again. I think I know what he's going to say. He says it every time he talks to me.

"It's a wonder Miss Chelsea made it out alive and not a scratch on her. I mean, when all those other gals and guys were killed off." Mel has a way with words sometimes, and usually not a good way.

Somehow he always forgets Chelsea's broken ankle, but I don't care enough to point that out, it will only prolong the conversation. His tangents only play into my own reservations about what I saw that night. The picture in my head is of her running toward the building, but when something's on fire your instinct should be to run away.

"You're a sweet girl." Mel ends his interviews the same way every time, too. "It's real bad what happened. I don't know how anybody can deal with such a tragedy."

I am now even more desperate for that nap. "I'm sure you have everything you need in your notes, and I need to go." I finally press the end button and leave the phone on the bottom step. I collect the runaway grapes and chunky cracker crumbs and dump them in the garbage in the kitchen along with my dried-out cheese. I don't feel like eating anymore.

Later that night, I join my parents in the den. Dad sits reading the paper in his favorite recliner while Mom perches at the computer.

I'm just going to flat out go there. "Dad, Mel didn't tell me what you two were talking about."

He and Mom exchange a glance before he puts the chair into rocker position, and pushes the newspaper aside. “It’s not good news, honey. Several of the parents of the kids who died have filed a lawsuit.”

“What?” I pull up the nearby ottoman and drop onto it.

He lets out a sigh. “They’re suing the Manors saying that since they sponsored the party, they were negligent.”

“But it’s been months since it happened. Now suddenly they want to go to court?” I search his face, hoping he has some kind of answer that makes sense.

“If you can believe it, they wanted to wait until after Kayla’s funeral.” Mom joins me on the ottoman. “I guess they figured it would somehow appear more respectful.” She frowns at the word.

“Who’s doing it? Which parents?” I have to know. Then the implications sink in and I fight the beginning of tears. “Mom, they were all friends.” I lean into my mom’s shoulder. “Who would do this?”

My parents exchange another cautious glance. “Dad —” I fixate on his face, trying to discern his hesitance. “Tell me.”

Mom drapes an arm around my shoulder like

she's preparing me.

"I'm not sure if this is the complete list," Dad says. "But Mel mentioned Lamberts, Browns, Martins, and . . . Mrs. Montgomery."

I erupt when he mentions Blake's mom. "What is she thinking? Blake probably saved Chelsea's life, and what, she wants the Manors to pay for it?" The sarcasm flows briefly, but then the news smacks me again. "Blake would never want this, none of them would. Don't they see that?" I collapse onto my mom's lap.

Mom brings me the phone Friday morning. I'm in bed, but I can't remember how I got here last night. I don't even open my eyes to see what time it is because it feels too early to have a coherent conversation with anyone.

But I do, only because it's Mrs. Ames. "Taryn, I was hoping you might come into school today."

I squint at the clock. 7:00 AM. I was right. Too early.

"Sorry to call at this hour." It's as if she can read my bleariness through the phone. "I left a message the other night, and, well, I'm wondering if you had a chance to think about what I said Monday."

I clear my throat, but it doesn't help. The words

are still tough to say. "I'm sorry, Mrs. Ames, but taking Blake's place as president is too hard. It's the last thing I want to think about."

"I understand. I really do."

I dig down deep in my comforter. I feel a "but" coming and I need to brace myself.

"I just wonder if you'll be okay if you don't."

I'm put off by her question. Like I need the constant reminder that Blake isn't here by pretending I can take his place? "What do you mean, 'be okay if I don't?'"

"Ideal High has experienced a tragedy. Have you considered that we can't be the same because of it? Right now you have the chance to make a difference."

Time out. Way too early in the quote-unquote grieving process for this conversation. And too-cheery catchphrases like "Make a Difference!" are dead to me now. "I know things will never be the same, Mrs. Ames, but I don't know how to fix anything."

"We can't change what happened, but we change because of it. We turn something horrible into something good."

I grip the edge of my blanket into a fist, but keep my words even. "This is not a made-for-TV movie. This is real life. Have you heard about the lawsuit? This is the nightmare that keeps on giving." I can't even muster a drop of sarcasm.

"I want to discuss that, too. I'm sure your parents have told you to be careful what you say. Things could get a bit sticky here at school."

"We talked about it last night. All those families are the Manors' friends. It makes no sense."

"I know. It's going to be really tough on Chelsea." Mrs. Ames' heavy sigh carries through the phone. "Everyone's still grieving. Maybe this will blow over and the lawsuit dropped when everyone comes to their senses."

I didn't think about Chelsea and the situation this put her in. Becca's parents are among those suing and she and Chelsea were best friends.

Mrs. Ames is still talking. "We'll get through it. We're having another faculty meeting first thing this morning, but if you'd like to talk some more, I'll be in my classroom by noon."

"Mrs. Ames, I can't serve on student council."

There's a pause before she replies. "I know. I'm still here if you want to talk . . . about anything."

"Thanks." I end the call, then roll onto my back to stare at the ceiling. How can those parents do that to the Manors? It was just an accident. But Mel keeps probing me for details. And what's up with the bullied-kid-revenge theory? I wish I had asked Mrs. Ames about that.

I turn on my side and stare at the stuffed dog on my bookshelf, the miniature version of Bugs, the Bulldog, Ideal High's mascot. It reminds me of football games and school activities, of friends, and Blake. Of last year. Now I just want to be invisible. Like Jackie.

My thoughts drift to yesterday. It's strange that Jackie came to Kayla's funeral. I picture her hurrying down the halls at school. She always hurries, always pulls at the edges of her hat, always looks at the floor. I pull at my comforter again, bunching the fabric in my hands. Jackie is invisible, but just like that guy's brother, Tim — she's a target. Even ignoring and excluding can be a kind of bullying.

The principal's words from Monday's memorial linger. "Here at Ideal High we have a long-standing tradition of pride, unity, and respect." Unity? Respect? Not hardly. *Ideal to your face,* well, not even always that.

I roll onto my stomach and plant my face in the pillow. Too bad that Tim's brother is such a jerk, otherwise I'm curious. But it doesn't matter. It doesn't change what happened.

Senior year is over before it begins. All that lies ahead is one long, painful test of my endurance. Maybe I should have joined the rest of them and become a balloon dot disappearing into the sky. Another classmate they grieve and memorialize before moving on. The thought has crossed my mind more than once while under the shelter of this comforter.

But I'd want pink. A single pink balloon wending its way toward heaven.

The alarm clock blares from my nightstand. I lift my head to stare at it, the irritating beep-beep continuing till I finally reach out to fumble with the snooze button. I play with the settings, checking the alarm several times. I promise I haven't set it since the last day of school in May.

Now what? Get up at this crazy hour on a no-school day? I grab the home phone from in between the sheets and shuffle barefoot to the kitchen to place it in its charger. Sleep is impossible anyway the way my thoughts are boomeranging from one side of my brain to the other.

Mom stands in front of the blender where something green whirrs inside. "Nice to see you so early this morning," she says over the noise.

I increase my volume, too. "I talked to Mrs. Ames and now I can't get back to sleep. She invited me to come over to the school." A pitcher in the fridge contains grape juice, the fake sugary kind I'm guessing my dad made. I pour myself some.

"Sounds like a good idea, honey." Mom wipes her hands, then flips off the blender. "Oh, I talked to Tracy. Don't you worry about it one bit. I'll help out in the morning at Donut King."

"Was I supposed to be worrying about it?" I stare into my juice glass.

"Oh, Taryn, no, that's not what I meant. You have enough to worry about."

I take a sip before looking at her. "I feel bad for her. I just can't —" Last spring it was Tracy's morning sickness, now fast forward a few months and it's her swollen ankles.

Mom touches my shoulder. "It's fine. I'll help for a week until they can hire someone."

Okay, now I feel horrible.

"You and doughnuts, Mom? Really?" Our mother is opposed to doughnuts as a rule and pretty much freaked out when her granola-girl daughter married Perry King, the heir-apparent of a dozen Donut Kings across the Greater Texas Panhandle when his dad retires. Perry the Prince, I call him.

"I'm not planning to be employee of the month, but if it will get Tracy off her feet it's worth it. I want those babies staying put for a while longer."

Mom lifts the lid off the blender to peer inside.

I down the juice and set my glass in the sink. "Just smile when you hand them to customers, okay? Doughnuts make people happy. At least I remember when they did."

Mom looks at me like she's trying to decide what to say. She knows a little bit about how Blake and I officially became acquainted.

"Taryn, if you're up for it, we could go to Lubbock tomorrow and do some school shopping. You know, go to lunch — our tradition?" Her tone is hesitant. I think she worries she pushes too much.

"School Monday, ready or not." I say it without feeling.

"Feels like it's coming too soon, doesn't it?"

"That's an understatement, since anytime is too soon." I tap my fingers on the edge of the counter.

"Sometimes all we can do when facing a tough thing is to push through it —" Mom stops. I think she gets that I've heard this before, that she's said it before.

Normally, right here is where I'd say I'm not buying it, but like I just told her, school's coming whether I'm ready or not.

"Look, honey, grieving is different for everyone. I told you to take all the time you need and I meant it. As much as I want you to be okay, you're on your own timetable with this." She reaches out to rub my shoulder and doesn't say anything else for a moment.

She's searching for words and I don't have any.

Finally, she continues as if she never stopped. "You might consider, though, that the distraction of school will actually help."

I start tapping my fingers again. "Staying home doing nothing hasn't."

"Is it okay if I say I agree? In fact, go over to the school today. It'll be good for you." She sets the lid on the counter and stirs the goopy green stuff. She knows she's letting it sit too long.

"Except Mrs. Ames just wants to talk me into being president."

"I spoke to her." Mom puts the lid back on before continuing. "I told her maybe your being president would be too much to expect right now."

That's been exactly my point.

"I mean, of course, you could under different circumstances. Hold on a second." She pulses the contents of the blender, then pours herself a large glass while finishing her thought. "Now I wouldn't be surprised if Chelsea quit the cheer squad. You've both been through a horrible experience. Worse than most people face in a lifetime."

"Chelsea's not quitting cheer."

"I only meant it would be understandable given the circumstances." Mom gestures towards the blender. "Do you want some?"

I make a face. "No, I'm good." I leave her in the kitchen sipping her green drink and head back to my room. What do Chelsea and cheerleading have to do with anything? High kicks and hair-tossing don't compare to student body president. But maybe Mom's right. Under different circumstances I could make a difference like Blakc had wanted, couldn't I? I groan audibly. Make a difference. There's that phrase again.

I stand in the doorway of my room gazing at the unmade bed, debating. Maybe I don't need to waste time going over to the high school. Why be subjected to Mrs. Ames' reminders of what Blake had planned for this year? More replayed-memories of desks pulled up close to the teacher's as we dreamed and schemed. I pick up the dress shoes that lay just inside the door where I dropped them the day before.

I can't do it without Blake. There's no way. I toss the shoes in the direction of the closet.

Suddenly I want, no need, to see our Junior Prom photo. After the tragedy I'd moved it from its place next to my alarm clock into the top drawer of my bedside table. I retrieve it, then drop onto the bed with it cradled in my lap. Half of my paisley comforter hangs off the bed. I gather it up and pull it around me in an embrace while I study the photo. I can't help smiling at our goofy grins and crooked king and queen crowns.

Blake's face in the photo. It's looking at me, questioning me. If I don't, then who will care enough to fix any of the school's issues with bullying or anything else? Chelsea joked about running for president, but seriously, there is no way. Everything has changed and yet nothing would change.

Finally, I set the frame back in its place and let my comforter slide back to the floor. I step over it to grab my robe before heading to the bathroom for a shower. I never could say no to Blake.

6

Shampoo. Rinse. No repeat. For the first time in forever my shower's quick. Whatever is swirling in the recesses of my brain terrifies and intrigues me at the same time. I can't be president. I just can't. Can I?

I dry off, then pull on a T-shirt and jeans and jam my feet into my favorite flip flops. I avoid eye contact with the mirror. I'm not ready to look too deep. After drawing my wet hair into a ponytail, I grab my bag and check the time on my phone. I forgot Mrs. Ames can't meet until noon.

I guess I could make my bed — that'll kill two minutes. I quit making it about seven funerals ago. What's the point when you're just going to get right back in it?

I untwist my top sheet and straighten it out flat. I pull the comforter up off the floor and drape it over everything, then arrange my pillows. Okay, one minute down. Now what? I sit on the edge of the bed letting my gaze find Blake's picture-perfect face again on my nightstand. What would he really say to me if he could?

That decides it — I'm going to the cemetery.

But I have to find something first.

My zebra-striped backpack lay on the floor by my desk, right where I dropped it on the last day of school in May. I kneel next to it, hesitating. What junior year memories does it contain? Holding my breath I unzip it and gingerly pull out the spiral notebook that sticks out on top. At the back of it Blake and I began a list of ideas for the new school year.

I run my fingers across the cover. The only sign of wear is at the top left corner where I doodled the words "HOT CHEETOS" in black ink. Underneath it Kayla added the words "are hot," scratched in with the end of a bent paper clip.

I open the notebook to reveal Trigonometry problems. Flipping through, I reach a blank page and yank the used ones out in one motion. Bits of spiral-notebook-paper edges flutter to the floor, but I have what I want. I toss the pages on my desk, grab a pen, and hit the lights.

In the kitchen Mom rinses out the blender, and from the bangs and dings I hear coming from the den, Caleb is up and already on the computer.

"Mom, I'm going to the cemetery. When I see the look on her face I reassure her. "Don't worry, I'm fine."

She places a hand on my shoulder. "You're sure you want to go alone?"

"I'm okay, really." I pull car keys from my purse and head to the door. I think I hear her breathe a sigh of relief.

The autumn-colored Corolla roars to life. I never understood why my sister drove an orange car, but now that it's mine, I love it. Tracy and the Crown Prince of Pastry have purchased a fully-loaded minivan to haul their babies around in. Lucky me, I get her hand-me-down.

It's the only good thing to happen this summer.

It isn't orange, anyway, it's a nice, reddish-brown color, like the color the leaves will turn when October comes.

Fall. School. What will that feel like?

Cheering at football games, going to dances — that was last year. The thought stops me as I pull up to the light at Thornton Avenue and signal a right turn. I did those things with people who are gone now.

I grip the steering wheel. Senior year without them will be more than unbearable, but I have no choice, do I? The making of memories goes on, for good or for bad. A horn honks behind me. I make the turn and relax my grip one finger at a time. My green-smoothie-drinking Mom has tried to teach me a few relaxation techniques over the years.

I don't have any answers to surviving senior year, but one thing I know. I am done hiding. I cowered under my paisley comforter all summer and everyone felt sorry for me, patted my arm, and told me they couldn't believe what happened. The victim role was expected and I played it all summer.

What would the Taryn of last May say to me — *this tragedy happened in your life, but it is not your life?* The quote from Kayla's funeral. *It should not become the center of everything you do.* At the next light, I pull the spiral notebook and a pen from my purse to scribble down the quote. I want to remember it.

I stay on Thornton, passing through several intersections before pulling to a stop at Wellman Boulevard. I allow my thoughts to drift to the last time I visited Blake's grave. Mom has reason to be concerned. Mrs. Montgomery called to tell me Blake's gravestone had been set, and even though daylight was fading, I begged my parents to let me go see it. Once there I sat and outlined his name with my finger and cried till heavy clouds followed suit with torrents of rain. Though drenched and cold, I didn't move from the spot, and it was where my parents found me when they arrived at the cemetery.

They piled me into the backseat of the van under a heavy blanket, and caravanned home with Dad driving the Corolla. I guess I didn't stop shaking until I was back in my bed, bundled tight in my comforter.

The arrow pointing the way to Ideal City Cemetery comes into view. I eye the notebook lying on the seat and a knot of nervous energy tightens in my chest. Is reading our list going to be a mistake?

I turn the radio on, suddenly needing a distraction. Recognizing the opening guitar riffs of a familiar tune, I ramp up the volume. When is the last time I even listened to the radio? First I hum along and then I'm yelling out the words of the chorus, not caring what the guy in the bug-antennaed pest control truck next to me thinks. Anyone who agrees to drive around in that lime-green thing can't judge other drivers, plus it feels good to let loose of what's been cooped up inside for so many weeks.

I crack the window open, allowing the summer-morning air to mingle with the music. I inhale like I haven't breathed fresh oxygen in a long time. No feed lot odor from the north on the breeze today. Perfect. Music and oxygen, where have you been all my life?

Finally, I turn onto Winslow Drive and slow

way down as I get closer to the cemetery's red brick entrance.

I flip the radio off and drive in silence through the front gate. A bright blue, cloudless sky provides the perfect backdrop to the strange calm that settles over me. For the end of August, the morning is pleasantly un-warm, a switch from yesterday. Or maybe I'm never up this early in the summer. The breeze can't muster much strength, so the American flag hangs nearly motionless. Rare for any time of year in West Texas.

I park in the same spot as before and gather up the notebook and pen, and a water bottle. I'm not sure where Kayla's grave is, plus I'm not thrilled with the thought of stumbling upon fresh dirt so newly-laid over her casket. I make a beeline for Blake's.

Beloved Son, Friend to All. I run my fingers across his name several times. Hello, Blake Austin Montgomery. I kneel in front of it and take my time brushing away leaves and dirt from around the headstone. Only then do I sit back and let my eyes rest on the notebook.

I can't move. I just sit and stare at it.

This is dumb. It's just a notebook, just some scribbles on paper.

I reach for it and hold it tight to my chest. I

finally speak out loud to the headstone.

"Remember this, Blake? Remember we were going to make something of our senior year? Why did you —?" I stop. It kind of spooks me to hear my voice. The cemetery is too quiet, plus the question is pointless anyway.

I open the purple notebook to the back and read our list, remembering sitting with Mrs. Ames, picking her brain about student council, and listening to Blake's ideas — he so practical about what could be done, me just happy I was a part of it with him.

I slide my finger down the column: Tutor Club, Spirit Club, an Anti-Bullying campaign. Would any of these help someone like Timothy Wade Jenks? I remember how his brother spoke his full name so decisively into the microphone.

Do pledges to an anti-bullying campaign magically translate into someone feeling less isolated or does it just stop the public teasing and encourage the ignoring? Like the way everyone treats Jackie Weir.

When I can't sit cross-legged on the ground another minute, I stand up to stretch. The last time I was here it was too dark to read any of the other headstones, but now the names demand my attention.

I start down a second row of gravesites and immediately the name WEIR jumps out at me from a small, rounded headstone. The man died on his fortieth birthday. I cover my face with my hands and exhale. Jackie and I were about ten that year. I drop to my knees to straighten a vase of silk flowers that lies toppled over. My heart feels heavier now at the thought this could be her dad. At the thought that kids at school go through hard things that no one ever knows about.

As the sun rises higher, the early morning coolness gives way to higher temperatures, and the heat and the surrounding sea of headstones combine to stifle me. I can't make people be Jackie's friend. I can't fix what happened to Tim.

I could have been president, but not now. Not like this. Not when I'm barely able to join the ranks of the living.

I tiptoe back to Blake's grave. When I flip the notebook's cover back to close it, the words of the quote I scribbled on the first page mock me. *Sorrows, disappointments, and even tragedies are events in life, they are not life itself. They should not become the center of everything you do.*

I tear the page from its wire binding and fold it over and over into the smallest square possible before wedging it in between the headstone and an attached vase. The quote isn't true. Not even close.

After grabbing the rest of my stuff, I trek back to my car, weighing the pros and cons of going over to the school to talk to Mrs. Ames. Maybe I just need to explain myself one more time, then I can be done with this whole president thing — start the school year, be done with the school year.

When I climb into my car, I press my forehead to the steering wheel. Unfortunately, graduation is so far away.

I don't know how long I sit there like that, but when I hear voices I raise my head to look out the window. I spy a circle of women in my side-view mirror, maybe four or five of them, on the cemetery lawn behind where I've parked. They're seated on portable camp chairs except for one who stands at the head waving her arm. I roll down my window and a sing-songy chant fills the air.

"I command . . ." I turn around to look out my back window. I swear she's holding a wand or something.

Back behind the leader of the group I notice a small ice chest and then something all too familiar, a golden yellow box with a crown and words imprinted in black: DONUT KING.

Let's command the universe and then we'll have doughnuts. Perfect.

If the whole idea wasn't so disturbing, I might have laughed out loud. But I've already learned commanding the universe is a waste of time. Seven funerals and ten and a half weeks of burying myself under my comforter have shown me that.

A noisy rumble draws my attention to the entrance of the cemetery. I watch an old Chevy with peeling paint sputter and misfire then turn at the first lane, away from me. That's the car from yesterday at the church. It has to be. I'm mesmerized as Jackie Weir climbs out of the driver's seat with a bouquet of yellow baby roses. She stops at the first gravesite and drops to her knees.

Whose grave is it? I have to know.

I start keeping time. One minute, two . . . five, ten. How long is she going to kneel there? I'm melting without the air on, but I'm afraid she'll notice me if I turn on the engine.

She's getting up. It's been fourteen minutes give or take. Wait. What if her next stop is the Weir grave in the row next to Blake's? I duck down in my seat till she gets in her car and, thankfully, drives out of the cemetery. I inch my car forward to the spot she left and step purposefully to the row of graves. The rectangular line cut in the grass means it's new, but there's no headstone, no name. That's no help at all, but it has to be Kayla's.

The cemetery ladies are done commanding the universe. I see them digging into the doughnut box and passing around water bottles. One of them gestures my direction and they all look. I slink back to my car.

Nothing to see here, ladies.

After the short drive to the school, I wait at Mrs. Ames' desk. It's not too long before the door opens to reveal the familiar round form of my former teacher-turned advisor and friend.

"Taryn, I'm glad you came."

I wait until she gets settled. "I'm sorry to disappoint you, Mrs. Ames, but I'm not —"

"Don't worry, I'm not even going to bring it up." She crosses her arms and places a hand at her neck. "We're prepared to move forward. We'll hold a new election, in fact, we already have a candidate." Mrs. Ames points to a bin at the corner of her desk. It holds one thin sheet of paper.

Emblazoned across the top line in capital letters, I read the name: CHELSEA LYNN MANOR.

7

After Chelsea's name jumps off the application and slams me between the eyes, neither of us says anything. If Mrs. Ames notices my emotional recoil, she doesn't react. Maybe she realizes I need time to wrap my head around it. Like just the idea of needing a new election at all is hard to take. Of course, it is, but this twist? I don't even know what to say.

But it gets awkward. I should say something.

"Thanks for understanding," I manage to mumble before escaping from the room. I'm in my car and home before I can think too much about anything. Angling the Junior Prom photo away from view, I drop on my bed and snatch up the covers.

I wake up in the dark, my ringtone blaring. I silence it and look to see who's calling. It's my brother. "Hey, Caleb."

"Mom said you would pick me up, where are you?"

There's just enough light from my alarm clock to see there's a note stuck to it. I pluck it off and turn on my lamp. *We're going over to Carter's. Please pick up Caleb from Donut King. He should be ready about 8:00. Thanks, Mom.*

A daunting request for such an innocent-looking sticky note. "What are you doing at Donut King?"

"Taryn, are you coming?" Caleb's not in the mood for questions. How many times did he call and I didn't wake up?

I feel bad, but still I grasp at any idea that will keep me away from the doughnut shop. "Is Tracy there, can she bring you home? Are you with a friend, can his parents pick you up?"

"Can't you?"

I get that I'm making this harder than it has to be. "Okay, but wait for me outside."

When I pull into the parking lot at Donut King there's a small knot of Ideal High students sitting at one of the outdoor tables. I purposely find a spot on the other side, away from them and the huge gold crown logo across the front of the store. I text Caleb. I'm not sure what happened to waiting outside.

Someone knocks on my car window with their elbow. "Taryn, open up."

Caleb's on one side and a Donut King employee on the other. Both are carrying a stack of doughnut boxes. I twist to lean between the seats to open both passenger doors, and instantly the sweet-glaze aroma of doughnuts and memories suffocates me.

Caleb sticks his head inside the car. "We need to drop these off to Perry's sister on our way home."

I sink back into my seat. "Of course we do."

I inhale sharply and grip the steering wheel. And Tracy thought I could work here again. I can't even sit in the parking lot. I roll down my window slightly, needing a gulp of fresh air. But Donut King air is not going to help. It's as fresh and sweet as day-old doughnuts tonight.

"No, let's turn them longways, then they won't slide." The boxes are in, but Caleb and the employee are contemplating best-placement scenarios and I'm about to pass out.

"Just get in so we can go." Caleb needs to hurry. The kids from school have left the table and are walking down the sidewalk in our direction. Jen Foster leads the way in her wedge-heeled flip flops.

"Taryn? We were just talking about you." Jen shuffles over, bringing the rest of the group with her.

I think I'd rather succumb to the doughnut fumes inside my car, but I roll my window down some more and try to hold my breath.

"So our question is, what did you do to Tim Jenks to get him so mad?"

I slump in my seat. "What?"

"Yeah, did you mess up his doughnut order, put too many marshmallows in his hot chocolate . . . what?" Paco laughs. "Or did you give him pink sprinkles instead of purple?"

Jen slaps him on the chest. "You're so inappropriate."

I feel like I walked in in the middle of a movie. "I don't know what you're talking about."

Jen moves closer and I can see she's been crying. "Didn't you hear? Paco was just telling us that Tim Jenks started the fire. They found his car out there hidden in the bushes."

"Where did you hear that, Paco?"

"J.T. hears stuff from his uncle. He works for the sheriff's office."

"But his brother said he died in the fire. Why would he —?" I can't even think straight. "Why do you think I made him mad? I didn't even know him."

Jen narrows her eyes at me. "C'mon, Taryn. You served him a doughnut every Friday."

8

Chelsea Manor shows up the first day of school Monday morning with a posse and enough posters and propaganda to elect Congress. After her poster-taping committee finishes, her face and slogan assault me around every corner.

"VOTE FOR CHELSEA! THE MANOR TO WHICH YOU ARE ACCUSTOMED!"

It's not what I need after the way my weekend went.

Jen said Tim Jenks bought a doughnut and hot chocolate at Donut King every Friday morning from March through May. An employee told them that. She also said they were kidding about thinking I made him mad, that they were only making up random reasons for what Tim did.

Allegedly.

Over the weekend I read everything I could find in the paper or online about the fire. Tim isn't even mentioned until last week and it's only in connection with "his brother" interrupting the memorial. There's a fuzzy postage-size photo of Tim. A headshot of him laughing and looking at someone or something off-camera. He's got a bunch of dark wavy hair and a wide mouth, and he didn't look familiar.

I slide into my alphabetically-ordered seat in the last row of homeroom. If I thought the Chelsea-posters were bad, it is nothing compared to homeroom without Blake. I turn away from his seat. I don't want to know who dares to sit there.

I also don't want to think about the fire not being an accident. All weekend the thought consumed me. I've finally reached the point of numbness and now what? I rage against someone who's not even around to hear it?

Someone started the fire. On purpose.

No.

Morning announcements blare from the speaker in the corner of the room — the usual warnings about tardiness and unexcused absences, and where to get parking permits. Mrs. Ames' voice comes over the P.A. to give the particulars about elections. Paperwork is due in the office or her classroom by day's end for all those interested in running for president, vice-president, and secretary/treasurer. The speech assembly will be Friday with voting to follow. Winners announced next Monday.

There's a pause and a fumbling with the microphone, then Chelsea's voice grates through the sound system. "Cheer Workshop starts a week from today for those trying out for cheerleader. If you make it past workshop, then you perform at the assembly Thursday." More fumbling with the microphone. "Winners posted that Friday."

Mr. Myers ends the announcements with a similar speech to the one he gave at the memorial: "pride, unity, and counselors are still available." It should be our new class motto.

The guy in front of me plants a student planner on my desk. Something's different. That's Jackie Weir's seat and Jackie isn't in it. We keep the same homeroom all three years, without exception. Where is Jackie and why is this guy in her spot?

I stare at the planner and tell myself to quit worrying about seating arrangements. Don't think about who is sitting in whose seat. Don't think about am I really ready to be with people? Do normal things like sit in homeroom?

There's absolutely nothing normal about realizing that my maybe-boyfriend isn't in homeroom because he moved out of town. He's just gone.

The kid in front of me lays his head on his desk, his shaggy hair draping over his crossed arms where his head rests. He should have trimmed it. Not that I can say much about prepping for the first day of school. I did my best, for my mom's sake, to pick out some clothes when we went shopping Saturday. To me the thought of trying anything on seemed unbearable, so we just dragged it all home and it sat in a heap until this morning. I ended up pairing one of the new tops with my favorite worn-out jeans. It just felt right.

The spiral-bound planner, all new and sparkly in bright red and blue, draws my attention again. I finally decide to flip through it at the blank year ahead of me. When I find May I circle the word with red ink. Graduation.

The bell rings and the guy with the shaggy hair bolts awake then grabs his backpack and shuffles out of the room in slow-motion. Sleepwalking through senior year might be my best option, too. I'm certainly in no hurry to get to first hour English. The room's nearly empty when I stuff the planner into my backpack and head for the door.

"Taryn." Jen grabs my arm the second I step into the crowded hall. "Hey, those jeans look familiar." She tightens her grip as we get caught up in the flow, then drops her head close to mine. "I was just in the bathroom in the other hall. Did you write that about the fire?"

"Write what?"

"About Tim Jenks."

Her nails dig into my flesh, but it's nothing compared to what I feel clawing at my stomach. "What does it say?"

"You'll have to go see." Jen disappears into a classroom just as the bell rings. AP English is next door, so I'm there before the ringing stops, but now I'm only thinking about getting to that bathroom.

I tap my fingers on my desk, cross and uncross my legs. Mrs. White outlines the semester in detail, and I can't sit still. All I get is that it's going to involve a lot of reading and writing. Will she stop talking and give us an assignment or something, so I can ask to go to the bathroom? I really need it to be empty and now's the best chance for that.

The clawing rises to my chest, sucking the air from my lungs. The funerals and the memorial are behind me, but did I really think the tragedy wouldn't taint these walls once school started?

Please, Mrs. White. Take a breath.

"Taryn, are you okay?"

I look up and the teacher is at my desk with a concerned look on her face.

"No, I'm not. Can I —?" I don't wait for a reply before I'm up and booking it to the door. I don't care if I don't have a hall pass.

"That reminds me, everyone," I hear Mrs. White say behind me. "If you need to speak to a counselor, they're available all day."

I breathe a little easier once I'm out of class, but don't waste any time moving to the girls' bathroom in the other hallway.

At first glance the walls are clean, proving that any graffiti from last year was covered over. A clean slate for the new year. It must be in one of the stalls. I start with the first one and find nothing. Each one after that is scrubbed and painted as well. I ball my hands into fists and enter the last one. The walls are clean, but when I rotate around the door to shut it, the blood-red words scrawled on its surface burn deep.

WHO DESERVED TO DIE IN THE FIRE?

It's a list with one name on it.

TIM JENKS.

I've never written on a bathroom stall before, but I have to get rid of this so no one else will see it. I don't care if he did start the fire, it's just wrong to be saying this kind of stuff. Unfortunately, I have nothing. Not a pen to write with, not some keys to scratch it out. My backpack is sitting by my desk.

I make an attempt with liquid soap and paper towels, but that's a fail, so I head back to class. I'll have to try again later.

My schedule takes me away from the 200 building, so I don't get a chance till lunch time. I leave fourth hour with a few girls under the pretense of eating with them, because that's high school, it's all about having someone to sit with at lunch. But when one of them asks why I'm not going to be student body president, I put her off with a made-up excuse about not feeling well. That gives me a reason to bypass the cafeteria altogether.

When I get to the bathroom there's just one girl at the sink checking her makeup, but that's better than I can expect. I smile and pretend it's not weird that I'm skipping every empty stall and going for the last one. I slip in and press the door shut, then slide the lock.

I clamp my hand over my mouth to suppress a gasp. There's another name added under Tim's in black ink.

BECCA MARTIN. Scrawled in after the name is the phrase: think about it.

I bump into the toilet then back around it till I hit the wall, still facing the door. I can't think what Becca has to do with Tim, but it doesn't matter. I have to get rid of it. I can't let it become a thing. An actual list that people add names to.

I grab a pen from my backpack and drag it back and forth across the horrifying question. I do the same to the names, but my puny blue pen can do nothing to blot out what's there in permanent ink. I freeze when I hear the door swish open and closed. Good. I'm alone finally.

I could try scratching the writing out with my keys, but that would take forever. My best bet is asking for something from the janitor and hope he won't ask questions. Just hand over some harsh chemicals and a stiff scrub brush and nobody gets hurt.

I'm too late to get a decent lunch, so I grab a bag of chips to eat on the way to my next class, plotting the whole way how I'll get to the janitor's closet.

I skip a shower after sixth hour P.E., but nearly everyone does because it's the end of the school day. If I don't change out of my gym clothes I'll have to remember to bring them back in the morning, but I don't care. I have to hurry and find the janitor. I keep my head down and ignore the locker-room chatter as I move my school clothes into my backpack. Kirstie Kenyon squeals from the direction of the shower.

"Ladies, put it away or you'll be scrubbing those showers." The P.E. teacher, Ms. Herman, yells over the noise of girly voices and slamming lockers.

When I emerge from the changing area I see Angel Britton chasing Kirstie around with a spray bottle of cleaner. Maybe I can skip a trip to the janitor.

I head to the bathroom first, but I'll check the shower if I have to. In the corner a white wooden cupboard leans against the wall. I've never paid attention to it before, but now I rummage through to find, along with extra toilet paper and liquid soap, there is a whole shelf of cleaning supplies. Girls come in in bunches, forcing me into a stall to kill time. When the bathroom is quiet again I choose two kinds of cleaner and a package of scouring pads from the cupboard. There's no room in my bag, so plan B.

I shove the cleaning supplies into my backpack and lay the clothes over the top for the speed-walk back to my locker. Kirstie and Angel huddle near theirs, so they don't notice me pass. Fortunately, mine's in another section. I sit on the bench folding and refolding my towel, waiting for them to leave. Everyone else is gone except Ms. Herman who is on the phone in her office.

"That list is so creepy," I hear Angel say.

I grip my towel. So they've seen the writing in the bathroom, or at least heard about it. I wonder how many others have.

"Who do you think wrote it?" I can barely make out Kirstie's question.

Angel's not worried about volume. "Jen said it wasn't Taryn."

"I wish we had asked her about it."

"She and Chelsea are the obvious choices. They have the most reason to hate Tim Jenks," Angel says.

I hold my towel to my mouth, forcing myself not to react. I don't want them to know I'm still here.

"Seriously, though, doesn't everyone hate him?" Kirstie's not trying to keep her voice down anymore, and I can tell they're moving toward the door.

"Good point."

"But who would add Becca's name? That's just sick."

"A lot of people didn't like her, Kirstie. She was kind of stuck-up sometimes. Especially after she made head cheerleader."

"Angel, you shouldn't talk about her like that, now that she's . . . you know."

"I'm just saying."

I let out a breath when I hear the door shut behind them. After I wrap the bottles of cleaner with my towel, I lock up my clothes and hurry to the door. I make sure they're gone, then break into a run to get to the bathroom stall.

As I'm pulling open the door to the 200 building I hear a whistle.

"Looking good, Taryn." It's Travis and Paco coming out of the main office carrying boxes. I forgot I'm still in my gym clothes.

"Yeah, sweat's the new black." I lean against the door, hoping they'll just pass on by. Of course, they don't.

"Hey, we want to see that list in the girl's bathroom." Travis drops a big box by the door and Paco piles the two he's carrying on top.

I think my heart just dropped into my stomach. Everyone knows about the list. I'm too late to stop anything. "Sorry, guys, no." I keep my voice even, like it's no big deal. "Aren't you supposed to be at football practice?"

They're flying past me into the building before I even finish my sentence.

"It'll take a second." Travis throws back.

They know exactly which stall it is and they beat me to it. Somehow they cram themselves in together and immediately I hear laughing.

It's more than I can take. "It's not funny, you jerks. It's sick."

"No, you gotta see this, Taryn." They hurtle out and push me into it.

There's a third name.

JACKIE WEIR (BECAUSE WHO WOULD NOTICE)

I think I'm going to be ill.

"Take a picture," Paco says.

"Good idea. Taryn, here's my phone." Travis holds it up.

"You guys better get out of here." I step out, but keep the way blocked so they won't come back in.

"Oh, man, Coach is going to be wondering where we are with his boxes. C'mon, Paco." Travis yanks him toward the door.

"Text me a picture" is the last thing I hear before the door shuts behind them.

I return to the stall and stare at the list for a long time. In my backpack I've got supplies, but I don't think there's a bathroom cleaner strong enough to stop the damage that's already starting to spread.

Something has to be done, though. Stupid lists like this make high school kids do stupid things. As if seven deaths weren't enough . . . eight, counting Tim Jenks.

My cell phone vibrates and I pull it from my bag to check the text. It's from Jen.

I heard someone added another name.

I slip the cell back into the zippered pocket.

Here's my chance. Make a difference. Even in my head the phrase drips with sarcasm, but I walk straight to Mrs. Ames' room anyway.

I find her sitting at her desk. "I'd like to fill out an application for president."

She doesn't say anything, just pulls one from a drawer.

"Has anyone else signed up to run, I mean, besides Chelsea?"

I watch her shuffle through the bin. "Only one for president, and now yours."

A face-off with Chelsea is the last thing I need to start my senior year, but I quickly fill out the application and push it across the desk.

"Are you okay, Taryn?" Mrs. Ames looks concerned, or curious. Or maybe just confused.

I don't blame her. I am, too. "You said, 'everything back to normal as soon as possible,' right?"

9

I adjust my backpack, bracing myself against the late afternoon wind as I hike from the Language building to the office. The staff stays until four o'clock and I have a question for Phyllis.

"Where you been, sweetie?" Phyllis calls out the moment I see her. There's still an ache in her tone, though. "I thought I'd see you 'round school before today."

"Just had stuff to do." Sleep. A funeral. Decide to be president.

"So how was your first day back?"

"One down, too many to go." I force a smile. "Phyllis, do you know anything about Jackie Weir? She wasn't in homeroom today."

Phyllis frowns. "I sure do. That bitty thing withdrew Friday."

"Last Friday, like three days ago? Did she move?"

Another frown from Phyllis. "Personal reasons, I guess. Her records aren't being sent anywhere. You know what that means?" I shrug.

"She dropped out." Phyllis shakes her head.

I flash back to my earliest memories of Jackie when we were in seventh grade. Her white-blonde hair was thinning, but she didn't wear a hat back then. By freshman year, though, Jackie began wearing her denim hat everyday — then she seemed to withdraw from everyone. Or is that when everyone withdrew from her?

"Sad, that's what it is," Phyllis says.

"What do you mean?" I move in closer, propping my elbows on the counter.

"Well, I know she went through some hard spells, missed a lot of school, her momma was down here talking a lot to the principal." Phyllis's voice is uncharacteristically hushed.

"It seemed like she was trying to get back on track last year. She even had a tutor that was helping her get caught up in her classes." Phyllis shakes her head. "Poor thing. High school's hard enough without —"

"What do you mean?" I repeat the question.

"You know, her skin disease, Al'pecia. Guess it got to be too much."

"Everyone always said it was cancer." I grab my backpack when Phyllis turns her attention to a pair of girls who approach the attendance desk. I make a mental note to Google Alopecia.

"The nurse's office is across the hall to the

left." Phyllis directs with a swoop of her big arm. "Not sure if she's still 'round, though."

I wave goodbye like I'm going to leave, but instead drop my backpack and return to the counter with another question — one that has been tip-toeing around my brain for a solid week.

I speak up once the girls are gone. "Who is Tim Jenks' brother?"

"The one that interrupted the memorial?"

"Yeah. And what happened with him? He wasn't too happy after he talked to Mr. Myers."

"I heard he's in a tizzy because the principal told him maybe his brother is to blame for the fire."

"But how?"

"I don't know nothin', sweetie. Just that Timothy was a sweet boy. Wouldn't hurt nobody. He'd come by the office a couple of times a week just to say hi. He'd show me his latest drawing." She points to a bulletin board. "He gave me that one on the last day of school."

It's a pencil drawing of a woman — Phyllis — standing behind a counter holding a tardy slip with a sly grin on her face.

A door down the hall behind the attendance desk opens and a voice drifts our direction. Mr. Myers appears from around the corner. He has his cell phone up to his ear, but he tells whomever he's talking to to hold on.

"Time to close up shop, Phyllis," the principal says. "Survive the first day, Taryn?"

"Sure," I answer, but my eyes are rooted on Phyllis.

Mr. Myers jiggles his keys. "I'll see you bright and early tomorrow." I think he wants me to take the hint, so I follow him.

"Forgot my backpack." I turn to retrieve it from the floor. I glance across the counter one last time trying to make sense of Phyllis's words.

Something is messed up. Tim Jenks was not at Ritter's Crossing that night.

With the election assembly scheduled for first thing Friday morning, I am in need of some immediate inspiration for my speech's intro. Instead I sit at the family computer Thursday after school facing writer's block.

Last May I was voted in as VP of the student body. What's so different now? Okay, everything's different. I cocooned in my paisley comforter all summer, only coming out to attend funerals. I avoided talking to anyone and everyone. It was understandable after what happened and just because I said I wouldn't or couldn't be president doesn't mean I can't change my mind.

What does it matter? Everyone's probably voting for Chelsea anyway.

"D-i-s-a-p-p-o-i-n-t-m-e-n-t," I say each letter as I type. "No, it's stronger than that." I right-click on the word and synonyms appear.

"'Displeasure,' 'Distress,' 'Discontent.' Yes, yes, and yes. 'Frustration,' yes." I gesture to the air. "I'm frustrated. "I'm distressed!"

Mom pokes her head in the doorway of the den. "You're talking to yourself?"

I study the list of synonyms. "I'm 'displeasured!'"

"Displeasured?"

"It's not fair, Mom. Chelsea's got everyone on her side."

"First of all, you don't know that's true. Second, are you doing this for the everyone you're talking about?" She moves behind the computer chair to massage my neck. "Maybe because of them."

"What do you mean 'because of them?'"

"Taryn, don't get me wrong, I've always been happy you had friends and an opportunity to serve on student council." No one would guess it now, but my mom was picked-on in school. Her Ideal years were not her best.

"Maybe because of my experience at Ideal

High I've watched you, just to make sure you and your friends treat everyone with respect, no matter who they are."

"You constantly reminded me, how could I not." I close my eyes when Mom starts kneading my shoulders.

"I'm proud of you. I can't say that about everyone, but Kayla and Blake . . . I remember you telling me about Blake's ideas when you two were elected."

"Can we not talk about them, please?"

"And Chelsea —"

"I don't want to talk about her either."

"Fine. But you know the school's not perfect, right? I don't think much has changed since I went there. Oh, they were nice to your face, but, watch out."

I can't help cringing. The "ideal to your face" tradition goes back a long way.

"Mom, that's why I'm running — to make a difference, like Blake wanted to." I wish there were a less clichéd way to say it.

Mom ends the massage and slides the ottoman next to me. "Is that enough? What about what you stand for?"

"What do you mean?"

"Find what it is that speaks to you."

"Are you saying pull out the yoga mat and get in touch with the universe?" The wand lady from the cemetery comes to mind. "Sorry, my speech is tomorrow. Unless the universe is receiving instant messages now, there's no time for that."

"Write your speech — a really great one — but then pay attention to what you see and hear at school. You'll know before long what to focus on."

I don't tell her what I saw at school today. Whatever that list in the bathroom stall means, I want to stop it. No more victims at Ideal High.

"Thanks, Mom." I wiggle the mouse and stare at the screen. *Disappointment* is all that stares back.

Mom hits the backspace button to quickly erase it. "Think of it as a persuasive essay. Piece of cake." She starts for the door. "And speaking of cake, we're not having any, but dinner will be ready in twenty minutes."

"Like you would ever let us eat cake!" I call to her retreating form. My mother — the queen of yoga, goopy green shakes, and Momerly-advice.

I spend a couple hours after dinner at the computer writing and rewriting my speech. Finally, I click print, hoping it will sound better read out loud in front of my bedroom mirror and not the cliché-buffet it really is. *Taryn cares about you!*

Taryn will make a difference! Taryn will make Ideal High the best it can be! If I am going to beat Chelsea, my speech needs to catch the attention of the student body and the same tired phrases aren't going to do it. I grab the pages from the printer and march to my room.

"Fellow Classmates and Friends . . ." I rehearse to my reflection. Totally overdone opening. Universe, where are you?

I pull into the high school parking lot early Friday morning and park in the first row next to the only other vehicle in the vicinity, a lime green exterminator truck with bug-like antennae. I check my hair and makeup one last time in the rear view, and then check my watch. Exactly twenty-eight minutes till the election assembly begins.

I slip out of the front seat with my backpack, careful to avoid hitting the truck. The wind instantly whips through my hair, testing the limits of my mega-hold hair spray, but today was no day for a ponytail. I got up extra early to curl it.

I lock my car and smooth my bangs out of my eyes. I went more casual this time, so instead of wearing a jacket and nice pants like I did for May's election, I chose mid-calf white denims and paired them with a royal blue button-down shirt. Flats, no killer heels for me this time, complete the look.

"I keep running into you."

I look up and find I am toe-to-toe with Tim Jenks's brother. "Literally." I can't hide my disgust at seeing the guy with whom I'd suffered three unpleasant encounters.

"Yeah, sorry about that. Guess I was in a bad mood." He shifts the bug-spraying equipment he holds in his arms to pull ear buds from his ears.

"Which time? Or are you just always in a bad mood?" I can tell by the way his brows go up that my assumption gets to him.

"And today?" I ask when he doesn't answer.

"I'm good."

"Right." I analyze him from the top of his green-logoed cap, personalized work shirt and pants, down to his black steel-toed boots. I linger on the gold-embroidered name across his left pocket — *Levi*. The blue-eyed stranger has a name.

I pull my backpack up to my shoulder. I'm so lame. His brother died. Of course, he'll have bad moods. Do I think I'm the only one working through the stages of grief around here?

But if his brother did start the fire? I want to push the thought away, but curiosity gnaws at me. I drop my bag and abandon hopes of beating Chelsea into the auditorium.

"Do you mind me asking about the memorial? I'm curious why you say your brother died in the fire. I was there. I saw what happened."

"Did you?" The light in his eyes flares and shows in his tone. He pulls at his cap. "Sorry. I still have a hard time talking about it."

"But if someone's made a mistake, I agree, it should be fixed."

"I know. How else are people going to know the truth unless I talk about it?" Our eyes lock for a nano-second, then Levi attempts to move around me, forcing some awkward dance moves as I shimmy and he twists, and I almost make him trip over my backpack. Finally he succeeds in setting his equipment in the back of the truck, but he takes his time. When he finally speaks again, I can tell it's difficult.

"Tim worked weekends as a dishwasher at the country club, and he was working the night of your party." He spits out the word "your" like it has a bad taste, then his voice softens as he talks about his brother. "He never made it home. He wouldn't answer his phone, so we called his boss and all she said was he left work late."

He walks back up to the side of the truck. "The police said they couldn't do anything until he was missing twenty-four hours, then they got the call about the fire and they were too busy for us. It wasn't till way later they found his car just past Ritter's Crossing with his keys and wallet still in it."

I'm frozen in place, but when Levi pauses I chime in. "I never heard anything about his car until last weekend." What I really want to know is where Tim's body was found. I hope Levi will go there because I'm afraid to ask.

"Well, isn't it obvious why? Once everyone realized the Ideal High cheerleaders and their boyfriends were in that burning building they didn't care about anything else. That's all the news focused on."

"But I was there. I didn't see —" I don't know what else to say, but what I've already said a hundred times: *I was there. I know what I saw.*

"Did you know Tim?" Levi looks right through me, almost daring me to prove I wasn't one of the bullies who made his life miserable.

"I didn't know him personally. I mean, we weren't in the same grade." It's the truth. I don't have to admit that I saw him picked on. And did nothing. But really it was just a few times.

"He had a learning disability, so that made him a little slower at things. He got messed with a lot," Levi says. "My mom wanted to home school him, but Tim refused. He didn't understand why the kids teased him. He'd get mad, but he always thought it would be different the next day, you know? We lived in Lubbock, but she finally transferred him to Ideal, thinking the smaller school would be better." Something flares in his eyes again. "That was a big mistake. He was only here a month, at the most, when that jerk, Zeke Miller, beat him up."

"I'm so sorry." And I mean it. "I wish things had been different here, but why does Mr. Myers think Tim started the fire?"

"How do you know so much?" He narrows his eyes at me.

"I just do." Now Levi studies me before replying. "It doesn't matter. I'm never stepping foot on Ideal High's campus again."

I look down at his black work boots and gesture dramatically toward them.

"Okay, after this, I'm not stepping foot on campus again," he says.

A horn honks and suddenly I'm aware that everything has changed around me. Now the parking lot is nearly full and students line the sidewalks. The courtyard in front of the auditorium doors is a traffic jam of students streaming inside.

"No!" I gape at my watch, the time jolting me back to reality. "I have to give a speech in two minutes!" I pull my backpack up by a strap. "I'm running for president, like, right now!" I say to Levi's bewildered look. I set off for the auditorium, my bag banging my thigh with every step.

After sliding my backpack behind the stage curtain, I slip into the empty seat next to my impeccably-dressed opponent.

Chelsea looks at her watch. "I thought maybe you'd conceded."

"I thought you were kidding . . . when you said you were running." I'm still out of breath.

"It's a good thing I am."

I clamp my mouth shut, hoping I can keep what I feel like saying from leaking out. Somehow in the next few minutes I'm supposed to stand in front of the entire student body and give a coherent speech. I should be practicing one of my mom's relaxation techniques, not mincing words with my least favorite person.

I gesture between us. "Is this what you meant at the funeral when you said we need to talk?"

"No, but that doesn't matter now," she replies, and then suddenly Mr. Myers is announcing Chelsea Manor first on the program.

Her perfectly-crafted speech focuses on continuing traditions, traditions that have been a part of Ideal High School for over seventy years. She mentions it at least three times.

Seventy. Seventy. Seventy.

Applause at the conclusion of her speech startles me and it's then I first single out the faces of friends in the crowd. It isn't difficult because an entire section of them are on their feet yelling "Chel-SEA, Chel-SEA" in the familiar chant.

I peer at the ceiling. Here I am, exactly where I don't want to be — on stage in front of the whole school without Blake.

The auditorium grows quiet and Mr. Myers motions for me to go ahead. Apparently, he has already announced me and I zoned it out. Grateful for a podium to lean on, I stand and scan the crowd, searching for my voice. My speech can't compare to Chelsea's. Maybe I personally can't compare to Chelsea. Why would anyone cast a vote for me when perfection sits behind me in a designer suit?

I could state the obvious — she's head cheerleader, she doesn't have time to be president. Or go for humor — Chelsea Manor sounds more like an upscale subdivision than a president.

What about the lawsuit? Do you want to elect someone who is being sued over the death of seven of our classmates?

Pull it together. Forget Chelsea.

I glance at my speech. The words look foreign, kind of like my Anatomy notes so far this week, though I practiced in the car on the way to school. I exhale deeply. Cliché, I know, but what else do you do when you need to stall. I study the postage stamp-sized auditorium windows. Cloud cover blocks the sun today.

A door scrapes open and Levi Jenks, cap in hand, slides inside and parks himself at the back wall. In that instant, a memory flashes of Levi at Stan's gas station on our way home after the funeral. He said I was part of his problem. I should have confronted him about the comment, but after talking to him about Tim, I think I know what he means.

And I know what I need to say.

"I want to tell you a story." I take a long breath, hoping to control the tremor in my voice.

"It's about a boy." I continue, but still tentatively. "A boy not that different than you and me."

I speak right into the microphone, gaining some momentum. "He wanted to go to school, but because he was a little slow people made fun of him. He even got beat up because of it. He kept showing up every day, thinking that day would be different. Maybe he would have some real friends. I don't know the whole story of what happened to this boy, I hope to find out," — I direct this comment to the back wall — "but one more thing you need to know is that he was a student here at this school, our own Ideal High School."

I pause, then realize there's another person's story I want to share. "I could also tell you a story about a girl. She was a little different, too. She walked these halls hoping to hide in the crowd, so no one would whisper comments about her under their breath when she passed. I don't know much about her either, except to say she dropped out Friday, before school even started for the year." I scan the crowd, but the faces blur in front of me.

"The rumors are true. I didn't want to be president. Not after what happened." My emotions catch in my throat and I take a moment to breathe again. "Eight students died. They're not faceless names we add to lists on bathroom walls. None of us are. We cannot be the same people we were before the accident. We can't be the same school. What we need is no more ideal just to your face, but a new Ideal High tradition."

A pin-drop stillness hangs in the air for a moment before the auditorium explodes in applause. All I can think about, though, are my new projects: bringing Jackie Weir back to school and finding out what happened to Levi Jenks' brother.

And getting the janitor to paint over that list.

10

A-l-o-p-e-c-i-a.

I stretch in the chair, arching my back and my toes, waiting for Google to do its thing. Finally, I am doing something besides lying in bed. Even if I lose the election to Chelsea, I can still instigate change at the school. Miss Cheerleader might try to block me every step of the way, but what will stop her from doing that even if I'm president.

I click a link and begin to read about Jackie's skin condition.

Alopecia areata is a hair-loss condition which usually affects the scalp, the website states. *The body's own immune system attacks the hair follicles and disrupts normal hair formation.* I skim-read down the web page to its ending statement. *Definitive cause unknown.*

Jackie's not sick or contagious, but no one will get near her. And none of it's her fault.

I start a new search. B-u-l-l-y-i-n-g. A drop-down box appears with a list of more specific topics. *Bullying in schools.* I start there.

City schools target bullying. I click on the link.

A school in Ohio is cracking down on bullying. *Bullying in schools has become such a major issue affecting the health of the nation's kids that the American Academy of Pediatrics now urges doctors to . . .*

I skim the article. "We have a policy on bullying," a high school official is quoted as saying. "We do not tolerate it."

Right. I click the back arrow, and peruse the links again. I choose another option. A video plays showing a woman standing in front of a large white board.

We must learn to recognize the signs of bullying because victims often hide what is happening due to embarrassment, the doctor-of-something says. *They don't want to appear weak or look bad in front of their peers, or even their family. That is why it goes unreported.*

I try to imagine the reaction Jackie might receive if she ever went to the principal. *Everyone ignores me or calls me "Tacky" under their breath when they pass me in the hall.* What could Mr. Myers even say?

The expert steps to the white board to discuss bullet points. *The victim may appear unusually angry or sad. They may appear anxious. You may observe them withdrawing from friends and family.*

They may lose interest in school work.

Or they'll drop out altogether like Jackie, or be slammed day after day like Tim. The expert's list continues, but my thoughts focus on the two of them. How could things have been different?

I select a new link titled *Bullying and Suicide*, but when a list of recent stories in national news pops up, I click out of it. I don't want to go there. Instead I open a new Google search box and type in Tim's name. Two items pop up besides the news article I read last weekend about the interrupted memorial.

The first one is a blurb about sixth-grader Timothy Jenks winning first prize for his entry in the elementary school's Reflections contest. The theme that year was "Dream Big," and his drawing was of a moon landing with an astronaut meeting several intricately-drawn aliens.

The second is listed under the title Freedom Junior High News. Maryanne Jenks complains to the school board after her son, seventh-grader, Tim Jenks, is punched in the face by fellow student, Dallas Hardy. *"The bullying has occurred non-stop since the start of school without any consequences," Mrs. Jenks says. Hardy's parents stand by him, saying, "He's a good kid, but we teach him to stand up for himself."*

Monday morning I gather with the candidates for office in the outer area of the school's broadcast booth to hear the election winners announced. Mrs. Ames sits on camera next to Mr. Myers as he reads the names, and the video is transmitted to the entire school. "We're pleased to announce our new student body president — Taryn Young."

I won?

The noise in the room combines to drown out the rest of the announcements for me. I think I hear Jen Foster's and Kirstie Kenyon's names, but it's kind of a blur.

"Let's hear a few words from your newly-elected president." Mr. Myers motions from the other side of the viewing window for me to come into the booth. "The other officers can join us, too."

Fortunately, Ms. McKinney opens the side door and points me toward the table where the school administrators sit because I'm still back at "I won?" I take a seat next to Mrs. Ames who smiles and pats my arm.

"Go ahead, Miss Young." Mr. Myers turns the microphone to me.

"I don't know what to say." Finally, I look into the camera as my brain kicks into on-air mode. "I appreciate everyone who helped me with the campaign and congratulations to the other new officers." I glance at the video monitor that shows what's being broadcast and see Jen and Kirstie standing behind me.

"I'm excited to get to work and hope that you are, too, because it will take all of us to make Ideal, well, ideal." I bite my lip. Yeah, I'm the first person to ever say that.

I lean back in my seat and slide the mic toward the principal. Just as quickly I pull it back. "I want to encourage anyone who has an interest in cheerleading to come to tryouts. That's what Ideal High should be about. All of us having the same opportunities academically, socially . . . whatever. So don't forget tryouts begin today after school in the gym." I push away from the table as the crew shuts down the equipment.

Mr. Myers shakes my hand. No congratulations for winning the election, just a stiff handshake and tone to match. "Mrs. Ames will keep me informed."

At least Mrs. Ames is happy for me. "You'll do a great job, Taryn." She leans in before continuing. "And, I thought you'd want to know. The writing on that bathroom door has been painted over."

That's a relief.

"New officers meet after school." Mrs. Ames herds everyone out behind the principal.

Chelsea steps into the open doorway to block

my path, moving far enough into the room to allow the door to swing shut behind her. "Excuse me." She folds her arms and leans forward.

She's starting already.

"I think I'm in charge of announcements about cheerleading tryouts."

"Check it out." The cameraman motions to the rest of the crew. He turns the camera on us, pretending to frame the shot.

I ignore Chelsea's comment, reaching for the door instead. "Excuse me, you're in my way."

Chelsea doesn't budge. "I hope you know all you have are geeks and losers on your side. Apparently, there are a lot more of them at this school than I thought."

"Why did you even want to be president if you think so little of the student body?" I throw back at her.

"You tell her, sistah," the equipment manager calls from behind the sound system. Chelsea glares his direction.

"Thanks for the vote of confidence, Carlos." I offer a weak smile.

"Oh, I don't have any confidence, but I did vote for you," he replies.

"Proves my point!" Chelsea storms out, letting the door slam behind her.

I look up to see Mr. Myers waving his arms in front of the plate glass window that separates the broadcast booth from the outer area. With wide eyes the principal frantically gives the signal to cut. Finally, he throws open the door.

“Cut the camera!” he roars. The scene between me and Chelsea has just been broadcast to every classroom of every building on Ideal High’s campus.

11

Geeks and losers. Chelsea said it, not me, but still everyone brings it up in every single class, all day long. I'm sick of it.

I leave P.E. with Kirstie because we're both heading to Mrs. Ames' room for a quick meeting. Angel, who has changed into spandex-everything for cheer tryouts, walks with us partway, but doesn't say anything. It's totally not like her. Is she jealous because we're on student council and she's not? About halfway across the courtyard, she stops and turns around.

"See you at tryouts, Kirstie. Don't be too late or they might take off points. You don't want to hurt your chances."

I can tell Kirstie purposely doesn't react.

Angel turns to me. "How about you, Taryn? You trying out?"

"Yeah . . . no. I can't do a cartwheel to save my life."

"Exactly. Not everybody can be a cheerleader, right?" Angel looks at me, like, *hurray, someone gets it,* but I'm not going to let her suck me in. I'm not getting in the middle of whatever is going on between her and Kirstie.

When Angel leaves to join a group of girls heading to the gym, Kirstie's relief is evident. "I don't know what her problem is. She knows they don't keep track of points on the first day. And 'not everybody can be a cheerleader?' She should know. She tried out last year and didn't make it."

I don't say anything. Maybe everyone's a little on edge because it's still so strange being back at school after the deaths of so many of our friends. We wouldn't even be having cheer tryouts again if it weren't for the fire.

Mrs. Ames and Jen Foster are already waiting in room 212 when we come in. "Pull up some desks, girls, and we'll get started." Mrs. Ames has been the student council advisor for years, so I'm counting on her to keep things moving when I don't know what I'm doing. Like now. She goes over meeting procedures and officer duties. Jen ran unopposed for VP and Kirstie beat out J.T. for secretary/historian.

Finally, our advisor sets aside her papers and looks at each of us in turn. "As class leaders, you have a huge role in making this school year a good one despite the tragedy. I hope you will take this charge seriously. Taryn, do you have anything you'd like to share right now?"

A flashback of sitting in this same room with her and Blake last May slams up against my brain. I swallow hard, forcing myself to speak. "The fire — " I spit the word out to get it past my lips. "I think we're forced to change because of it. It's a good time to ask ourselves what we can do to make this school better for every student."

Jen sticks her hand up to interrupt. "Why should we care that some girl dropped out? Isn't that her problem?"

I stare-down Jen for a moment before responding. "I think she dropped out because she was getting picked on. Maybe that's the old way of doing things, so let's start a new tradition of treating everyone with respect." If Jen wants to talk about Jackie specifically, I'm happy to go there.

"Respect is part of the school's motto. What more do you want?" Jen doesn't try to hide a cynical tone.

"I want people to actually follow the motto then. If kids are bullied for being different, how can they succeed?" I state it as deliberately as I can.

"Well, they should get some new clothes, fix their hair cute, so they're not so different." Jen flips her hot-iron straight hair with a wave of her hand.

Did she really just say that? I let her have it.

"You embarrassed Jackie Weir in front of everyone at Kayla's funeral and the next day she withdrew from school. Explain that, Jen." I see Kirstie's jaw drop, but I don't care. Might as well get it all out on the table.

"Since when are you the queen-of-treating-people-nicely, Taryn? You don't care about Jackie Weir any more than I do. And don't put her in the same category as that guy who started the fire. She's not going to lose it and pull a 'Tim-Jenks.'" Jen drops both her hands on the desk and leans forward. "Why are you talking about a murderer in your election speech anyway? That's messed up."

"Okay, girls." Mrs. Ames attempts to insert herself into the conversation.

"Everyone keeps saying that about Tim, but it doesn't make it true." I rub my temples in an effort to calm down. "My point is, we should help everyone feel included, or at least accepted."

"Accepted?" Jen purses her lips. "Seems like if anyone wants to be "accepted," then they best be enrolled as a student, don't ya' think?"

Jen does not want to know what I think. Not here in front of Mrs. Ames, and Kirstie, who has chosen to stay silent. She's probably counting the seconds till she can escape to the gym, even if it means more of Angel's attitude.

I lean forward in my seat and stare daggers at Jen. "I want to convince Jackie Weir to come back."

"What?" Jen is flippant, but without the obligatory hair-toss to go with it this time. "I didn't sign up for that."

Talk about being on edge because we're back to school after the tragedy. I was planning on Jen as my best ally and here we are having it out at our very first student body officers' meeting.

She's not done, though. "I'm sorry, but we have to plan the Howdy Dance, and Homecoming is right around the corner. I don't see where begging someone to come back to school fits in."

Avoiding Jen's glare, I focus on Kirstie. "I'd like to have a committee with students from each grade level to oversee clubs and programs that will bring the student body together. We'll have teachers recommend students and that way we'll get a good representation from the whole school. It won't be a popularity contest." I look hard at Jen now. Maybe I should speak more slowly and with smaller syllables. If it isn't about being popular it's most likely a foreign language to her.

I shuffle my notes. She's right, there is a lot to do, but Levi's comments about his brother keep coming to mind. It's too late for Tim now, but there are others just like him walking the halls of Ideal

High. Jen will never get it if she can't see helping Jackie.

Jen doesn't say anything, so, poor Kirstie, she finally sees her chance. "I'm supposed to be at cheer tryouts. Can I go now?"

"Of course. Let's let this settle and we'll meet again in a few days." Mrs. Ames tries to wrap it all up in a neat little package, but she's clearly relieved Kirstie has given us an out.

Kirstie grabs her belongings and is gone, leaving Jen and I to head to the door in silence. Once we're out of the classroom, Jen stops me. She moves from aggressive to passive. "I don't get it, Taryn. Like, now suddenly you care about Tacky Jackie? Why?"

Heat flashes along my jaw line. "Don't call her that."

"I'm serious, who's next? Those Goth-throwbacks? Taryn, you can't save everyone."

I tighten the grip on my backpack. "What's wrong with trying?"

Tuesday night after dinner, I spread books and papers in front of me on the bed to do homework. Both college scholarships and parent-offered privileges depend on good grades in spite of the time school-president requires. Plus, I'll do anything to keep from thinking too much about today.

Jen Foster and Kirstie Kenyon resigned from their positions. That's what Mrs. Ames said when I met her after school. I don't know which feeling was stronger — relief or bitterness. All I know is I'm in trouble. The Howdy Dance, always held the second weekend of a new school year, is only days away.

I position pillows behind me, wondering why Jen and Kirstie ran for office in the first place. Obviously, they assumed Chelsea would win, but I can't help thinking if Blake had been leading the meeting yesterday they would have hung on his every word.

Why aren't you here, Blake? I push my books to the floor and maneuver under my comforter. I should not be doing this. I have no business being the president of an entire student body. One minute I'm smuggling doughnuts into homeroom for the cutest guy on campus and the next I'm on stage asking people to choose me to lead the school.

And in between a horrible thing happened that took away my reason for all of it. Thanks, Universe.

I lay for a long time, clutching my comforter to my chin, but nothing new comes. I guess the Universe is as stumped as I am about what to do without a single student body officer to work with.

On Wednesday, every hour of school crawls by. I figure everyone knows that the vice-president and secretary bailed on me. At lunch I hide in the courtyard to eat alone. I don't feel like talking to anyone. Really, I guess I'm avoiding Jen and Kirstie. Fortunately, in P.E. Kirstie hangs close to Angel and I never have to make eye contact.

After class is over, I slip back into the gym and find a spot in the bleachers where I can watch cheer tryouts. At a table front and center, Chelsea sits with Ms. Hightower and the head of the P.E. Department, Ms. Herman, watching the dance routine in progress on the gym floor. Dressed in a Bulldog cheerleading uniform and a ponytail tied with red and blue ribbons, she looks the picture of head-cheerleader-ness perfection. Today is the final tryout. Thursday morning a list will be posted of those making the final cut and after a cheer assembly, the student body will vote.

The routine ends with all the girls displayed in various poses before collectively running to the far side of the gym to wait for instructions. One at a time, Ms. Hightower calls the girls out for their solo routines while Chelsea and the two teachers scribble observations on sheets of paper in front of them.

Boos erupt from the stands when a short, but muscular girl runs to the center of the gym and begins her cheer routine. It's Persimmon Glick, the student with the most unusual name, but she looks way different than last year. Her now pink-streaked hair is pulled back in short, thick braids, and her eye make-up overdone in jet black. A thick metal cross flies out from under her sports tank after her first leap. She's really not that bad. Obviously, she's had some gymnastics training.

Besides shushing the crowd once, the panel does nothing to stop the interruptions. When sporadic boos begin again, I can't take it. I slide off the edge of the bleachers and inch my way forward. I look back, trying to determine the offenders and spot a couple of jock-wannabes laughing and pointing where they sit along the wall on the top row.

Without thinking, I dart to the judges' table and kneel down. "Isn't someone going to do something about those jerks?" I whisper too loudly.

"We've asked them to be quiet," the P.E. teacher replies, not taking her eyes off the routine.

Suddenly, one of the guys yells out in a deep voice, "Next!" Flustered, the girl at center court fumbles and stops mid-step in her dance routine, then pleads for the music to be started over.

"Ms. Hightower?" My tone surprises even me. The P.E. teacher turns to the cheer advisor and shrugs.

Ms. Hightower stands and motions for the music to stop, then addresses the stands. "Please refrain from inappropriate comments."

I stand up, too. "That's it?"

"We're handling this."

"How? By letting them stay?" I gesture toward the gym floor. "She shouldn't have to put up with this." I say it louder than I mean to. Someone claps randomly.

"Listen to the prez," comes from the same guy who yelled "Next," followed by an offensive comment from his buddy.

"Excuse me, are you talking to me?" I gesture to the jerk in the stands.

"Taryn, you're making it worse," Chelsea hisses.

"She deserves a chance!" The phrase explodes from my lips. The gym gets quiet. Persimmon drops her red and blue pom poms and dashes out the side door, her cheeks nearly matching her hair color. All eyes turn to me with one big accusatory glare.

"That's all I'm saying." I shrug back. My tone is much quieter now. "Everyone deserves a chance." I duck out the gym doors, mentally shaking myself. I go from being elected president to melting down in front of a gym full of people. I round a corner and nearly run right into Phyllis who hurries past without saying a word.

"Phyllis, are you okay?"

She stops and turns around. "Oh, baby, I didn't see you. It's my boy. My neighbor says he got off the bus with a busted lip. He won't answer the phone. I've been talking to the school, but they don't know nothin' about it."

"I'm so sorry."

"I tell you what, you get Ideal straightened out and the elementary school's next. I'm sick and tired of my baby getting picked on. The year's just starting and it's the same old thing." Phyllis continues toward the parking lot muttering as she goes.

I give her some space before I head to the parking lot, too. I climb into my car and then berate myself all the way home. What compelled me to take on cheer tryouts? All I wanted to do is stick up for Persimmon, but I made it worse.

Phyllis shouldn't put such faith in me. I still haven't made an effort to contact Jackie Weir and really I have no idea how to convince her to return to Ideal High anyway. And what happened to Tim Jenks is still a mystery.

I crank up the volume on the radio in an effort to drown out my failure. I remember when I thought last summer would never end, and now, suddenly, time seems to be moving so fast. I need results and yet I haven't taken a single step forward. More than several backward in fact and I'm not helping my case by interrupting cheer tryouts.

I slam on my brakes, but the hood of my car sticks out well past the stop sign into the intersection. I wave a weak apology to the driver crossing in front of me, then sink into my seat till the driver behind me honks. I make a right turn and pull immediately into the gas station at the corner and put the car in park. Fumbling through my backpack till I find last year's IHS directory, I punch in the number for Jackie Weir.

Time to take a baby step forward.

12

The number I try is disconnected, so I find an address on my phone and study the directions. I run into the convenience store for a mini bag of Hot Cheetos and a bottle of water, and then jump back in my car, afraid I might lose my nerve if I don't go right now.

I head out to Ranch Creek in search of Jackie's house on Sage Lane. It's one of the smaller-than-Ideal spots on the map that feed into the high school. The kids from here are called cowboys, though there are plenty of city kids that receive the same label. They generally dress the part with boots and plaid shirts and the hideously large, shiny belt buckles associated with rodeos.

As I fidget on the Weir porch after pressing the doorbell, I wonder about belt buckles and what Levi's looks like. The times I've seen him, his shirttail is always hanging casually over the top of his comfortably-worn jeans.

I lift the hair off my neck and wipe away the dampness. No breeze today. A wooden rocking chair sits motionless next to the door, and a tin milk-jug-turned-planter holds fake yellow daisies.

My eyes flit across the porch to the trim, summer-brown front lawn. Many of the homes on the street appear vacant and long-past cared for, but the Weir house doesn't fit that stereotypical image of Ranch Creek. Its appearance reassures me somehow. Maybe despite the constant rudeness Jackie experiences every day at school, she comes home to a happy, smiling family. Well, minus the one brother who yelled at her to get in the car after the funeral.

Standing motionless on the porch, I hope it's true. If Jackie's torture doesn't end when the school bell rings . . . that's more than I can think about right now.

The Indian summer-heat and my nerves urge me to give up the attempt, but I try the doorbell again. As an afterthought, I reach inside the screen door to knock, but nothing stirs. I am more than ready to deem my trip an un-success, but I press my face to the narrow window alongside the front door anyway, wanting to satisfy my curiosity about how Jackie Weir lives.

Peering through the sheer curtain on the other side of the glass, I note the dated, but neatly-kept interior. The rumble of an ATV startles me as its rider pulls up front and cuts the engine.

"Is that how you get your information?" Levi Jenks yells from the gravel beyond the lawn's edge.

I cringe. "No. I'm looking for somebody. What does it look like I'm doing?" I call back.

Levi opens his mouth to reply.

I cut him off before he can say anything. "Don't answer that." I smooth my hair back behind my ears and rub at the spot on my forehead where I pressed against the window. "I guess nobody's home."

"Good guess."

Levi stays put on his four-wheeler, so I step off the porch and walk across the grass. He looks just like the guys at school in his Tech baseball cap.

"You know Jackie?" I ask when I get close enough to speak in a normal tone.

"Do you?" Levi cocks his head at me.

"Well, I . . . sorta." Until recently Jackie sat in front of me in homeroom, but I'd never said two words to her till Kayla's funeral. It's an unspoken rule. Don't talk to the invisible girl.

"Why are you looking for her?" Levi says.

I know what he's thinking. Who has ever come looking for Jackie Weir?

"I want to ask her to come back to school."

"Why do you —"

"Why do I care?" The same question Jen asked

earlier in the week. “I don’t know. I just want to do something decent as president. Is there anything wrong with that?”

Levi’s brows crease. “Of course not. It’s very noble, or something.”

“Maybe I didn’t care before and now I do. So what?”

“That’s your answer, ‘so what?’ Not very convincing.” He adjusts his baseball cap.

“Do I have to have a reason?”

“No, now you care. Whatever.” Now he pulls his hat off and rakes his fingers through his hair before putting it back on.

“Thank you.” Why do I always get irritated around this guy? I force myself to relax enough to take note of Levi’s appearance. First time ever I’ve seen him in a T-shirt. In place of boots he wears actual tennis shoes. And he looks good. And the ATV inviting.

“I am curious, though,” Levi begins.

“What? Now you’re going to say I need a reason?” I throw my hands up, purposefully pouring on the drama.

“Sorry, I’ll stop talking about it.” He revs his engine like he’s thinking about leaving.

If he isn’t going to offer, I have to make the first move. “Give me a ride and I’ll tell you whatever you want to know."

A grin slides across his face and he revs the engine again. Gravel flies as the back tires spin in the dirt. "Climb on."

I position myself behind him, but now I'm not so sure about this. Where do I hold on?

"Do you want the 'grandma' ride or the —"

Levi's words are lost in the growl of the engine and the wind that whips my hair as we peel out onto the roughly paved road. Quickly, I'm forced to grab hold of his middle, choosing safety over any sense of respectability.

The pavement ends a few houses down, but the four-wheeler doesn't hesitate as we hop onto a dirt path. I grip tighter, if that's possible, and bury my face in his back in an effort to hide from the dust stirring up.

Levi yells something I can't make out. Maybe a comment about the condition of the trail ahead because soon it's less bumpy and the dust stops almost completely. I lift my head to take in the dry brush and quiet creek that the path follows.

"Haven't you been on one of these before?" Levi calls back when conversation becomes possible.

"Not even a 'grandma ride,'" I say to his shoulder blade.

We slow around a smooth bend, then picking up speed, shoot across the creek over a makeshift wooden bridge, each jolt of the quad pushing me into Levi's back. Here the trail opens up and the ATV, too, as Levi increases our speed. I mold my body with his, making an effort to move with him. I'm determined to prove I can handle whatever he and the four-wheeler dish out.

Despite the warm temperature and the sweat spreading where our bodies touch, I can't suppress a squeal as we race along at increasing speeds. A heady energy surges through me and I feel the school issues that plagued my week slough off in a rush of air. When is the last time I felt like this? Certainly not since last May.

"Ya' ready?" Levi says. The ATV idles briefly, before we're off again, heading straight for a sloping dirt hill.

"For what?" I don't have time to catch my breath before we hit the first incline. I twist his T-shirt in my fingers and hug his back.

Levi slows the four-wheeler down, taking the next one at a bunny-slope beginner's pace by comparison. "You okay?"

I tilt my chin toward his ear. "This is great. But do you ever ride anything less . . . energetic? Like a pony? A skateboard, maybe?"

Levi laughs. "We could try one of those."

I like how he says we, and that surprises me.

It's all too soon when we roll to a stop alongside a spigot next to a huge cinder block shed. I slide off the vehicle, grimacing at the line of sweat across his waist where I clung so tightly. "Sorry about that."

Levi laughs his big laugh again. "Sweat happens." He lifts a shirt sleeve to his face to wipe his forehead, then flips the water on till a decent stream flows. He motions me toward it. "Go ahead."

Kneeling down, I fill my cupped hands and drink. When I finish, Levi moves in beside me. I scoop a handful of water and playfully toss it toward him, but he doesn't even care. Instead he fills his hands with water and dumps it over his own head and down his back, then holds his mouth under the spigot for a long drink.

I stand there watching him till I feel self-conscious that I'm enjoying it too much. "Well, it's no fun splashing you if you're just going to pour it all over yourself."

"You could throw me in a cold lake right now and I wouldn't care. I'm so dang hot." He lies back in the rough grass with his knees bent and arms outstretched.

I drop next to him and sit cross-legged. Cupping a hand over my eyes to block the late afternoon sun, I study Levi as subtly as possible. I decide to let his last statement slide without comment.

"I guess if we were smart we'd find some shade," he says, but doesn't move.

"Shade is good," I murmur. I weigh the irony of the situation. There are hefty issues I could be discussing with Levi Jenks, but here we sit, just chilling, talking about shade.

"Okay, come on." Levi gets to his feet and reaches a hand out to pull me up.

I take it, but protest. "We don't have to, really."

"No, c'mon." He tugs me toward him. "I can find us something better to drink." He doesn't let go, but leads me through the yard up to a patio at the back of a house. His house, it turns out. It occurs to me that I haven't even wondered why he showed up in front of Jackie's. Makes sense now. He lives in the neighborhood.

He pushes together two patio chairs then disappears through the back door. When he returns he's carrying two cans of Coke. "That's cool you're president." He holds one out to me.

"I guess. It's harder than I expected." I take the can and open it.

"But the school year just started, right?"

"I guess," I say again. "I can see that trying to change things isn't going to be easy, even when it's for something better." I look up from my drink. "I still need to figure out what better is exactly."

Moments pass, but it doesn't seem awkward. "I liked what you said in your speech," Levi says finally.

"Pretty brave of you to show your face in the auditorium again." I drop my gaze. "I saw you sneak in the back." I take a long drink and hope I didn't just get too personal.

Levi makes a face. "Kind of stupid, huh?"

"Why did you?"

"I don't know. Just curious." Levi downs the last of his Coke and sets the can on the nearby redwood table. "Anyway, it's nice you talked about my brother."

"Maybe I can help someone like him." I lean over to place mine next to his.

Levi nods, but doesn't say anything. We sit in silence till he speaks again. "I was a terrible brother."

A mixture of pain and tenderness crosses his face, but I can't think of what to say to his quiet admission.

"I should have protected Tim. I should have

had his back. Maybe he'd be alive today."

"You can't say that. He was just in the wrong place at the wrong time."

"Interesting coming from you who doesn't believe he was there that night."

I squirm in my seat. "Everyone's saying your brother was there and that he started the fire. You know that, right?"

Levi's expression darkens. "Yeah, but they're wrong. Tim wouldn't do that."

"No offense, but that's easy to say." Someone put his name on a bathroom door saying he deserved to die in the fire, but I don't mention that part.

Levi seems to think about my comment. Suddenly he turns in his seat to fully face me. "Remember you said you'd tell me whatever I want to know?"

"Yeah." I lock eyes with him.

"You didn't see Tim, but what did you see the night of the fire?"

My carefree four-wheeling and heart-to-heart with a gorgeous cowboy grinds to a halt. I sink back into the molded plastic chair. I see Levi again as the intruder at the memorial. I relive the echoes of his boot steps on the stage floor, his jarring question, *What about my brother?* He doesn't even believe I know what I'm talking about when I describe what happened at Ritter's Crossing.

"Are you okay?" Levi reaches out to touch my knee.

It isn't fair. Today is the first time I really enjoyed myself since forever.

"You just caught me off guard. When I said I'd tell you anything, I thought we were talking about Jackie Weir."

"I'm sorry," Levi says. "I know no one likes talking about the fire." He slides his chair in front of me and leans forward with his elbows to his knees. He runs a hand over his chin before looking up at me. "I have a confession to make."

My heart races to my stomach, not sure of what to expect, a something-good confession or a something-bad one.

"I've wanted to talk to you for a long time," he continues.

The instant realization hurts. "About the fire, right?" The words catch in my throat. Even after the ride on the four-wheeler, all we have between us is the fire.

"Yeah, but there never seemed to be a good time, you know. Whenever I saw you before —" His voice trails off.

I purse my lips. I can't look at him.

"Anyway, I was hoping you'd help me talk to Chelsea Manor, so I can get her take on what happened."

That's not a something-bad confession. It's even worse.

13

I don't look at Levi, but feel his deep eyes on me. He's sitting so close our knees almost touch, so it gets awkward pretty quick.

Finally, I have to say something because he's waiting for me to. "Chelsea and I don't talk." I stand up, pushing my chair back to put distance between us. "Anyway, I doubt I can help you. I'm part of your problem, right? You said so yourself." I look out toward the fields we were just joy-riding in and bite back rising resentment. The tragedy. It's the "center" of everything I do.

Levi seems to still be waiting, not accepting what I'm trying to say, so I continue. "I can see that what I thought I knew about that night is way off."

I don't care that he's confused when I reject a ride back to my car parked at Jackie's. He shows me where to cut through the block to return to Sage Lane, and I march through the tall grass without looking back.

When I arrive home, I lock myself in the bathroom for a shower instead of joining my family for dinner. I adjust the temperature to the hottest I can stand and grab the soap. It shoots out of my hand, so I reach for the shampoo instead. After dumping way too much, I scrub my scalp hard. I don't know what's wrong with me because I don't want a relationship. Certainly not with Levi and his tragedy-related baggage. What am I thinking jumping on his four-wheeler for a ride?

Bubbles roll off me in bunches and I scrub harder. I only want Blake, the one person I can never have again.

A stocky girl with obsidian-colored hair and the clothes to match barricades my locker when I arrive at school Thursday morning.

"I saw what you did yesterday at cheer tryouts." Apparently not a fan of introductions. "You know you made it worse."

"I didn't mean to. I just —"

Locker Girl interrupts. "Let me guess, you wanted to help?"

"Of course."

"Well, we don't need you.' She shakes her head, flashing an array of black-themed ear piercings. "Why do people like you always think you need to help people like us?"

"What are you talking about? I'm happy to help anyone."

"Ah. The campaign promises."

I drop my backpack at my feet. I didn't come to school today for this. Gazing up at the girl, I will myself to keep calm. "You know what? I feel bad about yesterday, I really do. But as far as promises for this year, if you'd like a say in anything you should get an application from your homeroom teacher to join the advisory committee."

"Yeah, right. No one would ever vote me onto a school committee."

"There's not going to be a vote," I explain, but the girl isn't listening.

"Obviously, you've never had to worry about this, but people like us, we try to avoid attention. How Persi thought she could try out for cheer and not have people mocking her, I don't know, but what I'm saying is, we get through the day by trying to make ourselves invisible. If someone gives us a bad time, we try to hide more."

I want to ask which *us* the girl is referring to. The *us* that are six feet tall and, well, stocky, or the *us* that dresses like the dead of night and has ebony as the color scheme of their makeup routine. Either way, there is no hiding for this girl.

Instead, I say, "You shouldn't have to come to school and hide." This seems to soften the girl's demeanor. A little. If that's possible.

The slamming of locker doors punctuates the silence that follows as the hall around us empties. I snatch up my backpack, deciding to forgo the needed book from my locker. “Can you tell Persimmon I’m sorry?”

“Fine.” The girl swings her own bag to her substantial shoulder. “You know, my homeroom teacher actually said he wanted to nominate me for that committee thing, but I shot him down.”

“No, you should totally do it,” I reply. Because what else can I say.

“You’re good. You almost say it like you mean it. And, by the way, Persimmon prefers being called Persi.” The girl turns on her military black boot heel and vanishes before I can defend myself.

Dangerously late anyway, I make a mad dash to homeroom, barely stepping into the classroom as the final bell sounds. I drop into my seat, feeling slightly more optimistic than when I awoke that morning, but not sure why. Maybe because Locker Girl didn’t take a swing at me.

Any optimism comes to a screeching halt when I notice students passing a cell phone back and forth. The glances, which I can only categorize as *furtive*, in my direction confirm it. I turn to the girl in the desk next to mine. “What’s on that cell phone?” Her nod drips with sympathy.

After homeroom and a numbing hour of English — vocabulary words from the latest ancient literary masterpiece inflicted on us — and more cell phone-sharing while our teacher isn't looking, which is always — I go to the nurse's office feigning a headache. Lying on a paper strip centered on vinyl-upholstered furniture does nothing to calm the anxiousness gnawing at my insides. I really do feel sick. I turn to the wall and pull my knees to my chest, the paper complaining with every muscle moved. I picture the cheer routine splayed across the internet for all to see. How had my good intentions backfired? I only wanted Persimmon to be treated fairly. Persi.

Sounds from the next sick room drift through the walls. A girl's pathetic plea, "Stop texting me," is hard to miss even though I'm not in the mood to eavesdrop.

I twist onto my back again to stare at the yellowed popcorn ceiling, wondering if my new no-name locker friend ever hides here. The crackling groan of paper underneath competes with the voice inside my head. The one from before that said I am done hiding.

"I told you I won't," comes from the next room. The same voice, but more insistent.

When I hear the bell signaling the end of

second hour, I sign myself out at the nurse's desk. With cell phone drama in the next room it's impossible to think clearly about anything.

I didn't notice it before, but Chelsea's name is scrawled on the top line of the sign-in sheet. She hasn't checked out. I can't help glancing at the closed door. It's quiet now. Do I want to know and do I care? No and no.

I step across the hall to the attendance office. Phyllis is absent from her usual post, so I slip past the counter unnoticed. Almost.

"Excuse me?" An unfamiliar voice stops me from behind.

"Sorry, I didn't see anyone. I'm looking for Mr. Myers or Ms. McKinney."

"Do you have a pass because it seems to me you've got less than a minute before third hour, then you'll be out of class without permission?" Office Lady says.

"It's really important. Please?" I'm not above begging, or flashing my title. "I'm the student body president. I need to discuss a matter with one of them." I appreciate Phyllis more with every second that ticks by. Where is she?

After a protracted sigh, the woman answers. "I'll see if one of them is available. Wait behind the counter." She points.

I pace while the bell rings and the halls quiet.

Finally, Office Lady returns. "You can take a seat over there to wait for Ms. McKinney." She seems annoyed that the school counselor agrees to speak to me.

"Where's Phyllis today?" I venture.

"I wouldn't know."

Ms. McKinney's office door opens and she crosses the length of the hall quickly. "Taryn, how can I help you?"

We return to her office and I start in on the cheer tryout mess, which, of course, is not news to the counselor. I tell her about the video being passed around the school.

"I haven't seen it," I admit. "But I know it's got to be horrible for her. Can you do anything to stop it?"

Ms. McKinney pulls open a drawer. "Take a look."

I lean across the desk and count at least half a dozen cell phones of various brands and colors filling the space. "These are the ones that have been confiscated so far today. And it's barely third hour." She pushes the drawer shut and I sink back in my seat.

"I know exactly what you're saying, but we can't control the content on the phones, only when during the day students are allowed to use them. Or at least try to."

I put my head in my hands. My fake headache is becoming all too real.

The counselor stands and moves from around the desk. "Been a rough first week for a student body president?" It's more a statement of fact than a question.

I stand up, too. "Ms. McKinney, what do you think about an anti-bullying campaign?"

"I know there are a number of great programs out there."

"Could we do something here?"

"Mr. Myers would have to approve it before we can even approach the school board for funding." Her tone stiffens a bit and I get the impression this might be a sore subject. Plus, the fact that she escorts me to the door tells me the subject is clearly closed.

At lunch I drag myself out to eat in the courtyard again, away from the free-reign use of cell phones. I'm halfway through my grilled chicken sandwich and a list of to do's for the Howdy Dance Saturday night when the redhead from the bathroom after the memorial approaches, followed by her mascara-borrowing friend.

"I just want to tell you not to worry about the

video," the redhead says. "Tomorrow there will be something new to talk about. You know that's the way it works."

"Yeah, someone'll do something dumb and you'll be off the hook," Mascara Girl adds. I digest her words while Red shakes her head and gives her friend a wide-eyed stare. "Not that you did something dumb. Sorry. That's not what I meant," she backtracks.

"I really wish that were true." I bite my lip. "Wait, do you mean it's me in that video?"

"You haven't seen it?" The pair exchange a glance, and Mascara Girl continues. "It's all you."

Red cuts in, "It's just up till you say 'she deserves a chance.'"

"Like really loudly," Mascara Girl adds. She's greeted with another glare from Red. Sorry, she mouths back.

Can this day, this week, this school year, get any worse? Even with the end of the school week there won't be a break from this nightmare. Friday night is the first Ideal High football game, an away game against Clearview. On behalf of the student body, I will be standing next to Chelsea accepting condolences from the opposing school to honor the Ideal High lives lost in the fire. Fortunately, the team captain, Travis, is part of the delegation.

Maybe he'll act as buffer, but still I consider the possibility that I am developing a really long, into-the-weekend headache.

I wake to the sound of cannon fire and screeching worms, and my father's appeal, "Caleb, no computer before school." I roll over. Worms Armageddon. Caleb's new favorite game. That explains the weird dream I just had.

"Ouch!" I clutch the nape of my neck. My whole body aches. I didn't exert myself that much in P.E. yesterday, did I? A burgundy and green-striped throw pillow works its way out from under my headache and plops to the carpet, joining a velour throw that obviously found its way there during the night. I haul myself into a semi-sitting position.

"H.D.A." Caleb chortles as he passes on his way out of the room.

"What?" I growl back.

"Hair-do Alert."

I pick up the throw pillow and allow it to live up to its name. It misses, but I wince from the tenderness the toss shoots across my shoulder. I don't remember falling asleep on the couch.

Dad appears in the doorway. "You better get moving." He stops. "Rough night?

"Apparently. What time is it?"

"Seven-thirty."

I fall back against the cushion, groaning.

Dad joins me on the couch. "Mom told me what happened. I'm proud of you for standing up for that girl at the tryouts."

Oh, yeah, that's how I got on the couch. I was up late talking to my mom.

"I made it worse."

"Maybe for now. But I bet it will make others think twice about how they treat people."

"No, Dad. It's a joke. It's all over the school. It's online."

"Changing the world isn't easy."

"Who ever said I wanted to change the world?" I mumble.

Dad leans over and kisses my forehead. "C'mon, I'm making French toast. It's not as good as your Mom's, but definitely less healthy." She's been gone every morning this week working at Donut King.

I hear him singing as he heads to the kitchen, "You picked a fine time to leave me, Michelle. Four hungry children and a crop in the field." Dad's from New York City and doesn't have a country bone in his body, but because he married a Texas girl he tries to make up for it.

I skip homeroom to talk to Mrs. Ames, which will work in my favor since I'm late anyway. All she can report, though, is that "things are being worked out" when I ask her about Jen and Kirstie's replacements on student council.

I avoid Ms. Hightower for the second straight day in a row, not easy to do with so many of my classes in the 200 building. I'm sure the cheer advisor has an earful for me after the interrupted tryouts Wednesday.

Chelsea's another story. She glares at me whenever I see her in class or in the hall which is too often, unfortunately, but after nearly three years of ignoring her, I am really quite good at it. No one else has forgotten the scene at cheer tryouts, either, but a few students even thank me for sticking up for Persimmon Glick. I mean Persi.

The aches from a night on the couch disappeared by sixth hour, but then squat thrusts and lunges do me in all over again. After class I gingerly gather my belongings. A dose of ibuprofen kick-started my day and I'm pretty sure I'll need another.

Gratefully, I'm one of the last to emerge from the locker room's dingy gray walls after class — the walls that hold the secrets of seventy years of high schools girls. Their triumphs, their disappointments.

At least that's the pep talk Ms. Herman gives us at the start of the school year. She was a judge at cheer tryouts, too, so I worried she might corner me in class. Turns out she didn't say anything about it, though she did make eye contact and give me a quick nod. I think that's her way of showing approval. It's hard to talk when you've got a whistle in your mouth.

Just outside the heavy gray door marked GIRLS LOCKER, a familiar array of framed pictures catches my eye. Photos of smiling girls' basketball and softball teams, followed by tennis and golf teams, and one from Ideal's first ever girls' soccer team give way to 11 X 14s of cheerleading squads and homecoming queens through the years. Only triumphs here.

I pause in front of a photo labeled with the year my mom graduated from Ideal High. A glitter-edged homecoming sash cuts across the neon-blue gown of a blonde-haired queen with a big-toothed grin and bangs that appear to stand on end. I've seen her yearbooks full of bangs like this.

I hear a tap-tap of heels I hope will keep on walking. It stops a few feet behind me.

"That's my sister, Ruth Ann. Homecoming Queen," Chelsea's mom says.

If I don't say anything will she go away?

"And before her, my oldest sister, Patty."

I glance at the photo to the left, a repeat of hair, teeth, and sash, but the gown is shimmering lavender.

"These photographs go back for over seventy years, can you imagine?" Mrs. Manor continues.

"Amazing." I suppress an eye-roll, but plot my escape, wishing to be anywhere but viewing the Homecoming Queen Hall of Fame with Chelsea's mother.

"It is amazing," Mrs. Manor repeats. She moves closer to my right and I can see she is crossing her arms. This is a subject she takes very seriously. "With poise and beauty these girls represent the very best of Ideal High's tradition of excellence and honor."

Right. That was honorable when last year's queen ended up in Lubbock's juvenile court by Thanksgiving Break. I want to say it aloud, but bite my lip and opt for silence again.

"Here's my mother. Such a beauty. And my aunt before her." Mrs. Manor reaches out to wipe a shadow of dust from a frame's edge with her index finger. She's probably in here every other week with a feather duster and some Windex.

"There's value in tradition." Mrs. Manor isn't through making her point. "It's what holds a school together. It's what holds society together."

The words drop into the awkward space that exists between us. My eyes wander over the expanse of frames, and then settle on one. "Congratulations. You must be so proud," I say.

"Of course we are. And we'll be proud of Chelsea, too." Mrs. Manor stares straight ahead. She keeps her tone casual, but her words dig. "You've got more than yourself to worry about, Taryn. Ideal High can rise and fall on one misguided president."

Indignation flares. She knows nothing about my plans as president. What kind of lies is Chelsea telling her?

I let out a deep breath. The desire to put distance between me and anyone Manor-related burns hotter than the need to fire back and prolong the conversation. Better just say my piece and be out the door.

"No, I mean you were homecoming queen, too. That's such an honor." I catch Mrs. Manor's wary expression and know she detects my sarcastic tone.

"Wait, fall of —?" I plant myself in front of the photo to pretend a closer look. The teeth and blonde hair match her older sisters' photos, but the dress, soft pink tulle, billows from an empire waist. I keep my eyes straight ahead. Chelsea told me the secret back when we were best friends in junior high. "Did they know you were pregnant?"

"Excuse me?" Mrs. Manor clearly bristles.

I know Chelsea's birth date. "You took the winning-homecoming-queen family tradition to a whole new level, Mrs. Manor."

Pulling my backpack tighter, I step deliberately toward the exit. I push hard on the door against the late afternoon breeze. I left Mrs. Manor positively *glowering*.

My English teacher will be proud of me. I found a use for one of my vocabulary words.

14

The stadium echoes with the drumbeats of hyper high school bands and the animated chatter of hundreds of fans. Friday night football is an Ideal City ritual and tonight, I have to admit, it almost feels normal. Almost.

I take a deep breath, willing the stadium's energy to fill me up. Then I feel guilty. I stop to lean against the railing that divides off the bleachers for our side. The familiar sights and sounds of a simple, uncomplicated football game seem reassuring somehow, and after this week, I need it. Just for tonight can't I pretend everything is okay?

I'm done wasting time over Levi Jenks and his brother. If I'm going to move forward at all, what happened the night of the fire needs to be kept locked away. Really, a safe with a lock isn't the best metaphor for what it feels like. It's more like a cancerous tumor that I keep drowning in chemo, so it won't grow so abnormously large that it consumes me.

It's just a miracle I've gone a whole two weeks of school without a comforter draped over me and a pillow under my head.

From field level, I scan the crowd looking for my parents, so I can meet up with them after the opening ceremony.

"Over here!" Chelsea appears on the sidelines carrying a large box overflowing with red and blue pom poms. Angel and Kirstie trail her with an ice chest between them. Others follow with poster boards, a banner, and more pom poms.

"Just drop it anywhere," the head cheerleader instructs. The new seniors on the cheer squad were announced this morning, and yet here are all ten girls decked out in full Bulldog uniform. Matching ribbons pull back ten swishing ponytails. How Chelsea pulled that off, I can only wonder.

I position myself at the sideline to wait for the principal and try to shut out the grating commands coming from Chelsea's mouth as the cheerleaders continue to set up.

Soon the stadium sounds taper off as the announcer welcomes the crowd and announces each team's entrance onto the field. Cheerleaders for each team scatter like mice to opposite sidelines, immediately beginning cheer routines to excite the crowd. Next the emcee introduces the schedule of the night's events beginning with the ceremony at mid-field, and the stadium goes quiet. The silence is *palpable*. It's an odd word, but one of my English teacher's favorites. I think it fits.

We get the cue to start walking. Flanked by Mr. Myers on the left and Travis and Chelsea to the right, I keep stride, crossing to the center of the field where we greet our contemporaries from Clearview High. It's like I'm on stage again at the memorial, yet another vulnerable moment because of the fire. Even though the faces of the crowd are too far away to be in focus and there's, thankfully, no Jumbotron of Blake's smile behind me, it feels the same.

We exchange, in turn, words of condolence and appreciation. Chelsea and I accept bouquets of white roses tied with royal blue and red bows that remind me of Kayla's casket. I have to get used to this. Every rival school wants to show Ideal their support.

I try to look past the flowers that were thrust in my face to see the people now on their feet in the stands. They may not have been there the night of the fire, but they were all affected. The tragedy didn't just happen to me or to Chelsea, or even Ideal High. It happened to our community. I don't have to feel alone when surrounded by all these people who get how tragic it is.

I breathe in the warm summer's-end air and look beyond the rows of bleachers. The last bits of daylight have dissipated, giving way to a dream-like dusk of varying shades of blue. Warmth flows through me and I wonder if somehow Blake, Kayla, and others are watching. I steal a look at Chelsea as we return to the sidelines and wonder if she's feeling it too, but she is all business as she calls the squad to formation.

I hand the flowers over to Mom for safekeeping, then head to the snack bar. I'm craving Flamin' Hot Cheetos all of a sudden.

Principal Myers falls into step beside me. "I'm sorry I haven't been able to meet with you personally this week, Miss Young." He coughs. "Ms. McKinney said you asked about an anti-bullying campaign?"

I'm surprised the counselor mentioned it to him.

"While it's a good idea for most schools, it's not really necessary at Ideal. We're small-town. We don't have the problems a Lubbock or, heaven forbid, a Dallas school has.

"That might be true, but that doesn't mean there isn't bullying going on. What about Jackie Weir?"

"This year will be different after what we've been through. Don't concern yourself —" Mr. Myers declines to finish his thought, but instead continues past the snack bar to meet up with the principal from Clearview.

"Don't concern myself?" I mumble to his back. It's the same thing he said outside his office when talking about Levi's claims at the memorial. I think this is the type of productive discussion I can look forward to from him all year long. No wonder Ms. McKinney didn't want to talk about it. She probably gets shut down by the principal every time.

I really need those Hot Cheetos.

The crowds on both sides cheer as the ball soars high on the kick-off, carrying with it the expectations of two communities of fans. I watch Ideal return it for a few yards, and then arrive at the snack bar counter just as the front window slides open to receive customers.

"Hey, how's it going?"

I turn to see who slipped into line next to me.

Levi Jenks. He's freaking everywhere.

He's dressed in his standard blue jeans, plaid shirt, and boots, with a baseball cap covering his close-cropped light brown hair like last time. But, regrettably, I find I'm drawn to how his blue eyes light up the darkening night.

"You left pretty quick the other day," he says in response to my silence. His voice drops. "Sorry I asked about the fire. I should have known you wouldn't want to talk about it."

I study his face. "You know all those times I've seen you, you never formally introduced yourself."

Levi pulls at his cap and twists the toe of his boot in the gravel, but a smile tugs at the corner of his mouth. "You mean when I was running you over in the office or spraying you with rocks at the gas station?"

"Yeah. And running on stage."

He looks away. "I'm trying to forget about that. It's not usually the kind of thing I do."

"Why did you do it?"

A gangly kid in a dark green apron frowns from behind the counter. "Hey, do you want to order anything or not?"

"Oh, sorry. Flamin' Hot Cheetos. Do you have any?" I pull a few dollar bills from my pants' pocket.

"Nope." The boy gestures to the wall behind him where bags of chips are clipped in columns on a pegboard. "This is all we got. Besides, I heard those are banned."

"Whatever. I'll just have a bottle of water."

Levi pulls out his wallet. "I'll buy you any chips you want."

"I'm fine. I don't want any." After Levi buys bottled water for himself we wander over to lean against the fence where we can see the game. Clearview, who intercepted the ball several plays back, is now threatening to score.

I unscrew the cap on the water bottle and steal a sideways glance in Levi's direction. I thought I was done with him, yet here he is again. Might as well dive in. "I've been online, but not one thing tells me where your brother was, you know, found."

"Yeah?"

"I'm just saying, they found his car, but that doesn't put him in the Gin Co. building."

Levi leans in close. "His body hasn't been found."

I don't know why, but the words, his tone, suck the life out of me. I have no reply. And I am even more confused.

"But we know he was there because —" Levi turns his gaze to the far end of the playing field when our fans' cheers intensify. Ideal High successfully defends our goal and Clearview prepares to kick a field goal.

I watch the kick with him, a bit half-heartedly, I admit, as it's blocked by one of our guys. I glance at Levi a few times, wondering if he'll resume the conversation.

Suddenly, he ducks his head and pulls me toward the bleachers. "Let's sit."

"What's wrong?"

"The principal's right over there. I'm not his favorite person."

"He can't do anything to you. We're at Clearview."

"I know. Still, it's better to just blend in with the crowd, don't you think?"

"I guess." I slide into the bench beside him. "Why are you here anyway? I thought you didn't like Ideal High School?"

"I graduated from Lubbock High last year, but my family going way back went to Ideal."

I take a long drink from my water bottle and keep my eyes on the field. Soon I'm biting my lower lip and rolling the half-full plastic container between my palms. I cross my legs, uncross them, then cross them again. When my leg begins to shake in time to the band's drum beat, Levi reaches out to stop it.

"Relax. It's not even that intense yet."

I can't contain myself. "You have to tell me, dang it." I point the water bottle at him like a weapon. "You can't start a conversation about your brother and not finish it."

"I think you brought it up," Levi says.

"But you started saying something and didn't finish."

“Okay.” He holds up his hands in mock surrender. “But first.” He pulls my water bottle away, and then takes a deep breath before starting in, his voice lowering again.

“Jackie Weir got a text from him.”

“Wait, what?” I say it a little too loud, and automatically switch to a whisper. “Jackie Weir? Got a text from him?” I think my brain hurts.

“Just, listen, okay?” Levi gives me a look. We’re talking about the death of his brother and I’m the one freaking out. But to think Jackie is somehow connected is beyond bizarre.

I sit on my hands to keep them still. “I’m sorry, I’ll shut up.”

“The text said —” He begins pointedly, as if waiting to see if I’m going to interrupt again. “He got left at the old gin at Ritter’s Crossing without his car.”

“But —”

Levi interrupts me. “I know you didn’t see him, and that’s what you told police.”

“Yes.”

The crowd around us jumps to their feet, screaming and applauding our first Bulldog touchdown. The band joins in, but we sit quietly. “Hey, it’s not my fault. I told the truth.” I pause. “At least what I thought was the truth.”

"I'm not blaming you. If you didn't see Tim, then you didn't see him." Levi shrugs his shoulders and takes a deep breath like he's trying to regroup. Suddenly, he pulls me to my feet. "C'mon, we just scored the first touchdown of the game. We can talk about it another time."

Can we? I'm amazed that I am standing shoulder to shoulder with the same guy that sent a chill down my spine when he interrupted the memorial service nearly three weeks ago. The same guy I started crushing on while four-wheeling. Blake is still in my heart, but maybe I need to figure this out.

I put our conversation aside, for now, and let the stadium's energy take over again. When we threaten to score again, I'm screaming the loudest of anyone. We celebrate two more Ideal High touchdowns, but a 21 to nothing win over Clear-view, isn't the only reason I'm feeling so good.

As we flow from the stadium with the crowd my phone buzzes. A text from my dad. Turns out there were several I missed. Oops. I never went back to sit with my parents.

"My mom and dad are wondering where I am."

Levi doesn't say anything, just looks at me. I can't tell what he's thinking. It's not until then that I notice people are staring at us.

I pull him off to the side. "Whatever happened to your brother, I'm sorry. I know how it feels . . . you know," I can't express the sudden heaviness that lands on my heart.

Levi nods. He seems to want to say something, but hesitates.

I stick out my hand and stare right into the depths of his blue eyes. "I'm Taryn. Now I can say I finally introduced myself."

Levi takes it. "I'm Levi, and I know who you are. Well, at least I know your name. Haven't quite figured you out yet, but I do know your name." He stares back, holding onto my hand longer than necessary before letting go.

"I'm sorry about the other day at your house. If we can leave Chelsea Manor out of the equation, I'd be glad to help you figure out what happened to your brother."

Levi gives me a half-grin. "Truce, then? No more me saying you're part of the problem and no more you . . . you . . ."

"Me, what?" I am curious how he thinks he'll finish that sentence.

"No more you taking the brunt of my craziness. I'll control myself."

"Thank you, I'll accept that. Though someone in your position deserves to feel a little crazy."

"The problem is, I don't think anyone else wants to hear about it. Half the town believes my brother started the fire, the other half is suing the Manors." Levi pulls off his cap and runs his fingers through his hair like he still wants to say something, but he's holding back.

"What?"

"Permission to mention Chelsea just one more time?"

I roll my eyes. "What am I going to do, hurt you?"

"As long as you're not holding a water bottle I think I'm safe." His eyes light up, then turn serious. "I found her number and tried calling her last night. She totally went off on me. Said to stay away from her and never talk to her about it again."

"Really?"

"It was weird, though. She's hiding something."

"Maybe she's not supposed to talk about it because of the lawsuit."

"Maybe, but it seemed like more than that. I think she knows something, but for some reason she's scared. I mean like freaked-out scared."

I think about what I overheard in the nurse's office that morning.

My phone buzzes again with a text. "My mom

this time and she hates texting. I gotta go."

He gives me a quizzical look. "Have you seen the guy sitting on the bull in the bucking chute at a rodeo, just waiting for the gate to go up? That's what I feel like. I'm so anxious about what happened to Tim, like I'm this close to figuring it out. My mom says I need to let it go. Get on with my plans for college, but I can't."

"The bucking chute, huh? Sorry, never been to a rodeo." I grit my teeth into a smile.

"By the look on your face, I'm guessing you don't want to."

"No, it's just that my dad teases me. He says we live in Texas, so we need to be accepting of things like country music and 'rodeoing,' as he likes to say. He's from New York City, so, truthfully, he knows nothing about either one of those."

"So I'm guessing you wouldn't want to listen to my playlist."

"If it's like what my dad makes up when he's pretending he knows country music, then no."

"I think I'd like your dad."

I hold up my phone. "He's still wondering where I am."

"Catch ya' later, then," Levi says.

Was it a question or a promise? As I walk away, I'm just not sure.

15

My mind wanders as I sit on my bed glancing through nominee forms on Saturday morning. Homeroom teachers from each grade submitted about a dozen names for the advisory committee. Most filled the lines with just quick one-word descriptors, but I still can't focus. I keep thinking about Levi and the football game — standing and cheering with him, laughing and talking with him. It felt good just to laugh at all, but why was it so comfortable doing it with him? Of all people. I decided I was done with him and now look.

I lean back and stare at the ceiling, picturing him yelling good-naturedly at the refs and his enthusiastic reaction to each touchdown. I try to square that with the Levi I've seen that is grieving and angry over the loss of his brother. One who interrupted a memorial service.

I push myself up so I'm sitting and rearrange the piles of paper in front of me, picking up the top sheet from the unread stack of seniors. *Gretchen Smith*. I don't recognize the name. The homeroom teacher begins by describing her as "having a deep concern for others and a flair for the unusual." The teacher gets all that by observing the student sitting at a desk listening to homeroom announcements? I read the teacher's name. Of course, he's the head of the drama department. Per the requirements, the nominee also received endorsements from two other teachers who both agree, though with differing word choice, that Gretchen is thoughtful, creative, and a hard worker.

My mind strays again to Levi. He so isn't my type, if I had a type. For sure I've never dated a cowboy. I reread Gretchen Smith's form, but it becomes a bunch of meaningless words. Last night Levi said we would talk another time, but, suddenly, waiting to randomly run into him again is not enough. When are we going to talk? When are we going to ride horses . . . or skateboards? He doesn't even know my phone number.

My cell vibrating along the surface of my nightstand startles me. I snatch it up, half-expecting it to be Levi to prove my conclusion wrong. If he can find Chelsea's phone number, he can find mine.

"You probably don't know me," a girl's voice at the other end says in one breath. "But did you hear what happened last night? A bunch of students went to Donut King after the game and there was a fight. Well, almost."

No wasting time with hellos, so I try to keep up. “Between us and Clearview?”

“No. It was some of the football players and cheerleaders, and kids from band. Some skaters even got involved.”

“What?” I’m confused. “What happened?”

“I was there with some friends, just sitting in a booth at the front with our hot chocolate. We were too full after nachos and all the other stuff we ate at the game to —”

“Then what happened?” I urge her to keep to the meat of the story.

“We decided we were going to leave, but then the entire football team walked in, practically. Jen Foster and some of the cheerleaders were pulling tables together, like for a big group, you know. Some of the band kids were sitting at a table out in the middle and Jen asked them to move, but they said no. That’s when the football team got involved and someone bumped their table and a drink spilled all over one of the girl’s laps.”

“Wonderful,” I mutter under my breath.

“That’s when a couple of King’s employees came over and told them to stop.”

“And that was it?”

The girl keeps talking. “Some skaters were in a booth close by and they started sticking up for the band, so the football players were ticked about that. You know there's always been a thing between the jocks and the skaters. Everyone was like, 'You deserved to die in the fire.' 'No, you deserved to die in the fire.' It got a little crazy."

I reach for my pillow and hug it to my chest. "I'm glad I went home with my parents."

The girl is silent at the other end of the line.

"Are you still there?" I ask.

"Um, yeah."

"What's wrong?"

"I'm sorry, I forgot they're your friends. I didn't mean to say anything bad about them, that's just what happened. I thought since you're school president you should know. Since you're trying to unite the student body."

Thanks for the reminder.

I think of the stack of nominee forms I just read through. Not a single one of my friends were recommended. Is it because the teachers didn't consider them, or did they refuse to be involved? Are they that much against me, that, like Jen and Kirstie, they won't even work on a school committee with me?

"Don't worry, after the past two weeks I've decided my definition of friend apparently needs some tweaking," I reply before hanging up.

I notice a missed text from my sister, Tracy.

What's the deal with your friends last night at Donut King? They need to get over themselves.

Exactly.

I stuff my phone into my pocket and stack the forms in a neat pile on the floor for later. Right now Howdy Dance prep will take the rest of my day and, maybe, the first school dance of the year will give the illusion of normalcy. I'll hold on to that.

I check my list. Tradition makes planning the dance easy because every year it's the same. Bales of hay and assorted farm implements as décor, the chemistry department's famous homemade root beer to drink, and the usual lame get-to-know-you games. Basically the junior and sophomore class officers and I are the makeshift committee. There wasn't time to enlist any other help.

After phone calls to follow up on assignments, and last-minute errands to run, I finally enter the school's cafeteria where the dance will be held. I drop my load onto the nearest table and survey the room. A couple of sophomores carry in hay bales from a side door and two girls are hanging the "Welcome, Pardners!" sign that is hung every Howdy Dance. This is the only night of the school year that it's cool to go cowboy.

"You look like…well, I probably shouldn't

say." It's her. The girl that confronted me at my locker.

"Excuse me?" I'm not in the mood for more of the same.

"Yeah, it's me. My teacher turned in my name for that committee thing after all, so I thought I better come check it out. See what's up with school dances and all." The girl is dressed in a jet black, lacy blouse, belted at the waist, black jeans, and black boots. She's holding a black felt cowboy hat, but it's the chains and leather straps circling her forearms that make the look really unique.

"I don't mean any disrespect," she continues. "It just looks like you're not dressed for the dance. Or are you?"

I glance at my faded T-shirt, holey jeans, and comfy flip flops. The backpack I dropped on the table holds a change of clothes.

When I don't reply, the girl keeps talking. "We don't really know each other, but I'm prone to saying what I think. Not a problem, I hope."

I look at her with deference. "Of course, not." And I already know that about her.

"My name's Gretchen. Give me something to do."

Gretchen Smith? A flair for the unusual. Check. But her homeroom teacher also said she has a deep concern for others. That could come in handy.

I retrieve my backpack from the table. "How about I go get dressed before anyone else has to see me like this?" I gesture to my outfit. "And you start setting up the sign-in table. It's all in this box: nametags, markers, tickets for the door prizes."

"On it."

I survey the room again and can't help frowning. "I just hope it's okay, you know? And not just tonight. I want this year to be okay for everybody." Suddenly I'm baring my soul to this girl?

"Why put that pressure on yourself? Do what you can, forget the rest." Gretchen picks up the box of supplies and heads to the front, her boots echoing across the cafeteria floor.

In the bathroom, I check makeup while buttoning the last of my plaid blouse. Hair's fine, but my face needs work. I pull the mascara wand from its tube, but a mix of voices stops me. I look at my watch. Maybe the DJ's here.

I fly through a ten-second application of mascara, then toss it into my backpack with the rest of my makeup. I push the bag onto a shelf in the bathroom. I will worry about it later — right now the voices are growing, in number and intensity.

When I get back to the cafeteria I find the principal, Ms. McKinney, and Mrs. Ames around the sign-in table in the midst of discussion with sophomore and junior class presidents. Gretchen stands nearby with an amused look.

"Taryn," a sophomore class officer hisses. He cocks his head toward the clump of administrators.

I slip noiselessly to his side. "What's going on?"

"They're talking about cancelling the dance."

"An hour before it starts?" I cross the width of the cafeteria. My boots are not lasting the night, I can already tell. When I get closer I shoot a glance at Gretchen who shrugs her shoulders.

I square my stance in front of the group. The boots make me feel powerful in an old-west-cowboy kind of way. Like, don't mess with me, I've got my boots on.

"Is there a problem, sir?" My question comes out too quiet, too hesitant. What happened to my western bravado? That was short-lived.

"Recent events might cause concerns at tonight's activity," Mr. Myers begins.

"Last night you said everything at Ideal High is perfectly fine," I say, remembering our conversation at the football game. I fold my arms across my chest and stand a little straighter. I don't have a pistol in a holster at my hip, so folded arms will have to do.

The principal sighs. It's then that I notice his

cheeks seem leaner and the skin around his mouth sags a little. He looks tired. “We’ll maintain tight security. Keep out any troublemakers. I guess the dance can go on as planned.”

“Thank you.” I’m not able to keep the sarcasm from my voice. I want to ask how the troublemakers will be determined, but Mr. Myers’ blank expression stops me. I don’t think he can handle me pressing the issue.

Later, after the dance gets going I grab a glass of root beer and head to a corner chair, a nice dark spot. It’s the Howdy Dance, but I don’t feel like being friendly.

“Is this a good turn out?” Gretchen stomps into my darkness with her own full cup. “I wouldn’t know. This is my first one.” She drops into a chair a few seats away.

“I think it is. Even without the troublemakers.” I roll my eyes.

“They must have all stayed home.” Gretchen’s laugh comes out as a snort. “Oh, Mr. Myers.”

“I know. He’s been principal at Ideal High since before that wagon wheel turned rusty, but he doesn’t get it. He talks about troublemakers, but he won’t admit we have a bullying problem.” I take a sip of my root beer then adjust my boots, trying to give my toes some wiggle room. "I hate these things. How can anyone wear them?"

"I hear you. I think I'm done." Gretchen begins pulling hers off. "Hope bare feet aren't too uncool."

"You're a senior and this is really your first Howdy Dance?" I make a face, though I know she's telling the truth. She isn't the rah!-rah!-school-dance type.

"Yes, ma'am, my first." She tips her hat and then pulls it off. "Stupid head accessory."

I survey the room. The large turnout of students is encouraging, though it's so easy to identify divisions among the crowd. My friends, for lack of a better word to describe them, are bunched together, dancing and talking in the middle of the floor, the band and chess club kids are toward the back, a group of cowboys hovers in a corner, and another knot of students close to the stage jumps up and down to the music.

Mrs. Ames passes by to inform me that according to her calculations, this is the most well-attended Howdy Dance she's seen in a long time.

"That's a good sign, right?" Of course, maybe they're all here to see if a fight breaks out.

Students pair up for a slow dance and I can't help thinking about Levi. Wishing he were here, no matter what size his belt buckle is. I know it's crazy, I hardly know anything about him. He said college plans are on hold. What is he doing now besides working for a pest control company?

I know the answer to that. Tim.

After the song ends, the couples go back to their groups. They're so predictable. Kind of like the fight last night. Jocks and skaters never get along.

Gretchen leans forward and picks up her boots. "I made my appearance, time to go."

"Come on, stick around. The dance barely started." I fake a cheery tone. "Besides, you haven't experienced a Howdy Dance until you've played the Lame Dance Games."

"I hope you're not serious."

"Unfortunately, I am. It's tradition. It goes so far back that we now refer to them with capital letters."

Gretchen drops her boots in her lap to rub her temples with her index fingers. "I'm getting a vision. A girl running for president. Something about a new tradition."

"Very funny." I pause for a second. "Okay, you want a new tradition? How about ending the rivalry between the jocks and the skaters."

Now it's Gretchen's turn to roll her eyes. "This may be my first Howdy Dance, but if it's anything like my old school, I do know a thing or two about jock/skater history. Keep dreaming."

I give my watch a dirty look. It's time. "Well, think about it. I've got to get this over with."

I step to the makeshift stage and accept the microphone. "Howdy, ya'll!" I give it my best fake Texas twang. "I'm Taryn Young, student body president. Thank you for coming and welcome! Later we're going to have the traditional Howdy where we'll introduce new students that are here tonight, plus give away some amazing door prizes, so hang around for that." The requisite smiling is going to kill me.

I consult an index card where I scribbled down the order of the games. "As always, we start with the 'Texas Tornado.'" Several students groan.

"It's lame, I know, but here's how it goes. I start by asking someone I don't know to dance. When the music stops we choose new partners, someone we don't know, and so on, till everyone is dancing. Got it?"

As the music starts, I scan the crowd looking for a dance partner. I spot a round-faced boy sitting alone and cross the floor toward him. The other students' raised-eyebrowed looks follow me, but I don't care. They match the one on the boy's face when I pull him out on the dance floor.

Sticking out my hand to shake his, I introduce myself, "I'm Taryn, what's your name?"

After several partners, I snag J.T. As we slow-dance I get his take on what happened at Donut King last night. He downplays the incident. "It was just the guys, you know? Pumped 'cause of the game. That's all."

"Don't you think it has something to do with them thinking they can push around whoever they want?"

"It wasn't a big deal." I can see J.T. doesn't like this topic because he changes it pretty quick. "I haven't seen you at our lunch table at all. Is the president too busy to eat?"

"To tell you the truth, I'm kind of feeling a little out of the loop." I look away.

"Forget about Jen and Kirstie and the student council thing."

"It's a little hard to forget when Chelsea turns everyone against you."

His voice gets an edge to it. "What'd Chelsea do? Have you been talking to her?"

"She's not happy about losing the election, I'm sure."

J.T. relaxes. "She told me she was relieved. Her mom freaked about school and traditions and said Chelsea needed to stand up and be the leader, had to run for president. You know how her parents are. Her mom is the one that's ticked off that you won."

"Don't worry. I've already added her to my list of people to avoid." I wince at the memory of yesterday's encounter.

"Yeah, now take me off that list, Tare." He gives me a side hug as the music dies down.

"I'm curious. What was Chelsea doing during the fight? It totally sounds like something she'd be in the middle of, but no one mentioned her."

J.T. hesitates. I can't read the look that flares in his eyes. "She wasn't there. She went home with her parents."

He's holding back. "What are you not saying, J.T.?"

"I'm just worried about her, that's all."

Later, after the howdy-shout-outs to new students and drawings for door prizes, I announce the last game to another chorus of groans. "Play along. You know it's your favorite." More groans. "Girls pick a pink slip of paper with a word on it from the table at the north wall and guys pick a blue slip of paper from the table at the south wall. Your word or words has a corresponding word or words, and whoever has it is the person you dance with."

"Give us an example," someone calls out.

"One might be 'Remember' and the matching words will be 'the Alamo.' You have to find the person who has your match and dance."

Everyone mills about, mostly talking, and then slowly accepting their slips of paper. I circle the outer edge of the crowd helping make matches. By the time, the DJ cranks up the volume on one of the latest hits, some have formed couples and are ready to dance.

"You don't have a word." I hold out a pink slip of paper to Gretchen. I'm surprised she's still here.

"No thanks." Gretchen waves it away.

"You said you're here to find out what school dances are all about." I press the word into her hand. "Go for it." I step away to encourage other matches before Gretchen can protest again.

Soon I hear Jen's voice over the music. "'Yellow?' What goes with yellow?"

"'Rose of Texas' coming through," J.T. calls out as he pushes his way through the mix of students. Obviously-relieved, Jen takes the offer of his arm and trots out to the dance floor beside him.

I wonder what that's about.

I'm distracted by loud voices near the refreshment table, so I head over. A skinny kid, looking barely tall enough to be in high school squares off with Chelsea Manor.

"I don't want to dance with you anyway!" he says. "Who wants to dance with a murderer?"

"What did you call me?" Chelsea's response reveals a tremor in her voice.

"I'm just calling it like it is. You took all those students into a burning building. One of them was my cousin, Keisha."

"Hey, lay off her. It wasn't her fault." J.T. appears nearby. He and Jen move in close to Chelsea who seems frozen in place. Angel and Kirstie flank her right side while Travis steps in front of her. The music plays, but the dance floor has come to a standstill.

"Keisha wanted to be a cheerleader more than anything, and look what it got her. Hanging around you was her biggest mistake."

"I said lay off!" J.T. leans in, his football player bulk looming over the kid's thin frame.

"J.T., stop! Don't make it worse." I reach the inner circle and pull at the football player's beefy arm before turning to the offender. "We miss Keisha, too, but tonight we're here to have fun. If you can't be a part of that, you should leave."

"Who deserved to die in the fire? Why don't you tell me that!" The boy spouts off, but backs away when Mr. Myers appears.

"This isn't over." His glare is aimed straight at

Chelsea. "Your court date's coming, cheerleader!" The crowd parts, allowing him to stride unencumbered toward the exit. A few boys trail behind, voicing their support for his accusations.

Chelsea's friends crowd in closer around her, but she waves them away. "Give me a minute." She's lost the color in her face, and I recognize the threat of tears. I watch Angel and Kirstie follow her to the bathroom, but she stops them and leaves the cafeteria alone.

I reinstate the match-up dance, then sit with another cup of root beer, stewing. How dare that kid ruin the dance. And to accuse Chelsea like that? The fire was an accident.

Was this the first time someone confronted her with such an ugly accusation? Probably not considering how she went off on Levi when he called her to ask about what happened that night.

I don't like it, but I have to admit I never thought about what she might be going through. Before the last chorus of the dance music fades away, I slip unnoticed into the bathroom.

I find Chelsea sitting against the far wall, her forehead resting on her knees. Her golden-white hair falls in layers down to where her hands clasp her legs around the ankles. Her boots are tossed off to the side. I wonder if I should say something about her sitting in the exact spot where a girl lost her lunch earlier in the week, just to announce myself, when she breaks the silence.

"What do you want?" She doesn't even look up.

"I know this won't mean much coming from me —" I stay put, letting the words tumble out. "I'm sorry about what that boy said and I'm sorry about the lawsuit. I know Keisha —" my throat tightens "— and the others wouldn't want it."

I allow myself a breath, then finish when Chelsea doesn't respond. "The fire. It wasn't your fault." I have my doubts about what she knows about the tragedy, but at the moment it seems the only thing to say.

Eons pass while she sits motionless and I stand rooted in place. Finally, she raises her head, but her glazed look unnerves me. "Do you have nightmares, Taryn?"

Why is she asking me this?

"I do," Chelsea continues, her tone low and raspy. "Except I'm awake and I'm watching seven of my best friends trapped in a burning building."

She leans her head down again, so her chin touches where her knees meet. "I couldn't save them. Why couldn't I save them?" I can barely make out the words.

"You broke your ankle," I remind her. Her tone is beginning to scare me. "The fire was an accident, remember?" I'm not bringing up Tim Jenks.

Chelsea's reply is a hoarse whisper. "Sometimes people cause accidents."

A chill rattles through me. The grating squeal of tires tearing up pavement races across my memory, followed by the baffling sight of Chelsea running toward the burning building. This time the recollection is filled with her wailing calls for help and Blake yelling, "Stay there." But he yelled it at her, not me.

"What are you saying?" I manage to whisper back.

16

Still reeling from Chelsea's cryptic remark, I dig down into my comforter. I try to relax, but sleep eludes me.

Though I danced a few obligatory dances and helped clean up after, my mind raced the entire time with questions that had no answers.

Chelsea would never put her friends in danger, so what could it mean, "Sometimes people cause accidents?" She clammed up and refused to offer a single word of explanation. The opportunity to ask was lost anyway because Kirstie and Angel gave up waiting and came in to check on her.

I roll onto my back and stare at the shadowy ceiling above my bed, the only light in the room coming from under the closed door. It doesn't make sense that Chelsea wouldn't have just said Tim started the fire. Her tone implied there's something more to it. Levi seemed to think it's not just the lawsuit she's worried about, and now I'm thinking he's right.

I shut my eyes, but sleep isn't a possibility as a fast-motion replay of the night of the fire forces itself on me. I try slowing it down as I gather up the shredded bits of memory and piece them together in a disjointed array of pain-filled remembering.

The end-of-school party was held out at the Lubbock Country Club where Chelsea's parents are probably the only Ideal residents to hold some clout. The future senior class ate, danced, played games, ate some more.

The cheesecake.

It was amazing.

A full-body cringe shakes me to the core. I pull the comforter up to my chin, balling up the edges in two fists. It hurts that an innocent beginning to the summer ended in such a nightmare. I take even breaths and finally let myself go back again.

Around eleven-thirty, Kayla and Keisha found me half-asleep watching Blake shoot pool. Then Becca appeared in the doorway. "Chelsea's ready to go."

"We're seniors!" Keisha squealed before they followed her out to the entrance of the country club.

I move onto my side, pulling my knees to a fetal position. Blake whispered those same words into my ear when he leaned in close after opening the car door for me when we were leaving.

Then he kissed me. A long-but-not-too-long, perfect kiss, the kind that hinted of a future.

I chew on my lip. That kiss betrayed me. There was no future.

Squeezing tighter into a ball, I shut my eyes tight, too. This is where my brain always hits the wall, where it rebels against remembering. That kiss. It meant everything was right with the Universe. Me and Blake a couple, newly-elected president and vice-president of the student body. Prom King and Queen. We talked that night about hanging out over the summer.

I roll onto my back and deliberately uncurl my body, as if I am lying on a yoga mat preparing to meditate. I've seen Mom do it dozens of times. Breathing deeply, I visualize each muscle unfolding, relaxing, and preparing for the unavoidable hurdling of the wall. I am ready to face the unfaceable.

Well, maybe.

Clutching the black and white comforter again for support, I let my mind wander. I was there that night. But what happened? What would cause Levi to interrupt a community-wide assembly with such boldness, claiming a victim had been completely ignored, and why would Chelsea say that sometimes people cause accidents if she was talking about Tim?

After we said goodbye, I watched out the

window as the newly-elected senior cheerleading squad piled into Chelsea's Dad's Hummer. Becca in the back with her boyfriend, Weston, Keisha and Vaughn, who were a couple, squeezed in next to Ashley, and Kayla up front with Chelsea.

Purposefully skipping over the kiss, I fast-forward to the drive home. The radio was blaring. Blake was laughing about something, but I lay back on the front seat, exhausted. The month of May had been crazy — filled with finals and research papers, class elections, Junior Prom, late-night weekends with friends.

Blake nudged my shoulder as we sped down the dense tree-lined county road away from the country club. "C'mon, it'll be fun," he said, but I missed what he was talking about.

"I just want to crawl into bed." My eyes sting with the bitter tears of remembering. I actually said those words, and my careless wish came true. The summer began and ended with funerals, and in between I definitely stayed crawled into bed. Within the safety of my four pink walls and paisley comforter, I tried to keep the dark scenes of summer at bay.

I kick my legs against the bed. Forget summer. Forget the funerals. I have to focus. We were driving, Blake laughing, I was having trouble staying awake.

It was foggy then and it's foggy now in my memory, but I remember when we got to Stan's gas station that the road to Ideal was still blocked off. We had to detour through Ritter's Crossing. That's when my cell phone beeped. It was a text from Kayla asking if we could stop and pick her up. They were going to play night games at the Ideal Gin Co. building that was pretty much all that was left of the abandoned town. She said she hated the place and wanted to go home.

I knew it had become a popular place to hang out, but I didn't get what was fun about running around the scary old cotton gin in the dark either.

Blake suddenly cursed out loud, jolting me again from my half-sleep. He pulled over to the side of the road and fumbled with his phone. "Chelsea, answer," he muttered over and over.

That woke me up.

We took off and I told Blake to slow down when he suddenly swerved a quick left onto the narrow shoulder and jammed on the brakes. Ahead I saw the cotton gin, the headlights pointed at the huge black letters, faded, but legible: IDEAL GIN CO. We always called it the Gin Co building, preferring not to judge whether it had ever been ideal. Maybe in its day. But not now.

I hadn't realized we were already so close.

"Stay here. I'll be right back," he said. He was gone before I had a chance to mention Kayla.

It was eerie sitting in the dark with just a sliver of moonlight casting shadows on the abandoned building. After about twenty minutes my mind had conjured up all kinds of scenarios about what was taking Blake so long and they all involved some version of him and Chelsea together.

And where was Kayla? I tried calling her, but she didn't answer her phone. It was so dark I didn't dare go looking for her.

A knock on my window made me jump. Kayla. I asked her if she'd seen Blake and that's when she told me not to worry, that she'd find him.

Using my cell phone as a flashlight I finally decided to go in after her.

It smelled like smoke inside the cotton gin. Then the world exploded. Literally. Blake pushed me out of the building, then disappeared. When I got to his car I heard, and felt, the second explosion. Smoke and flames billowed out the side of the Gin Co. building not more than fifty feet in front of me and I remember searing hot fingers grabbing hold of my stomach and twisting. My legs buckled and I fell against the car door for support, my head pounding.

Blake appeared and yelled something at me. Then he was gone again. For the last time. That's when I saw the Hummer. They were here playing night games. All of them were in that building.

I relax my vise grip on my comforter and breathe deep for a few minutes. Is this drive down nightmare lane necessary? There seem to be no new clues. Tim Jenks isn't anywhere in my memory.

I stare at the ceiling, the light twisting into ghostly shapes. If I could just pretend I'm watching a movie, pretend it's not real. But I've never been a fan of disaster flicks.

I remember hearing voices. Blake yelling at Chelsea, but other voices, too. Chelsea yelling at someone. I thought they wanted me to call 9-1-1.

Wait. I heard Chelsea screaming when we first pulled up, before the explosions and the fire. After I got back to Blake's car I spotted Chelsea crying and half-running along the shoulder, the headlights highlighting her jerky movements as she hobbled along, then she was gone, over the edge of the road, to where Blake had gone.

Wait. I close my eyes tight, trying to force a memory. I heard the squeal of tires from farther around the bend, and saw gray and white wisps of exhaust. Someone left the scene. It wasn't Tim, though, not if Levi is right and he died in the fire.

A knock at the bedroom door jars me back to the present. "Taryn? Are you still up?" It's Mom.

"I'm awake." I shield my eyes from the light that spills in from the hall when Mom cracks the door open.

"Brad Manor's on the phone. Chelsea didn't come home from the dance. They wonder if you might know where she went."

"Did they call Kirstie or Angel? Or Jen? She was probably with them."

"Jen said she dropped her off at home, but Manors haven't seen her."

"I don't know then."

"I'm so sorry, Brad," Mom says into the phone. I can tell she's concerned. "Taryn hasn't seen her since the dance. Let us know if there's anything we can do."

Mom ends the call, but almost immediately the phone rings again. "Hi, Brad." Pause. "What a relief. Thanks for calling us back. Goodnight."

Mom sticks her head back in my open bedroom door. "Chelsea's home. She said she went for a walk. I don't know why she would do that after midnight, but at least she's okay." Mom shuts the door behind her, bringing back the nightmare rerun.

Who started the fire? Who made the "accident" happen?

Thoughts whirl until the lines between consciousness and unconsciousness blur, and the endless hours of a restless night tick by.

No. Chelsea is not okay.

17

"Guess who we ran into last night." My dad's question is the first thing I encounter when I walk into the kitchen mid-Sunday morning. He's gathering drinks and snacks for a full slate of football games, I can tell.

"I can't guess," I protest. My eyes burn and my head pounds from lack of sleep. I only dragged my body out of bed because of a serious need for pain reliever.

"Zeke Miller. He was in town having dinner with his parents at the Grapevine. He said he's hoping to get some playing time in next week's game against UTEP. Won't it be great to have a homegrown hero playing for Tech again?"

"How is he even on the team? He didn't graduate," I manage to mumble, though talking at all is a chore. I chase the ibuprofen with a glass of cold water, before squinting into the open refrigerator. I think the fridge door is the only thing holding me up.

"He took care of that during the summer so he could get his diploma and keep the scholarship."

Nothing looks appetizing, so I push the door shut and lean against it.

Dad reaches around me to dispense crushed ice from the fridge door. "You know we've been in a drought." He speaks as seriously as if he is talking about the county's cotton crop. "I mean, it's been three long years since the McAffees played college ball."

"Don't say it, Dad. Let me guess this one. You can't believe Dan McAffee didn't go pro." I'm really way too exhausted to be giving my dad a hard time over his football obsession.

"Exactly." He ignores my jibe. "And then his brother gets injured. They were the hopes of Ideal."

He starts singing. "You picked a fine time to leave, McAffees. Four hungry children and a crop in the field."

"Dad? Please, stop." I rub my temples, praying for the drug to work its magic.

"We can root for Zeke, though, right?" Dad's arms are loaded with a variety of snacks. "Do you want to catch a game?" His eyes indicate his armful. "I'll share."

I grab the package on top. "Wheat germ and honey rice cakes do sound appealing."

"It's the best I can do." He shakes his head. "Your mom's stopped buying food for normal people. Even my secret stash has run out."

I cover a yawn. "You can have the rice cakes if I can have the recliner."

"How about until half time, then we switch?"

"Deal."

I fall asleep during the first quarter.

When I wake in the recliner, the television is off and daylight gone. I stretch almost the full length of the overstuffed chair. Best sleep I've had in a long time.

The doorbell rings, but I don't move. I listen for my parents or Caleb to get it. It rings again. Where is everybody?

Still dressed in pajama pants and a ratty gray T-shirt, hair looking like who knows what, I throw a wool plaid blanket across my shoulders and shuffle to the door. Inching it open, I peek out to find Jen on the other side of the threshold.

"Were you already in bed?" she asks when I open the door wider.

"I kinda just got up." Now I'm really wondering where my family is. The lights inside are off and the outside lights are on. What time is it?

"Do you want to get a shake?"

I gaze at her through half-mast eyes. My brain can't process any explanation for Jen Foster to be on my porch inviting me to hang out.

"Unless you're still mad about student council," she adds.

"That feels like a hundred years ago," I mumble back.

"So you're not mad?"

"I didn't say that —"

"Will you just come? We'll stay in the car. You don't even have to change."

"I'm not wearing a bra and I can pretty much guess what my hair looks like." Recliner-head has to be way worse than bed-head.

"I have to be home by ten-thirty," Jen pleads. I notice her eyeing my lovely appearance, her eyes lingering at my chest. "Who needs a bra? Brush your hair. I'll wait," she says.

I tug the blanket across my front and then attempt to smooth my hair back behind my ears. Seconds tick by, then for no reason at all — maybe just stupid curiosity — I decide to go with her.

"Give me a minute." I turn to climb the stairs, deliberately allowing the blanket to molt from my body like dead skin. I leave Jen standing on the porch.

I run a comb through my hair, pulling it back into a fast ponytail. After throwing on a comfortable sports bra, I replace the gray T-shirt, slip into flip flops, then grab my wallet. I find my parents in their room and tell them I'm going with Jen. "I'll be home by ten-thirty, I promise." Before leaving the house I snatch up the blanket, my protection from the night's cool wind.

As we drive, Jen talks nonstop about nothing, leaving me to wonder what her motive is. She literally hasn't spoken a word to me since resigning as vice president. When we pull into one of Burger Heaven's drive-ups to order, the aroma of char-broiling meat starts my stomach groaning.

"I haven't eaten a thing today." I rummage through my wallet adding up my few bills and coins. "Can you order me a cheeseburger, no onions? I'll have a chocolate shake, too."

Once my food and Jen's large Diet Coke arrives, she raises the driver-side window and deliberately turns to face me. Here it comes.

She speaks quietly. "Can I explain why I resigned?"

I nod, trying to look interested in more than my cheeseburger.

"When I got home that day after our first meeting, my mom told me she was diagnosed with lung cancer."

I stop mid-chew. Swallowing hard, I set the burger in my lap.

Jen continues, "I freaked out. I mean, that's

supposed to be the worst kind of cancer to get. I'm the youngest and the only one left at home. I feel like I need to take care of her."

"Jen, why didn't you tell me?"

"I didn't think you'd want to talk to me. I was so awful to you at the meeting." Jen stops to sip her drink, taking her time as if she's contemplating her words. "No offense, but I thought Chelsea would win. We planned to be student body officers together." She stops, and then adds as an afterthought, "Now I'm glad she didn't."

"Why do you say that?"

"She's psycho, Taryn. Something's really wrong with her. Kirstie said she's been losing it at practice. When they're in public she's all smiling and cheerleader-ish, but in private she's angry all the time or she's like spooky-quiet in her own world. Even Angel's mentioned it and you know she never says anything against Chelsea."

"I guess things are pretty rough for her. I mean, you saw what happened last night." I'm defending Chelsea? That's a switch.

"About last night —" Resentment shows in Jen's tone. "I dropped Chelsea off and I was thinking about my mom and feeling horrible. Up until then I didn't feel like I could even talk about it, but we were just sitting in my car outside her house and I told her my mom has cancer." Jen dabs her eyes with a napkin.

My eyes moisten, and the weight of the word seems to settle in around us when she says it out loud for the second time. It's quiet for a minute before Jen takes up where she left off.

"Anyway, she'd been kind of moody the whole night anyway. I can't blame her after what Keisha's cousin said, but then she just froze like she was possessed or something and then laid into me about how everyone has stuff to deal with, not just me."

"You know her dad called and said she was missing."

"I know. They called me, too. When she got out of the car I heard her talking to someone, but I left. I was pretty mad at her. Her dad called back and said she went for a walk."

Thinking about last night rolls my stomach. First Keisha's cousin's accusation and Chelsea's chilling pronouncement, and then my nightmarish reminiscing that didn't help one bit. I wrap my cheeseburger back in its foil and drop it in the Burger Heaven bag. I can't stand looking at it anymore.

Jen brought up Chelsea, so I have to ask. "Did Chelsea ever tell you what happened the night of the fire?"

"No, she never talks about it. She basically went into hiding all summer like you. I'd call, I'd go over, but nothing."

"About that —"

"I mean I totally understood, but everyone was freaking out. Some days I just wanted to hang out with my friends so I knew I was still alive, you know?"

I nod, but her words cut a little too deep. I never considered that hiding in my room all summer might have been a selfish choice.

"Do you want to know what we thought — me, Kirstie, Angel, everyone — when you and Chelsea wouldn't hang out? That, obviously, your best friends had died in the fire."

"That's so not true, Jen." Almost not true.

We sit in silence, then the rumble of a truck's engine pulling up next to the passenger side cuts through the quiet. My first thought is of Levi, but Jen's squeal proves me wrong.

"It's Zeke Miller. Roll down your window."

"Jen, I'm wearing a blanket."

"The button on this side doesn't work. Do it!"

I can't help replying like I'm narrating a movie. "It was in that moment that she realized her decision not to wear makeup had been a mistake."

"Taryn." Jen gives me a look.

"Rolling, rolling." With my free hand I push the blanket to the floor, though it's a toss up as to which is worse — the ratty tee or the wool plaid.

Jen leans across the car as far as she can. "Zeke, hi! What are you doing in town?"

"Hey, Jen, Taryn. What's up?" Zeke lifts his chin toward us. The epitome of college-football-player cool-ness.

"Just hanging at Burger Heaven, you know, like old times," Jen gushes. "How about you?"

"Just grabbing a Coke before driving back to school. It was my mom's birthday. I came down after the game yesterday."

"That was a close game. Ya'll should have won it," Jen calls, too loud for the short distance between the two vehicles. I wonder if she even saw the game.

"Idiot refs." Zeke's tone doesn't hide his irritation. He looks at me. "I heard you were student body president. That rocks."

"I guess you could say that." I can't help noticing the way Zeke's dark brown hair curls up at the ends, kind of like Blake's did, and the muscle that ripples across the arm he hangs out the window of his truck. Compliments of years of football practice, I'm sure. Blake didn't have muscles like that.

A tiny blonde on roller blades obstructs our view as she wheels to Zeke's window to take his order. She hangs on his door too long, leaning in to speak in a sing-songy voice that I can't quite make out.

"She's a freshman," Jen says, as if it's an insult. Finally, the girl flits away.

Zeke picks up the conversation. "Hey, I saw your parents last night."

"I know. My dad's all excited about you playing next week." I smile, trying to forget about my messy ponytail and no makeup, though it doesn't matter much. It's only Zeke.

"You better watch. It'll be on TV."

Jen leans across me again, inserting herself back into the conversation. "Oh, we will," she calls.

The roller-blading blonde stops on her way back from delivering another order to flirt with Zeke some more. I nudge Jen off me. It feels too gawkerish to be hanging out the window staring at them.

"Be right back," the blonde declares before gliding away.

Zeke leans out the window a bit and when he speaks again his tone is lower. "So, Taryn, what's the deal with you and that Jenks guy at the football game? You're hanging out with him?"

The question catches me by surprise. "I've talked to him some."

"After what his brother did? Why?"

Jen leans in. "Seriously, Taryn? That's so messed up." This must be the first she's hearing about it.

"There's nothing wrong with trying to figure out if the fire was an accident or not." I shrug my shoulders.

"Suddenly you're going all CSI on us? I think you of all people would want to stay a million miles away from him." Jen is clearly disgusted.

"No, I get it." Zeke's eyes get big like he thinks he's on to something. "You're waiting for just the right moment, then —" Zeke thrusts his left fist. "Knife in the back."

I gesture between them. "Stop. It's not like that. I don't know what it's like exactly, but it's not revenge, believe me."

"Someone's thinking about it. I heard his name is on a list on the bathroom door."

"The list is gone. It was just a joke." I'm so not comfortable defending Levi since I don't really know the facts either. How did we go from "my mom has cancer" to this?

Zeke narrows his eyes at me. "He just better watch his back. He's nobody's favorite person."

His drink arrives with a side order of more flirting, so I tug on Jen's arm. "Can we, please, go now?" I'm done with this conversation.

"Fine. It's time anyway." She starts the car just as my cell phone chirps. It's a text from Mom.

"It's 11:00, Jen." I groan. I should have been watching the clock, apparently.

Zeke revs his engine. "We should hang out sometime."

Jen is quick to lean across me again. "I'll hold you to it. Call me."

"Jen, please. Just drive. Besides, how do you know he wasn't saying that to the freshman?"

Jen wrinkles her nose. "Don't insult me." We leave the parking lot with Zeke's truck on our tail. He revs his engine again and pulls right up on the bumper of the VW Bug.

I hold onto my burger sack to keep it from slipping off my lap and watch him in my side-view mirror. "What's he doing? Lubbock's the other direction."

"Relax." Jen is clearly enjoying the football player's attention. After a block of tailgating, Zeke pulls up next to us and flips a U-turn before the light. Jen giggles and taps her horn at him, then makes a show of adjusting the rear view mirror to better watch him speed away. "You know we're seniors now. We totally should be dating college guys."

I roll my eyes. "Right."

When we pull up to my house, Jen touches my arm before I can escape from the car. "Taryn, if you want my advice, stay away from Tim Jenks' brother. Haven't you been hurt enough? Just let it go."

I'm kind of touched by her concern, actually, even though she has no idea what I'm feeling. I gulp down some of my runny chocolate shake to avoid having to say anything.

"Oh, and at lunch, when we talk about seeing Zeke tonight, don't mention that you've been hanging out with that other guy. I don't think it will go over well at our lunch table."

Ah, priorities.

18

Chelsea. Saturday night.

There's definitely something going on with her. I towel off after my shower Tuesday morning and then reach for my blow dryer. But why should I care? Chelsea and I haven't been friends for a very long time.

So stupid to get all emotional worrying about her and reliving the fire. If anything, Saturday's late night rerun proves I don't want to replay those memories ever again. If Chelsea still suffers because of it that's her deal. My dilemma is choosing between the yellow-striped tee and the brown one with the *fleur de lis* design down the side.

I slip into first hour English class, barely beating the bell. I settled on the stripes, but it took too long to decide. I raced to school, took the worst parking spot ever, and then ran like a crazy person just to get to first hour. I completely missed homeroom.

I reach into my backpack for my three-page English essay. Crammed in next to it are

Constitution worksheets for American Government and an Anatomy assignment covering cells and tissues. After neglecting most of my homework until Labor Day, I stayed up past midnight to get it all finished. It didn't help that thoughts of Levi kept crowding out cell membranes and the Preamble, but it was more fun thinking about him than anything else that happened over the weekend.

I pass my essay forward, then notice Chelsea's empty desk at the front of the third row. Annoyingly enough, my eyes stray to it throughout the class's entire discussion of short story structure. When Mrs. White finally releases us to read a selection from our textbook, I pull out my spiral notebook and focus on a to-do list.

I have to meet new officers after school, and it's time to start planning homecoming. I'm much too busy to worry whether Chelsea comes to school or not.

At the top of the list I write "Talk to Gretchen." I want her to ask some of her skater friends about Friday night. I'll catch up with her at lunch.

The main topics of conversation on campus are the incident at Donut King and the confrontation at the dance between Chelsea and Keisha Lambert's cousin. By the time I'm heading to the cafeteria for lunch, I've had my fill of both. I hear Chelsea's name has been written in the bathroom stall, on the painted square covering the others, but I'm past caring about the list. It's a joke now, so as long as it stays that way, I'm not worried.

"Hey, Taryn." Jen calls from the end of the salad bar. After paying the cafeteria cashier for my pizza, I follow her over to where our group eats lunch, where I should've been sitting the past two weeks.

"Remember, don't mention Tim Jenks' brother." Jen barely gets the words out before we're greeted by the table.

"El Presidente! She graces us with her presence." Paco gestures toward me in a mock bow. "Good times at the Howww-dy Dance Saturday."

Good enough to want to forget. But their words serve to loosen the knots in my stomach. I fit in here. Even without Blake. And even though I won the election and not Chelsea.

"Travis thanks you for the hook-up he made with the Jolly Goth Giant during the matching game," J.T. continues. The stomach knots quickly return. He's referring to Gretchen.

"Very funny." Travis throws a straw like a dart, barely tapping J.T.'s forehead.

J.T. won't stop. "You had 'Amarillo' and she had 'yellow'— the perfect match. He tried to get out of it, but Paco's Spanish-translating skills set him straight."

"No, I had 'yellow' and you had 'rose of Texas,'" Jen insists.

"There were two yellows. Why do you think J.T. came runnin' so fast? He didn't want to get stuck with you-know-who." Paco laughs. "Travis just didn't run fast enough which is sad, seeing as how he's the quarterback." He nudges Travis with his shoulder. "You got sacked, buddy."

"I didn't dance with her, so shut up." Travis jabs him in the chest with an elbow. I feel the air being forced from my lungs as if I'd been the one hit. Poor Gretchen.

"Taryn, hi!" It's Angel, with Kirstie following behind. She's calling from across the far end of the long table, her voice shrill. They clip-clop over in their chunky heels to join us with their matching salads and Diet Cokes.

"We haven't talked to you in forever." Angel is over-friendly and I'm not sure I should trust her ideal-to-my-face tone, but I accept a side-hug anyway. Kirstie winces at me, and it almost looks like a smile, but she doesn't say anything before they fold themselves into seats next to Jen. Kirstie hasn't spoken to me since the student body presidency fell apart. Yeah, P.E.'s been awkward.

Angel douses her salad with ranch dressing. "Jen says y'all ran into Zeke Sunday night."

Jen launches into a full-blown embellishment of our encounter for the benefit of all the girls at the table.

"Hey, there she is, Travis," I hear Paco say. "Plenty of empty seats by her, too." I feel my cheeks flush. They're still talking about Gretchen. I glance at the corner table where I've seen her eat before and a tightness criss-crosses the hollow of my stomach. Persimmon, with the pink hair, sits opposite her. I lean in, feigning interest in my pizza and Jen's lively description of last night. Gretchen can wait.

Jen chats non-stop which is typical. She barely glances at me, so obviously I don't even need to nod in agreement or anything. Still I try to listen because it's easier than thinking about Gretchen. Easier than wondering why I don't say anything in her defense when the guys talk about her. I hung out with her a bit at the dance and it was fine. She's funny. She's smart. As funny and smart as anybody at this table.

I imagine her sitting here, or try to anyway. Jen with her white-blonde streaked hair, pencil-straight jeans, blinged-up heels, and designer makeup elbow to elbow with Gretchen in her army surplus cargo pants, black jacket, and boots. And the on-purpose dark-themed makeup. Day and night. Night and day.

"Chelsea —"

I turn my focus back to the lunch table when I hear her name mentioned, but Angel and Kirstie have started their own conversation and aren't sharing it with the rest of us. I don't care about Chelsea one bit anyway.

Jen finally stops talking about Zeke and decides to jump on my bandwagon for some reason. She points a finger at the football players. "You guys can't say that kind of stuff in front of Taryn. She wants us to be nice, remember?"

"Thanks, Jen." Now I feel worse that I didn't stick up for Gretchen.

When the bell rings signaling the end of lunch, I follow Jen to the trash cans and add my tray to the teetering pile growing in the dishwasher's window. A quick glance toward the corner reveals that Gretchen's table is empty and immediately fingernails of guilt claw my insides.

After leaving the cafeteria I turn toward fifth hour, falling in with a group of students headed the same direction. The bits and pieces of conversations floating around me center on the topics of the day and I'm relieved that not one of them is me.

After the three o'clock bell signals the end of the school day, I hurry to Mrs. Ames' classroom from the locker room. Finally, we're going to have a real student body officers' meeting.

"Taryn, do you know if Chelsea Manor's alright?" The redhead from the bathroom after the memorial stops me outside the 200 building.

"Chelsea? I don't know. Why?"

"I saw what happened at the dance. It was horrible."

"I wouldn't worry about it," I mutter back. I'm not the keeper of information about Chelsea Manor, and I don't want to be.

"But she wasn't at school today," the girl continues.

I reach for the door, hinting I don't want to have this conversation. "Maybe she's sick."

"The whole thing is sick, don't you think?"

I could write a hundred-page essay about everything that's wrong with what happened to me and Chelsea and this school, but I just agree with her and duck inside the building. I'm still in my running shoes because I didn't take time to change after P.E., so I jog down the hall and open the door to room 212.

My apology for skipping a shower doesn't make it past my lips.

"Good news, Taryn." Mrs. Ames beams at me from behind her desk. Two student desks are pulled up close. Obviously one's for me, but Chelsea sits in the other with a look that beats out any conceited, full-of-yourself look ever given. And I do mean ever.

"We've got you some help," Mrs. Ames' finishes.

And now I'm going to be sick. Or at least paralyzed because my jaw locks on the first word that comes to mind and it's totally not like me to say stuff like that. Plus I find I can't will my feet to move from point A to point B because B is the desk next to Chelsea.

I swallow the inappropriate word and begin to mumble something about how I thought there would be replacements for both Jen and Kirstie. And what's your definition of good news, Mrs. Ames?

I don't actually express this last part out loud, but I'm sure it's blinking in neon letters across my face.

"No one else ran for vice-president, and I contacted J.T. Webb, but he wasn't interested in serving as secretary/treasurer anymore." Mrs. Ames stands up. She must sense I'm going to need some help walking across the room.

"So —" I have no words.

"Fortunately, Chelsea is willing to step up and serve as a student body officer because there's no time to hold another election." We're still talking about Chelsea like she's not here. And I wish she wasn't.

I think fast. "I had a good talk with Jen the other night. I know I can convince her to come back."

"Chelsea is more than willing."

And I'm more than willing to run screaming off the nearest cliff if I could find one, but instead I do the respectable student-body-president thing and shuffle over, plop down at the desk, and open my notebook. Ready or not I'm diving into a student council agenda with my favorite teacher and my worst enemy. I'm glad I didn't dress for the occasion.

Mrs. Ames leads off and I say a silent thank you for at least that much.

At Kayla's funeral I was all "Yay, back to avoiding Chelsea" and now I'm rerunning our recent encounters and they're adding up to too many in just a week. She tells me only geeks and losers are on my side. She tells me I'm making things worse at cheer tryouts. She didn't say a word to me as we walked across the football field Friday night, fortunately, but Howdy Dance on the bathroom floor was more than memorable.

Chelsea seriously wants to put herself in front of the whole school as a class leader? I gnaw on my lip. Sounds a little too much like me. The fraud who became president.

"Taryn, have you studied the nominees?"

Both Mrs. Ames and Chelsea are looking at me.

"The nominees? For the advisory committee?" I shuffle through my notebook. "I have the seniors. I gave juniors and sophomores to their class presidents, but said we needed them back by the end of the week." I hold them out to Mrs. Ames. "I marked my picks in red."

"Chelsea, why don't you do the same and we'll see what you all have come up with. That will give us our homecoming committee."

Nobody moves, so I guess they're waiting for me. I set the forms in front of Chelsea.

"So you want these back by the end of the week, too?" she asks.

Chelsea's looking at me, but I'm caught off guard. It's the first thing she's said directly to me since I got here.

"Sure," I reply quietly.

But I'm confused by how quiet she is.

Normally, she's hissing at me or commanding the cheerleader universe in her high-pitched shrill. Maybe she missed class today for a reason. She really is not well.

Or Saturday night. The Howdy Dance. If that still has her freaked out, it's understandable.

We cruise through the agenda 'cause Chelsea's agreeable to practically everything, or at least she's not disagreeing. She's still not saying much at all. While Mrs. Ames outlines the budget for homecoming, our last item of discussion, I debate whether I want to bring up Jackie Weir.

Mrs. Ames looks up from her notes. "Sound good to you?"

I muster an answer. "Great."

Chelsea leans in. "Can I add something? There's a girl named Jackie Weir who dropped out right before school started. I feel bad for her. Do you think there's something we could do to help her come back?"

Last week I'm upset that Jen can't comprehend helping a fellow student out, but when Chelsea brings it up, I'm thinking, no, Jackie's my deal.

I'm messed up. I get that.

I make sure Chelsea knows that it's Jackie I was talking about in my election speech, and that I've been to her house, and have a plan which I really don't, but since when did she get so charitable?

I didn't say that last part out loud.

But I can't let her win. I can't let her be the hero. "That's interesting that you bring up Jackie. Did you know Tim Jenks texted her the night of the fire?"

19

After the meeting, Mrs. Ames joins me on the sidewalk. I have no idea where Chelsea disappeared to. She basically had a mini melt-down when I mentioned Tim texting. She mumbled something about it being off-topic before she made a quick exit. Poor Mrs. Ames. I think she was feeling caught in the cross-fire again.

"I'm sorry about the meeting, Mrs. Ames. I didn't know Chelsea was so sensitive." I lie.

"No apology needed. You two have been through so much and, still, there's no closure. But it finally feels like things are moving forward with student council. You should feel good about that."

"I'm tired, that's what I'm feeling." The effects of my late night homework session are beginning to hit me. I look past Mrs. Ames, to where half-a-dozen football players huddle at the far end of the parking lot. Practice must have ended early.

"I'll talk to the Special Education teacher about the Paw Pals Club. It's a great idea. Those kids will love being included." Mrs. Ames looks tired, too, but she smiles anyway.

"Yeah." My reply is cut off by shouts erupting from the direction of the football players. Together we stare wide-eyed as a skinny kid raises a skateboard above his head and swings it like a bat, producing a sickening smacking sound as it makes contact with the side of J.T.'s head.

Instantly, Mrs. Ames is on her walkie talkie. "Security!" she barks.

"J.T.!" I sprint down the sidewalk.

My knees give way and I fall more than kneel alongside the prone figure of my friend splayed on the black pavement. Trembling fingers caress his face, but I'm careful to avoid the mass of sticky brown fluid and gravel merging near his head. Opposite me, Paco presses a Bulldog-logoed towel to the other side.

Some students take off on skateboards with several football players barreling after them. A few remain, unsure whether to stay with their injured teammate or pursue with the others.

A faint moan accompanies the slow rise of J.T.'s linebacker chest. "You're okay," I say it more to myself than him or anyone else. Challenging the adrenaline that pulses through my system with a rhythm akin to blender blades, I force even breaths, despite the bitter taste surging in my throat. I lean in close. "Hang on. Help's coming."

Mrs. Ames relays first aid instructions from a 9-1-1 operator. “Just keep pressure there, Paco. Taryn, keep talking to him.”

Bracing myself against the mingling stench of blood and sweat, I bow again toward J.T.’s ear. “I’m right here. I’m right here. I’m right here.”

A security guard arrives, and soon the Ideal paramedics. After checking J.T.’s condition, they load him onto a gurney, then whisk him away to the local emergency room.

Mrs. Ames is on the phone trying to reach Mr. Myers.

The security guard takes down names and Travis pulls me to him. “You’re shaking,” he says into my ear.

“I can’t stop.”

“He’s probably taken bigger hits on the football field. He’ll be okay.”

“Sure, he’s a Bulldog,” Paco chimes in. Others grunt in agreement.

“Why would someone do that? I mean, a skateboard?” I shudder into Travis’s shoulder a bit deeper.

The security guard moves in. “That’s exactly what I want to know, so, you —” He points to the beefy football player at his left. “Start talking. I’m going to have to write a report.”

"Well, Glenn —" The football player makes a show of reading the name embroidered on the guard's work shirt. His friends snicker. "It's like this. We were just tryin' to have a respectable conversation, and all of a sudden, skateboards are flying."

Another player slaps his teammate on the back. "That's right, dude." More scattered laughter erupts. Why doesn't Mrs. Ames do anything? She's still on her cell.

I pull away slightly from Travis's hold and search his face. "What happened?"

Just then the pair that followed the skaters rounds the fence into the parking lot. "We let 'em get away," one says, trying to catch his breath.

"But we scared them good," his companion adds.

They give each other a high five, then sober when they noticed the additions to the group. "Hey, Taryn."

"I need your names, too." The security guard positions himself in front of them, pen poised.

"Anyone use Billy Bob?" the one Taryn knew was Isaiah Powell says. "That's my name today." He runs his fingers through his short dreadlocks.

Jerks. Twice the size of any of those skaters.

Mrs. Ames interrupts my thought. "Okay, guys,

why don't you go on home. I'll talk to Glenn."

"Wait a minute now. No one goes anywhere until I say so." He makes all the boys sit down along the sidewalk, no small feat when it's one gangly security guard versus a bunch of pumped up football jocks. Finally he turns to me. "Now what about you, little lady? Are you involved here?"

The teacher pulls me to her side. "Taryn was with me. Sit tight, boys, I'm still trying to reach the principal."

Travis protests. "C'mon, we need to go to the hospital to make sure J.T.'s okay. Mrs. Ames, tell him."

Standing there in the school parking lot with the West Texas wind whipping around us like dust devils, I suddenly feel very small and the issues at Ideal High loom too far beyond my reach.

"Can I leave?" I ask in a little-mouse voice. "I want to go to the hospital." The thought jars me, reminding me of Blake — how, when the paramedics determined I was okay, I wanted to go to the hospital to be with him. But there was no point. The smoke inhalation was too severe. He died at the scene.

"Ride with me, Taryn." Travis pulls out his keys and looks at Glenn. "I didn't do anything. Paco and I barely got out here, right, Paco?"

"Then you'd have to bring me back to get my car." I pull my own keys out and walk away.

"Tell him I'll be there in a sec," he calls after me.

"Me, too," Paco says.

Once inside my car, I leave a message on my mom's phone before pulling out of the school's parking lot onto Bulldog Lane. I don't care if I am still wearing my P.E. clothes. I'm going to see J.T.

After eating my warmed-up dinner, I sit at the edge of my parents' bed telling them about J.T. plus how horrible I am for not sticking up for Gretchen.

"I'm so lame. How can I fix anything if I can't even make myself acknowledge her in front of Jen and the football team?"

"Try again," Mom encourages. Of course. "You have to start somewhere. It's not just the gap between the football players and the skateboarding kids you need to bridge."

"Try again?" I groan. "Even if it's a lost cause? What's talking to her going to fix anyway?"

"Good ideas are never lost causes, honey."

That's the phrase rolling around in my head when I finally go to bed. Unfortunately, it sounds too much like a Make a Difference-platitude.

Yes, my year is going to be bearable. Minus the

war between the jocks and the skaters, and the fact that I'm ignoring a new semi-acquaintance, and I have to serve with Chelsea on student council, my year is going to be very bearable.

At lunch the next day, I huddle with Jen and some of the guys to share updates about J.T. Angel and Kirstie show up to the table, fashionably late, as always. They act nice enough to my face, but beyond that I have no idea. Chelsea's absent again today, and I hear them whispering about it when they sit down. They actually seem relieved.

Angel notices me watching them. "So Taryn, what do you think about Chelsea being a student body officer? That was a surprise, I bet." Kirstie fidgets with her salad and doesn't look at me.

"You could say that." I could also say I was surprised when Kirstie resigned, but I don't.

"If she keeps missing school, though, she's not going to be on student council or the cheer squad," Angel seems pretty proud of her conclusion.

"Chelsea's having a rough time. Give her a break, Angel." Travis speaks up.

"I'm just saying." Angel starts in on her salad.

Talk turns to bad-mouthing the skaters and I squirm a bit but don't say anything even when asked. Let Travis and Paco try to explain what happened yesterday in the parking lot.

After listening to them for half the lunch period, though, I feel like I have to ask. "So why was the kid swinging the skateboard so mad? What'd J.T. do?"

Travis and Paco exchange a look. "Nothing," Travis says. "J.T. just jumped on his friend's board."

"Pretty extreme reaction if that's all it was, don't you think?" I press.

"Yeah, but he shouldn't have said that stuff about Chelsea." Travis stuffs a pizza slice in his mouth.

Paco mumbles and nods. "And J.T.'s name being on the list." He's got his mouth full, too.

"Wait, J.T.'s name is on the bathroom door?" I'm not getting much of my sandwich eaten.

Travis chugs his milk before answering. "Nah, the kid was just talking. He doesn't know anything."

Next to me, Jen stabs her salad hard with her fork. "We all agree the list is stupid, right? I mean when names are written there and those people weren't even at Ritter's Crossing that night, it makes no sense."

I know what she's saying, but the way she says it creeps me out a little. "First of all, there's no list.

It was painted over, remember? Second of all, I hope you're not saying it was okay to have anyone's names on it, Jen. Whether they were there or not, it doesn't matter. No one deserved to die."

"Except for Tim Jenks." She points her fork at me. "Didn't you see the press conference last night? They found fireworks in the backseat of his car."

"There was a press conference?" Last summer I avoided all the news about the fire, but now I'm obsessed. "What else did they say?"

"That's all, pretty much. Basically they're taking it as proof that Tim started the fire. No one knows why he did it and they wouldn't speculate."

"But they haven't found his body yet. How do they know Tim was there?" Levi's already told me how, but I'm not in the mood to reveal anything incriminating to the table, so I don't say anything about Jackie's text.

"Taryn, come on." Angel decides to add her two cents. "There's something disturbing about you sticking up for him."

Jen glares at me. "You're listening to his brother's lies, aren't you?"

Everyone's eyes on me. They don't know Levi and how he cares about his brother, how he's grieving.

"I'm not sticking up for him. I'm just —" I

stop. I want to believe Levi when he says his brother wouldn't do something like this. I shake my head and decide to finish my lunch. No one sitting here was there that night. What do they know?

Wait. I stop mid-chew.

I down the rest of my water then wipe my mouth with a napkin. "I have a random question. Why weren't any of you at the Gin Co. building that night? Weren't you invited to play night games?"

"Whoa." Travis holds up his hands.

"I'm appalled. Are you implying you wish we were?" Angel's fierce look says it all. "Kirstie, are you hearing this?" Kirstie's been so quiet through the whole conversation I almost forgot she's here.

"What are you saying, Taryn?" Jen asks.

"Nothing, never mind." I thought such a simple question would deserve a simple answer.

The bell rings and we gather our stuff. When I stand up to leave the table, Kirstie looks right at me. "We were invited. We just got there too late."

I guess I'm not the only one who feels bad for still being alive.

As the day passes I feel a little less guilty about not taking time to talk to Gretchen yesterday. Besides, any hope of ending rivalries was broken upside of J.T.'s head.

In Government, a student drops a note on my desk. "Someone told me to give you this." The note reads, "J.T. Webb punched Kenny Grimes, so Trek Lyons smacked him with the skateboard." It's from Gretchen. I don't know what good the information does me, though. It won't undo what's done.

The next morning Gretchen is barricading my locker. It's a rerun of last week, except she has Persi with her this time.

"To the bathroom. Right now." She practically drags me there, with her friend bringing up the rear.

There's a crowd around the bathroom door, and more inside, but she pushes through it. It's the army boots, I know. No one wants to get in their way. Soon I'm thrust into the stall and staring at the inside of the door.

Kenny Grimes and Trek Lyons have been added under Chelsea's name, and then J.T.'s, scrawled in different handwriting, under theirs. On a list that's not really there anymore, but is somehow still gathering names.

I don't move even when Gretchen says my name.

"Taryn?" She says it again.

I push open the door. Everyone in the bathroom has stopped talking and is staring at me, waiting for my reaction. They probably want some grand pronouncement, some great plan for how I'm going to fix this. How I'm going to unite the school.

I've got nothing.

Gretchen speaks first. "Did you get my note? You were right, we have to stop this before someone else gets hurt."

"How, Gretchen?" The bell rings, but nobody moves.

"What do you mean, how? We tell Mr. Myers. Kenny's afraid to say anything. Trek won't either, but we can. C'mon, I'll go with you."

I stall. I'm not ready to report anything because I just don't know. I haven't heard the straight scoop from any of the football players. I've heard Travis's and Paco's lame excuses, but I haven't talked to J.T.

Jen buzzes through the crowd and ends up next to me. "Let's get out of here, Taryn. You don't have to listen to her."

She pulls on me, but I don't move. I think Gretchen's stare-down is keeping me stuck in place. "Jen, please. Gretchen, I'm sorry, but—"

"If we don't speak up, nothing will change," Gretchen says.

Jen finally yanks hard enough to get me moving, but not fast enough to avoid Gretchen's wrath.

20

I drag myself into the house after school and drop onto a kitchen stool with a bag of Hot Cheetos. I made a special stop for them at the store. It was one of those days.

A note sitting on the counter reads: *Lasagna's in the freezer. Bake for 2 1/4 hours at 400 degrees. Love, Mom. P.S. Thanks for picking up Caleb from cross-country.*

Caleb! I completely forgot. Mom's spending the day with Tracy finishing the nursery for the twins. I check my watch. Twenty minutes late already. I grab keys, fish the wallet from my backpack, and make a dash to the car just as my cell phone jangles my ringtone.

"I'm on my way," I tell him.

"I'm not at school. I walked over to Webb's. They live down —"

"I know where they live." I drop the phone onto the passenger seat. It looks like ready-or-not, I'll get the chance to talk to J.T. When I ask him what happened he'll gloss over it as thick as possible, but he won't lie. Not to me.

Dang. I left the Cheetos on the kitchen counter.

I only hope this will go better than the scene with Gretchen in the bathroom. Her stinging rebuke still lingers. I tried to explain that I want to talk to J.T. first, but she blasted me. "At the dance didn't you ask me to talk to the skaters?"

It didn't end there. "You're the genius student body president who wants to create the perfect school year," she said. "No, not perfect. Ideal. The ideal school year. Wasn't that your platform?"

Persimmon of the pink bangs and perpetual braids stared wide-eyed right along with me, and how many others, I'm not sure. Gretchen's final questions particularly haunted me. "Did you think it would be easy?" she demanded. "Did you think change wouldn't require hard things? Like maybe you'd have to associate with members of the student body who aren't bleached-blonde and perky?"

It didn't help that blonde and perky Jen wouldn't keep her mouth shut. "Taryn, who is this person?" she kept asking. "Why are you even listening to her?"

I maneuver a quick U-turn and pull up close to the curb in front of Webb's red brick home. Maybe I'm not in the mood to talk to J.T. after all.

An unfortunately shirtless Mr. Webb ambles over to the passenger-side window carrying a garden hose with power sprayer attached. I dutifully roll down the window and wait while Mr. Webb puts the nozzle to his lips for a drink. Swishing the water like mouthwash, he promptly spits it on the grass, then sticks his head in the window's opening.

"Good to see you, Taryn. Keeping things in line over at IHS?" Is he making inane conversation or is this a sarcastic reference to the incident this week? The one his own son was involved in.

"Trying," is the only reply I can muster. The sight of J.T.'s bulk looming suddenly behind his dad's dispels the awkwardness.

"Tare! What up?"

"I'm here to pick up my brother." Apparently taking it as his cue, Mr. Webb tosses the sprayer on the grass and heads for the house. J.T. stuffs himself into my small front seat and shuts the door.

"I thought I'd see you at school today. Didn't you say the doctor cleared you?" The bandaged side of his head is away from me, but my eyes keep straying to it. I know he didn't suffer any serious injuries, and boasted about the sweet scar he would have after stitches were removed.

"I've been getting some threats and my dad wants me to hold off going back."

"Threats from who?" I ask, though I can guess the answer.

J.T. swears. “Those weasels on skateboards.”

“One of those weasels, as you call them, is suspended.”

“Yeah, and he’s ticked about it.”

“Wouldn’t you be? I mean if —” I stop, wondering if J.T. will fill in the blank.

Instead, he swears again. “I’m going to have to miss a game. We’ll beat Rustin easy, but it’ll kill me not to be out there.”

Rough, J.T.

“They’ll get what’s coming.”

“What?” I spit the question at him.

“You know. We’ll pay ‘em back.” He arches his shoulders.

“J.T., you cannot be serious. You guys are retaliating?”

“If that’s your nice way of saying ‘paybacks,’ then, yeah.”

“There’s nothing nice about it, J.T. You need to end it, not keep it going.”

“Oh, we’ll end it. Don’t worry.”

I swivel in my seat till I’m fully facing him. Blood pounds at my temples. I can’t wait a second longer for him to fill in the blanks. “What are you talking about? You started it, you jerk!” I hit him hard in the shoulder with an open palm.

J.T. pulls away from my outburst. “Hey, I just

got out of the hospital." He leans against the car window. "Taryn, you don't get it. This goes way back. It didn't start because I jumped on a guy's skateboard."

"I heard it was more than that. I heard you punched him." I dig my fingernails into the arm rest thinking J.T. should be grateful I don't have a hold of his arm. "Why don't you get that we need to be different after what happened at the beginning of the summer? Fighting and rivalries aren't helping."

J.T.'s look gets an edge to it. "Taryn, you don't know what this is about. Besides if I really wanted to hurt him, he'd be in the hospital right now. I barely popped him."

Caleb opens the car's back door.

"Never mind." I fall back in the driver's seat and grip the steering wheel. Forcing my fingers to relax, I take a deep breath, but it does nothing to unsqueeze the tightness across my chest. I think I'm finding out what I've known all along. Things are going to get worse at Ideal High before they get better.

Mr. Webb's doughy face appears in the passenger window again. "Sorry, it took a bit to get them off their video game. You know how it is."

J.T. waits until his dad leaves before trying to defend himself again.

“Not now, JT.”

“But —”

“I know how it is, okay?” I stare straight ahead and turn the key in the ignition. J.T. climbs out of the car and swings the door closed. I watch him in the rear view, still standing on the sidewalk even when I pull away.

Within seconds my phone beeps, signaling a text. From J.T. I touch the screen.

Why do you care so much?

Caleb speaks up from the backseat. “Don’t text and drive, Taryn.”

I tap the phone off and fling it to the floor. “Don’t worry, I’m not.”

“Cold cereal for dinner? That doesn’t sound like Mom.” Dad teases when he comes into the kitchen. “You picked a fine time to eat cereal, four hungry kids and a crop in the field,” he belts out in his best Texas twang.

“I didn’t get the lasagna in the oven in time. Sorry.” I sit hunched over a bowl at the bar, stirring soggy flakes into a whirlpool.

“I can do better.” Dad produces a pizza from the freezer and holds it up. “It’s vegetarian, but still.”

“I’m not hungry.” I carry my bowl to the sink,

flip a switch, and dump the contents down the disposal with a flush of tap water.

The sound echoes in my brain along with the questions that plague me. *Why do you care so much? Did you think it would be easy? That it wouldn't require hard things?*

"Taryn?"

I hadn't noticed Dad moving over to stand next to me.

"Are you okay?"

"Just some things I've got to work out." I finish rinsing the bowl and turn to place it in the dishwasher. "Plus homework. Tons and tons of homework." I can't remember anything about my day except J.T. and Gretchen, but I'm sure a fair amount of assignments await me, and they will hopefully provide the distraction I crave.

"I'm here if you need anything." He massages my shoulders like Mom sometimes does.

"I'll hold you to that, Dad." I relax into his plying grip for a moment.

Later, instead of digging into homework, I just stare at the computer screen. Maybe I can't do anything about J.T. and Trek Lyons, but that doesn't mean I can't try to help Jackie. Has it really been a week since I drove out to her house? Even thoughts of Levi have been pushed aside by the craziness of the last few days.

I punch in a new number I find for her. A girl answers.

I stumble over what to say. "This is Taryn Young. From school. Ideal High. Homeroom."

"Taryn Young?" It's Jackie.

"Taryn. From school. I wanted —" I silently wonder why Jackie would want to come back to Ideal High. Everything is so messed up. But I have to ask her about Tim Jenks.

"Why are you calling me?"

21

I enter school the next morning to find Ms. McKinney in the middle of a heated conversation with the head football coach.

"If Myers isn't going to do it, then you have to," the coach is saying. "Take care of Jenks, and take care of this." He gestures toward the office.

Take care of Levi? He didn't have anything to do with Tuesday's fight. I press flat against the foyer's brick wall and slide along its surface, grateful they are too occupied to notice me. Soon I have a full view of the glass-fronted office where Phyllis is working crowd-control.

"Taryn." Ms. McKinney walks my way. When she reaches me, she turns down the volume. "I haven't had a chance to talk to you since J.T. was hurt, but you can see we've got some parents with issues about Trek Lyon's suspension. Mrs. Ames said the two of you were out on the sidewalk. Do you know anything about what happened?"

I think about the look in J.T.'s eyes. About the paybacks he's planning. Maybe I don't know what's going on, but Gretchen's right. If we don't speak up, nothing will change.

I chew on my lip for a second. I'm done hiding. If I'm going to make a difference and turn good ideas into good causes, then I start right now.

"Ms. McKinney, I didn't see the whole thing, just the swinging skateboard, but I know that J.T. hit Kenny."

That's all that needs saying so I just walk away.

Once out in the courtyard, the sharp wind cuts across me. I bend into it and head to homeroom. My friends are going to dump me because I ratted out J.T., I let down Gretchen big time, and Mr. Myers will find a way to paint over the skater/jock incident like everything else. And Jackie hung up on me last night when I brought up Tim.

Fail.

Fail, fail, fail.

Maybe Jen and Kirstie had the best idea all along. Resignation. I'm not inspiring any unity, pride or respect so far among the student body. Maybe I really can't be president. Not under any circumstances.

But it's too late now.

At lunch the only vibes I get from Travis, Angel, and everyone else at the coveted A-listers' table are prickly ones. Not one of the football players will make eye contact. Even Jen is suddenly involved in a textbook or the latest shade of her fingernails when I come into close proximity. The fingernails are nothing new, but the reading of textbooks is way past obvious.

I grab a salad and take it to a corner of the courtyard. Eating with the wind at my back is challenging, but preferable to the stares and whispers behind cupped hands of the cafeteria. Not that I care what they're saying, I just need to regroup. Figure out what "not hiding" means. My plastic fork breaks and soon I'm slipping shredded lettuce and ham cubes into my mouth with my fingers. Finally, I dump my bowl into the trash, and decide to spend the rest of lunch hour in the bathroom.

"Taryn." Ms. Hightower points at me as I enter the school from the courtyard. "Just the person I want to talk to." The over-tanned teacher punctuates each word with a jab of her finger in my direction. "I'm on my way to my classroom, will you walk with me?"

Not if it's about cheer tryouts last week. I force a weak smile and wipe my palms down the sides of my jeans. They smell like ranch dressing, and that, or Ms. Hightower's request, produces an instant queasiness in my stomach.

Ms. Hightower holds the door open as we leave the main building to head to her classroom. We both pull back wind-swept bangs, and I remember my sticky fingers too late.

"Who's your Government teacher this year, Taryn?" the cheer advisor asks as we walk.

"Mr. Thomas."

"I should have guessed you were in AP Gov. Thomas is a good teacher." Ms. Hightower teaches sophomore and junior History, but I've never had her.

"Yeah." I reply. The small talk is brutal and we are only halfway to the 200 building. Is Ms. Hightower waiting till we get to her room before she attacks?

We enter the building and walk in silence to her room. At the door, the teacher gestures me through. "I want to show you something."

Once inside, she pulls a framed 8 X 10 from a bottom drawer of a file cabinet. Taking a tissue, she dusts the photo before turning it toward me. A variety of toothy blondes, brunettes, and a pair of redheads pose for the camera, decked out in red and gold cheerleading uniforms. I recognize the pretty, tanned face of Ms. Hightower beaming from the center of the group, her slender form matching the others.

"Did you know I was a cheerleader in college?" the teacher begins.

I nod.

"And at Ideal High, too. It was my dream. My older brother and my cousins were big football stars and all I wanted was to wear the uniform and cheer for them."

I nod again while discreetly pulling a tissue from off the desk to wipe my fingers. Everyone in the Texas Panhandle has heard of the Hightowers.

I slip the tissue into my pocket. My nerves jangle as I brace for the inevitable tirade about the sanctity of the cheer tryout.

Ms. Hightower sets the frame on her desk. "I used to display this proudly. Now it's an embarrassment, but not just for the reason you're thinking. I know I've gained weight, in fact, way too much since college."

I shift my stance, uncomfortable that the teacher speaks so personally.

"I started putting on weight my first year. The cheer coach gave me several warnings and then she, along with several of the girls I thought were my friends, forced me off the squad at the beginning of our sophomore year." Ms. Hightower stares off toward the back wall, unaware her American History students are trickling in from lunch to gather their belongings.

"They could do that?" I ask, hoping Ms. Hightower will make her point before the room is full of too many listening ears.

"Let's just say they made it very difficult for me to return."

I glance at the clock on the wall above the chalkboard and let out a slow breath.

"Long story short, Taryn, I couldn't stop thinking about this photo all week. I thought about the girl at cheer tryouts, just putting her heart into it, only to be made fun of. I thought of all the girls who don't have the skills or the popularity or whatever to be chosen as cheerleader, but would love to be a part of it, who maybe had dreams of being a cheerleader when they were little."

I might have pointed out that there was more to life than cheer, but I remember listening to Kayla, Ashley, and Keisha talk about it. I kind of get it. But really I cannot make this conversation any longer than it already is.

The bell signaling the end of the lunch hour rings. "Anyway." She stalls while seeming to gather her thoughts. "I heard what you did this morning and I admire you for telling the truth. That's why I changed my mind about your idea for a spirit club. Please, let Chelsea and me know how we can help."

I just stare at her. "Thank you," I say finally, though it comes out sounding like a question. I turn to exit with the last stragglers from the classroom, weaving my way through the clogged doorway of those trying to come in.

I wish I could run to the bathroom to wash my hands, but I'm going to be late as it is. At least late according to Mr. Thomas-time. He has a habit of starting class before the bell rings. When I drop into my seat a few rows from the front, he places a pop quiz in front of me.

"Nothing on your desks except a pen, people. You may begin once you receive your test."

I peruse the first few questions before starting in on number one. I got this.

Something smacks me on the back. I turn to find a catalog lying on the floor by my desk. An unsmiling Chelsea stares at me from farther down on the next row. So she's back in school today. I didn't see her in English.

"Ms. Hightower told me to give this catalog to someone," Chelsea says in a loud whisper. "She said you'd know who. It's for shirts for the Spirits, or whatever it is you're calling them." I read the title, *Cheer and Pep Club Uniforms*, before sliding it under my desk with my foot.

"Taryn, please report to my desk." When I

glance up I see that Mr. Thomas's lips are drawn in a thin line. He indicates the book on the floor. "And bring that with you."

He calls Chelsea up, too, and subjects us to a lecture about appropriate test-taking behavior, but that's not the worst of it. He has to put on a good show for the class, so he takes both our tests and rips them in half, then lets them flutter dramatically into the trash can. He thinks he's just scared the class into proper-test-taking etiquette, but they're probably silently cheering the class-president-and-head-cheerleader fail.

Thanks, Chelsea. I hate you.

22

"Taryn," Dad calls from downstairs. "Time to head out. Caleb?"

"Coming, dad," my brother yells back.

I slide a brush and a small mirror into my purse, then rummage through my backpack for my favorite lip gloss. After adding it in with the other items, I steal another look in the mirror on the inside of my bedroom door. The extra care I took with my makeup can't hide how I really feel about attending the football game tonight.

I pull at my red and blue Ideal High sweater and hope the black dress pants aren't too much. Just one more spritz of Sweet Pea-scented body spray, because maybe Levi's love of Ideal football will win out, and he'll show up to make the night bearable. I make a face at my reflection in the mirror. He said he wouldn't set foot on campus again and tonight is a home game. But it's been a full seven days since I last saw him. Not even a single glimpse of a pest control vehicle around town. I slip my purse over my shoulder and hit the lights.

Why am I even thinking about it? Obviously, I mean nothing to him and that's the way it needs to stay.

Dad whistles when I enter the kitchen. "You're all dressed up."

"It's the first home game. I have to represent the school." Truthfully, I'm worried about showing my face at all after what happened today.

"And you'll do a fine job, Madame President." He takes my hand and kisses it. I paste on a cheesy grin. If he only knew how un-fine of a job I'm doing.

"Where's Mom?"

"Remember? We're going to Carter's for a barbecue. She's already there helping set up."

I don't move. "I didn't know about this."

"I'm sure Mom told you."

"I could've gone to eat with friends," I whine. It isn't even close to the truth, like anyone would include me in their plans. I just want to get the night over with. Now I have to endure dinner, too, or get out of it.

"I don't want to go to Carter's, Dad," I force my point. "I can find something to eat at home."

"They really want to see you."

"They said that? 'We want to see Taryn.' Yeah, right," I don't bother to hide the sarcasm.

Caleb bolts down the stairs. “I’m going. Michael’s waiting for me,” he calls before slamming the door.

“Dad —” I plead.

He pulls me close. “I know it’s hard, but they don’t want you to avoid coming over just because Kayla’s gone.”

“They hate that I’m alive and not Kayla.”

“That makes no sense. Sure, they’re still grieving, but they miss seeing you.”

“You’re making this up.”

“Taryn.” Dad runs his fingers through his receding hairline with a free hand, just as his phone rings. He releases his hold from around my shoulder and takes the cell from his pocket.

“No, we’re still here.” He keeps the phone to his ear, but gestures at me. “Mom says bring some napkins. Do you know where they are?”

“Can I talk to her?”

He listens to the phone for a moment, then looks at me. “She says you’re going.”

I open the pantry, snatch a pack of napkins, drop them ceremoniously onto the counter, and march to the front door. Throwing it wide open, I’m immediately assaulted by wind that warns of a cold night. Holding back my bangs, I descend the few steps leading to the stone walkway, grateful for the warmth of my high school cardigan.

"Nice day for a barbecue," I mutter. I'm almost to the sidewalk when I see the Manor's pearl-white SUV parked in front of the Carter's house. The Manors are coming to dinner, too.

Dad catches up to me and says again, "You're going." If he didn't latch onto my elbow when he said it, I'd be back home by now. Instead, we make the short walk between our house and Carter's two doors down.

I never really explained to my parents why, back in ninth grade, Chelsea suddenly no longer came around, why there were no more sleepovers at the Manor's house, or why phone calls between me and my best friend became nonexistent. They asked plenty of times, but I always made up an excuse.

My bruised pride kept me from telling the truth about how Chelsea didn't choose me for the American History Bowl's A-Team. She chose Kayla, who we'd only known for a few months. I was relegated to the B-Team — super-geek Harrison's team — along with the Fletcher twins. Darius Fletcher constantly had his inordinately protruding nose in a tissue and Darwin had bad breath. Or was it the other way round? I refused to meet with them to practice, choosing instead to study on my own.

After a humiliating loss in the first round and Team-A's subsequent first place victory. I started being really busy when Chelsea called or wanted to hang out at school. We shared so many of the same advanced classes, but as time went by ignoring her became a habit, and eventually she moved on to a new best friend. Kayla wasn't my favorite person either, but with Carters as neighbors, it was impossible not to be sociable. She always pretended everything was okay, and so I let her drag me along to parties and school events.

My resentment at the thought of sitting across the dinner table from Chelsea Manor vanishes once I'm in the Carter's living room. Warm feelings of a happier time wash over me when Mrs. Carter draws me into an immediate hug.

"Taryn, it's been too long," she whispers. I stiffen when pleasant memories are hit head-on by reality, and my thoughts whirl between the two, each not wanting to give place for the other. Do I focus on the warm and fuzzy past or do I acknowledge the bleakness of the present. The present that means Kayla is gone. I wait out the long embrace, grateful that I don't have to say anything.

Finally, Mrs. Carter holds me at arm's length. "You look beautiful." The bit of wistfulness in her voice makes me squirm inside. "And Student Body President. That's wonderful. I'm so proud of you, Taryn." She turns to give my dad a quick hug. "Thank y'all for coming. We've missed our family get-togethers."

Dad nods.

"Well, let's finish getting dinner on the table." Mrs. Carter breaks the mood. "Andrew and Brad are in the office discussing that horrible lawsuit." She shakes her head. "I expect them to be done shortly. While we wait, could y'all help bring things from outside? With the wind up we're eating in, I'm afraid."

I follow my dad to the back patio and find little Hannah towing a red wagon behind her. Mrs. Carter is right. It has been way too long.

"How are you, cutie pie?" I scoop her up and take her into the kitchen where my mom is cutting watermelon. "Look who I found."

A door closes down the hall and Chelsea appears at the end of the hallway leading to the kitchen dressed in her Bulldog cheerleading uniform. Under her sleeveless top and pleated skirt, she wears a crimson red turtleneck.

"Kessie." Hannah unhooks her legs from around my waist and I help her slide to the floor. She toddles over to take Chelsea's hand and leads her into the kitchen.

Mrs. Carter's eyes light up. "I'm actually glad to have you both here. Hannah, will you help Mrs. Young set out the napkins? I want to talk to Taryn and Chelsea a minute."

She leads us into the living room. "Go ahead and take a seat on the couch. I want to show you something." She pulls a navy blue book from the drawer of a side table and carries it to an arm chair next to us.

"Can you sit here together?" She indicates the closest end of the couch, so I slide down to close the physical gap between me and Chelsea.

"I don't know if either of you knew this, but Kayla kept a journal, you know, a diary. I've spent the last few weeks reading and rereading it." She runs her finger over Kayla's name engraved in gold on the lower right corner. "You both meant so much to Kayla. Do you mind if I share some of it with you?"

I don't say anything. I just nod and focus on Mrs. Carter's face as she gently thumbs through the lined pages. Gravity is pressing a little too hard on my chest.

"Here it is." She smoothes the book open. "This was written August twenty-sixth, the summer we moved here."

Today was the first day of class at my new school, Crockett Jr. High. Remember all the terrible things I said about moving to Ideal, well, I guess it's not going to be as bad as I thought. School was pretty okay. There's lots of cute guys, even though a few actually wear cowboy boots to school! My friends back home will love that. None of the cool guys wear boots. At least that's what I was told. My science teacher, Mr. Harris, is so weird.

"Oh, sorry, I shouldn't have read that part," Mrs. Carter interjects.

"Don't worry, it's not news to us," Chelsea says.

"Everyone thought so." We speak over the top of each other.

Mrs. Carter continues, "*Anyway, I met some nice people. Taryn Young and Chelsea Manor are in most of my classes, and they invited me to eat lunch with them. Then I found out Taryn lives two doors down from us, so that's cool. I still totally miss Nikki and Brittany, but it felt good to finally make some friends. I miss Utah, but my Mom's happy she's close enough now to take care of Grandma.*

Later: Taryn, that I talked about before, just came over to see if I wanted to walk over to the park. Sometimes kids in the neighborhood get together and play basketball there. It was so fun. I met about five people that live around here. Taryn said Chelsea doesn't live that close, but they're best friends, so she comes over a lot. Next time she does, she said they'll come get me so we can hang out.

Mrs. Carter stops reading but keeps the book open. "There's more, of course." She strokes its pages.

I shift uncomfortably. Mrs. Carter's look seems to bore right through me. What else did Kayla write?

"You two meant everything to Kayla," she continues without missing a beat. "From that very first day of school, you were there for her. I just wanted to tell you thank you."

Mrs. Carter gets a faraway look in her eyes. "Kayla hated the idea of moving to Texas — well, that's putting it mildly. She definitely expressed her feelings about that in her journal." She pats the book and laughs, but there's sadness at its core.

I brace myself. Is Kayla's mom going to reveal more from the journal — embarrassing things about the academic team and my wounded pride, or unflattering comments I made about Chelsea over the years?

Instead, Mrs. Carter sets the journal on the end table. "I'm from here, but it wasn't home to Kayla until you helped make it that way."

"Jane." We hear Mr. Carter call from the kitchen. The smell of burgers cooking wafts in from the kitchen and the noises intensify as everyone gathers. I hear Mr. Manor teasing Hannah.

"In here, honey," Mrs. Carter calls back. She kneels in front of the couch and takes her time looking at us before speaking again. "With my oldest married and away at college, we don't get to see her as often as we'd like. Hannah needs you two to be her big sisters. The boys, too. Kayla's gone, but y'all are welcome here anytime." She pats our knees, and then dabs at her eyes. "I love you both and I look forward to watching you grow and succeed in whatever life brings you."

I nod, stone-faced. I don't hear a sound from Chelsea and I'm determined not to look at her. Besides, I don't dare break Mrs. Carter's gaze.

"Goodness, this is supposed to be a game-day barbecue. What am I doing getting all sentimental? Let's eat before we're late for the kick-off." She leaves to join the others.

An awkward silence settles in the living room, but immediately it's broken by Chelsea's sniffling. I fidget, not comfortable with what's streaming through my brain. The journal entry stirs up memories I built a wall against, of a time when Chelsea and I were as close as sisters. Our friendship then was so solid that even inviting Kayla to join our twosome back in ninth grade didn't threaten it. At least until the American History Bowl.

I pick at my sweater.

Chelsea's still sniffling.

Is it rude to get up and leave the room without saying anything at all? I risk a glance her direction.

"I didn't throw that catalog at you in Government," Chelsea blurts out, and it startles me.

"What?"

"I didn't throw the catalog."

"I know what I felt hitting me in the back," I stare straight ahead again.

"I asked Sam to pass it to you, but he threw it instead. He was trying to be funny."

"Real funny."

"I just wanted you to know."

"Now I do." More uncomfortable silence follows, interrupted only by Mrs. Carter exclaiming from the kitchen that the food is ready.

I stand up, not wanting to invite more conversation. I'm across the living room when Chelsea speaks again. "Taryn?"

I stop to look at her. Her eyes glisten and she seems to fight a losing battle against a runny nose, but her mouth twists into a half-smile.

“Remember when Mr. Harris started the lab on fire, but didn’t stop his lecture the entire time he was trying to put it out?”

I bite my lip and nod.

“He really was weird, wasn’t he?” Chelsea says.

“Yeah.” That’s all I say before bolting from the room.

23

I hold off my emotions until I lie safely under the black and white paisley of my comforter after the football game. I roll onto my stomach and dig my fingernails into the pillow, irked that Chelsea was so emotional at Carters. And why did she bring up freshman-year Science? That was forever ago.

She seemed her usual energetic, controlling self at the game. She ordered the cheerleaders around, met the opposing school's leaders at mid-field, then was bouncy and smiley when leading the Ideal High Fight Song after each touchdown.

She was also plenty perky when talking to Levi Jenks. I saw them across the parking lot after the game. It hurt that he didn't care enough to find me to talk to. No, just Chelsea. Even though it's only because he wants to talk to her about the fire, it still stings. I really wanted to ask him about the fireworks police found.

My pillow is streaked with mascara, but I'm too exhausted to find a tissue. Why are my emotions so out of whack? Chelsea and her dad didn't stay for dinner, so it was bearable after all. Someone mentioned the press conference and everyone agreed the lawsuit would be dropped soon. That's hopeful news.

She wouldn't say why, but Ms. McKinney took the principal's place with us on the field. Travis was quiet, and I assumed it was because he was mad at me for telling on J.T., but then he was given a microphone. He announced that the team was dedicating the game to Weston Brown, last year's quarterback, and one of the victims of the fire.

The announcement about Weston was followed by a huge display of banners, balloons, and even a fog machine as the team rushed onto the field. The cheerleaders outdid previous home openers and it made me wonder what they can possibly do for homecoming.

Zeke Miller showed up near the end of the game. Dad spotted him in the parking lot and cornered him for at least ten minutes talking about Tech football while I stood by and tried to smile at the appropriate times. He repeated what he said last Sunday, about how we should hang out sometime, but before I could say anything he said he had to go. I watched him catch up with Chelsea when she was getting into her car.

I roll over again, then flip the pillow onto my face. I am not wasting time thinking about former best friends, jerk football players, and cowboy-types that have no interest in me. Why can't my brain just switch to off and let me sleep?

I prop my pillow under my head and in the dim light coming from under my door, I reach for the Junior Prom photo of me and Blake from its place. Our cheesy grins and king and queen crowns bring back memories of the best night of my life.

Almost four months. Is that a long time or a short time when it comes to grieving a death? How about grieving seven deaths? Is the time multiplied?

Still clutching the photo, I turn my pillow over to find a dry spot. I should get up, wash off my makeup, and get out of my clothes, especially the sweater that's feeling way too warm now. Those things take energy, though, and sleep begins to be more than a suggestion.

Does mascara wash out? The thought flits across my mind and is gone. I don't know the answer to it or any others that are plaguing me.

Should Levi just accept that his brother started the fire? Maybe then he can grieve properly and move on. Like Chelsea talking about Mr. Harris. Seriously, move on.

I shrug my sweater off and slide my pants to the floor. Sleep is preferable to my thoughts running in circles.

I reposition my pillow. Focus on the present. That's the way to get over tragedy.

My cell phone buzzes on the night stand, dragging me out of a shadowy half-sleep to check the text. I don't recognize the number.

Answer your door.

I check the time. Nearly midnight. Plenty of my friends would think the night is still young, but not me. Not tonight.

The cell buzzes again.

Hurry.

I feel around for my bathrobe, but can't find it, so I shuffle to my dresser and pull out a long T-shirt to throw on. I step quietly down the hall with my arms wrapped across my chest, intentionally ignoring the light switch. It better not be Jen. But it wouldn't be. Not after what I did to J.T.

If it's Zeke. I groan. He said we should hang out. I flip the light on in the hall bathroom and squint into the mirror. After splashing water on my face, I take a tissue to the mascara streaks and smooth down my hair. I give up and head down the stairs.

I crack the front door open to find Chelsea standing on the porch shivering. "Can I come in? It's cold."

I open the door another quarter-inch, the wind

chilling my bare legs. "What do you want?"

"I need to tell you something."

"Look, I get that you didn't throw that catalog at me."

"Taryn. Please?"

"It's midnight, Chelsea. If it's about me ratting out J.T., I don't want to talk about it. We creamed the Harvesters 35 to 3, even without him."

Chelsea stands waiting, the wind throwing her long hair out in wild bunches, her eyes big as saucers. Either she's desperate or just determined. I open the door enough to allow entrance, then lean against it once it's shut. I ignore her glance at the living room and its inviting leather couches. The conversation is going no farther than the entry.

"I saw you with Zeke Miller tonight," Chelsea begins. When I don't respond, she continues. "I need to warn you about him."

"Warn me?" My eyes narrow. More than they are already.

"He's bad news. I'm telling you, Taryn, stay away from Zeke."

"Since when do you tell me who I can and cannot hang out with?"

"Taryn, you don't know."

"No, Chelsea, you don't know. I quit caring what you think a long time ago." Hurt fills her eyes, but I don't stop. "What if I told you to stay away from Levi?"

"Levi? I just met him for the first time after the game tonight."

"But you know who he is, right? I just thought it was strange that you were hanging out with the guy that interrupted the memorial service."

A new look of confusion and something else that I can't place appears in Chelsea's expression. "He's the one —?" She leans heavily on the banister.

"He's not that bad," I backtrack. "I've talked to him, too. He's just trying to figure out what happened that night."

"But —" Chelsea looks away.

What is going on with this girl? Anything about the fire freaks her out. "You were there, remember? The memorial?" It's like I'm talking to a two-year-old all of a sudden.

"It was a blur," Chelsea whispers. I think she's in one now. "What are people saying about his brother? What does Levi say?"

"He didn't ask you about the fire?"

"No. We talked, but —" she hesitates. "Someone wrote all over my car windows. He helped me clean it off."

"What was on your windows?"

Chelsea stares at me. “Are you serious, Taryn? You’ve heard the things people say about me. Keisha’s cousin wasn’t the first or the last. It’s everybody. Jen hates me. Even Angel and Kirstie are mad at me.”

I have no answer. Chelsea is far from my favorite person, but I don’t blame her for the tragedy.

Should I?

“Wait.” Chelsea drops onto the first stair, still clinging to the banister with one hand. “Is Levi the guy that called me last week? I told him to leave me alone.”

“Why won’t you talk to him? Is it because his brother started the fire?”

“Why would you think that?” Chelsea’s eyes widen.

“Where have you been? There was a press conference earlier this week. They said they found fireworks in Tim’s car.”

“How did fireworks get in his car?”

I’m confused. “Do you know something you’re not telling me, Chelsea?”

Now she won’t answer. She just sits there.

She’s making me crazy.

“Look, if you can clear up what happened, why don’t you? Even if it’s not what Levi wants to hear, at least he can quit wondering."

She appears to think about it at least. "Who told you the fire was his brother's fault? Did Zeke say that?"

"Zeke? No." I make a face at her. "That's what people are saying. In the newspaper. At the press conference."

"I don't read or watch anything about the fire. I can't handle it."

That I can relate to. I pace back and forth across the small entryway, wishing I had found my robe or at least grabbed a blanket. It's cold.

Finally, I stop in front of her. "If it was Tim Jenks' fault, you're off the hook. No more lawsuit, right?"

She doesn't reply. Instead she pulls her legs up close and places her chin to her knees. With her arms wrapped tight around her body and her blonde hair falling forward she looks like she did on the bathroom floor at the Howdy Dance.

I kneel in front of her on the tile, adrenaline pumping through me like it did that night. "Chelsea, why did you say that 'sometimes people make accidents happen?'"

Seconds tick by, then suddenly she's standing, checking her watch, and pulling her jacket close around her. "You're right, we should get our stories straight. But not yet."

"What stories, Chelsea?" But she is gone in a gust of wind, leaving me to sink to the stairs in exhausted confusion.

24

Saturday night, Dad sticks his head in my room where I'm sprawled on the bed reading a novel assigned in English class. "Mom called from Tracy's and said she'll meet us at the Grapevine for dinner. Wanna come?"

"Sure. If you want to take me away from *The Scarlet Pimpernel.*"

"A dermatologist could take care of that for you."

"It's a classic, Dad. And actually pretty good."

"I'll take your word for it. Ready to go?"

"Yeah, but are you sure you and mom don't want to go alone? Caleb's gone to a friend's house. I can find something to eat here."

"Normally, yes, but she wants to check in with you. A mom thing."

"Let me grab some shoes."

At the restaurant, once our salads are arranged in front of us, the grilling starts. My parents pepper me with questions about what's happening at school.

"It's almost October and I haven't been able to

make any changes," I lament when the questions stop.

"You can't expect things to happen overnight, honey." Mom pats my arm.

"I'm not asking for overnight." I say it a little too firmly, then stop when I feel adrenaline rising.

"Taryn, the students are hurting. It's only been a few months since the fire."

"You mean they're hurting each other." I stab at a cherry tomato, but it skids across my plate. "I thought the tragedy would somehow make everyone get along. They would realize life is short and treat each other better."

"That sounds like your campaign speech. Obviously, it struck a chord because they elected you, but be patient." Mom takes a bite of salad. "And you've done plenty. Senior Spirits. The Advisory Committee. Paw Pals."

"And you were just telling me on the way here about a tutor club," Dad interjects between bites.

I pick up the tomato and plop it in my mouth. Just one bite runs seeds and juice down my chin.

"Hey, my man, Zeke." Dad is on his feet patting Zeke on the back before I can even reach for my napkin.

"It's the Youngs again. Hi, Taryn." He nods.

"Is someone waiting for you or can you join us

for a minute?" Dad pulls out the chair next to him.

"I have a second."

I follow Zeke's eyes to the front of the restaurant, then turn my attention back to him when he drops down next to my dad and is immediately drawn into a discussion of Tech football. I pick at the remains of my salad, admiring again how Zeke's dark hair curls up at the ends and how he fills out his Red Raiders jacket.

I spear a large lettuce leaf and guide it into my mouth.

My dad places his hand on Zeke's shoulder and flashes me a look. "I've got a proposition for you, Zeke. How would you like to escort my lovely daughter to Ideal High's Homecoming Dance?"

I bite down too hard on my fork. What did he just say?

I finally pull the fork out, but now I look ridiculous choking down a huge piece of lettuce and my eyebrows practically lifting off my face.

"Dad!" I can't bear to look at Zeke.

"Honey!" Mom's as surprised as I am.

"Sure, I mean, do you want to, Taryn?" Zeke does the polite thing. I'll give him that.

I swallow noisily. "You don't have to take me to homecoming. My dad does not find my dates, I promise."

Dad gestures in front of himself. "In my defense, weren't you just saying in the car that you weren't planning to go with a date to the dance?"

"Dad." I rub my temples. "How does that translate to me needing you to find me one?"

"But Zeke's a good guy. I know he'd love a chance to be back at Ideal High, right?" He clamps his hand on Zeke's shoulder again.

"Yeah, sure." He looks toward the front of the restaurant again.

Poor Zeke. He's silently begging for his date to come save him. What if it's Chelsea? It would be just like her to warn me about him while claiming him for herself. Now I can't keep my eyes off the lobby.

"How about I call you, Taryn?"

I look at him. "Fine."

Chelsea emerges from another part of the restaurant. Then Levi appears. Zeke swivels in his seat, then stands. I do, too, beating him into the aisle.

"Be right back," I say to my parents. I head toward the entrance, suddenly worrying that somebody needs saving. Chelsea from Levi or Levi from Chelsea, maybe even Levi from Zeke. I'm not sure about anything right now.

Zeke taps me from behind. "Where are you

going, Taryn?" When I don't stop he passes me to get there first. He snatches Chelsea away from Levi in one motion. "Back off, Jenks. She told you to leave her alone."

Chelsea wrenches her arm away and turns her glare from Levi to Zeke. "Don't touch me." She stomps out the front door, completely ignoring me.

Zeke squares his shoulders. "Why are you going after her, dude? Just so you can shift the blame off your brother? That's cold." He follows Chelsea out the door, but not before threatening Levi with bodily harm if he doesn't keep his distance.

I lock eyes with Levi, certain that he can read my confusion, but the moment's lost when my dad appears. "What's going on? Are you okay?"

"I'm not sure." I look at Levi again. He leans forward, his head in his hands.

"Your food's ready."

"I'll be there in a second, Dad. I have to talk to someone." Dad eyes Levi, then flashes me a questioning look. I really don't want him to figure out who he is before I have a chance to explain everything, but there isn't time now.

"Taryn?" My dad leans in close. "That's the kid from the memorial." Too late. "I don't think you talking to him is such a good idea."

"Dad, I'm fine." I touch his arm to reassure him. "Can we talk about it later?"

"Mom's not going to like this."

One more "please" sends him back to our table.

I sit on the bench next to Levi and speak to his back. "So Chelsea talked to you?"

He sighs heavily. "For what it's worth, she said my brother was there." He pauses. "She said he started the fire."

That's pretty much exactly what I told Chelsea to say to Levi last night.

"I'm sorry." Instinctively I place a hand on his shoulder. "Maybe it's better just knowing. Then you can get past it."

He jerks upright and my hand drops to my lap.

"Will you get past it knowing my brother caused the death of a bunch of your friends? Will anyone?"

I bite my lip as the faces of Blake and Kayla appear in my head. "But it was an accident, right?" I say evenly.

"Of course. An accident. Nobody's fault, right? Except for Tim's." Levi stands and begins pacing the lobby. "Then tell me why Chelsea Manor can't explain her part in all of it? And why is that jerk, Zeke, trying to shut me up — along with the entire football team?" A mix of anger and grief shines in his steel blue eyes and I wish I knew what to say to erase them both.

"Zeke's just protecting Chelsea, that's all. And what do you mean about the football team?"

"SomeThey're threatening me, telling me to quit hounding the police about my brother."

I can't help groaning. "It just keeps getting better and better, doesn't it?" My eyes wander across the restaurant, hoping diners are focusing more on their entrees than the craziness that is center stage in the Grapevine lobby tonight. My eyes stop on Mom who is gesturing from our table.

"Look, I have to go." I make eye contact with Levi again.

He stops in front of me and catches my hands in his. "Taryn, come with me to Ritter's Crossing. Show me what you saw, where people were, what happened."

I push his hands away. "I can't."

"Please, Taryn. They say there were fireworks in Tim's car."

"I already know about the fireworks, so what are you saying? No, wait, I don't care. I never want to see the burned-out Gin Co. building again."

"Tim was scared of them. He was when he was little and he never got over it. He wouldn't have them and he for sure wouldn't be lighting any."

"You're not listening to me." My face burns, just thinking about that place, that night.

"I can't figure you out. I thought you said you wanted to help me. Help my brother."

"Levi —"

"Taryn, eight people were killed in that fire. If one of them was your brother wouldn't you want to know what happened?"

I bristle at that. "People I cared about died, Levi. They weren't family, but close enough, so don't try to say I don't get it."

"Sorry, I didn't mean to imply that." He moves to sit beside me again, resting his elbows on his knees. He runs his fingers through his short-cropped hair. "The fireworks had to be planted by somebody."

"So you're not accepting what Chelsea said?"

"Would you? I still think she's hiding something."

"Why would she lie?"

"Then why didn't she say this before? She's just trying to shut me up."

"Forget what Chelsea says, if you don't believe her. Just look at the evidence."

"The evidence doesn't fit what I know."

I sit still for a second, hoping to diffuse the tension. Why is he taking this out on me? When I speak again, it's as calmly as I can. "Levi, maybe she kept quiet about him being there because she didn't want to hurt your brother more by having his name dragged through the mud."

But Levi isn't listening. He grasps my arm. "Taryn, please come to Ritter's Crossing."

Mom shows up. She's clearly not pleased that the guy that interrupted the memorial has a hold of my arm. "Your food is getting cold," she says.

I drag myself back to the table where I twist fettuccine in figure eights with my fork, wondering why I feel like what Levi said last week, "shoved onto a bull in a bucking chute." And, ready or not, the gate is going up.

25

Levi called me five times on Sunday and texted me three. He found my phone number, obviously, but now I don't want to talk to him. I am not going to Ritter's Crossing. Before heading to Lubbock with my dad and brother after school on Monday, I set my phone on the desk in my room and walk out the door.

Soon we're taking turns in the hospital's neonatal unit gazing at the delicate hands and fingers of Tracy and Perry's twins. Amid the tubes, tape, and miniature diapers that still look too big, they cling together. Twin pink bows top their doll-sized heads. Mom went straight to the hospital from the Grapevine Saturday night, and after several hours of labor and a Caesarian Section the pair of underweight, but healthy babies arrived.

I'm an aunt. I've got two cute little bundles to set an example for now.

"They're like little wrinkled aliens," Caleb states. "They're hooked up to these machines, getting all kinds of information, then when they come out, they're taking over the world."

"Exactly, Caleb. That's what kids do," Dad says.

"They can take over my world all they want. They are so cute," I chime in.

Caleb groans. "That's my limit on hearing the word 'cute' in one day. Can I go get something to eat?"

Dad sends him to the cafeteria with ten dollars, and I take another turn with the babies. "Your dad's sisters are nice, but I'm going to be your favorite aunt," I whisper.

Dad has to pull me away when nurses start checking charts and exchanging looks like maybe they have actual work to do to keep the newborns thriving.

When we get back to Tracy's room Dad announces he's going to the cafeteria, too. "Anybody want anything?"

"I'll go with you, Dad."

Dad touches my elbow, turning me toward the elevators. "You okay?" he asks when we reach the first level.

I step out of the elevator ahead of him. "Just kind of amazing how these new little people come into the world so easily and quietly. I wish leaving the earth didn't have to be violent sometimes."

"There are plenty of women who would say

birth isn't so easy. And I was there when you were born. Your mother was not quiet."

"But why does God do that? Why can't he take us back more peacefully?"

"Sometimes he does, but, really, would that make it any easier on those left behind?"

"It might lessen the nightmares, that's for sure."

Dad places an arm around my shoulder and pulls me close to his side "You're having trouble sleeping?"

"I'm talking about when I'm awake, Dad."

He exhales heavily.

Poor dad. "At least I don't do drugs," I offer.

"What?" He frowns in confusion. "Where did that come from?"

"I've put you through a lot the last couple of months, but at least I don't do drugs."

"Taryn, you haven't done anything. Yes, the summer was rough. It killed me to watch you suffer, but I'm proud of you. Leading the school, helping others." He leans in to kiss my forehead. "I love you, honey. I'm so proud of you."

"You said that twice, Dad."

"Well, it's true. Now as for your original question, maybe it's not God that dictates violent deaths. Maybe choices people make play a part.

Like the person who engages in risky behavior."

"I hope you're not hinting that the lawsuit has any point to it."

"No, but we're all human and sometimes we do things without thinking and those things end up hurting people. Not on purpose, of course."

His words remind me again of Chelsea's chilling comment, "Sometimes people cause accidents." Levi's right. Chelsea knows something.

At the doors of the hospital cafeteria, Dad points out Caleb who has planted himself in front of a big-screen TV with a plateful of ketchup-covered fries.

I notice the gift shop farther up the hall where a display of colorful knick knacks invites customers in. An array of blown-glass angels shimmers in the late sun that pours in from the windows surrounding the lobby. "I think I'll take a walk."

"You don't want something to eat?"

"I'm good."

Dad kisses my forehead again before I continue on to the gift shop where the pretty pinks and purples of the baby girl section catch my attention. The high price tags soon lessen the fun of window shopping, so I wander back down the hall toward the bank of elevators, wondering if the nursing staff will allow me another glimpse of the babies.

I round the corner to find the elevator door closing, but a woman's bejeweled hand reaches out to stop it. I slide in between the gap. The woman moves to the back of the elevator, holding on to the rail that runs the length of it. She keeps her eyes to the floor, but her heavy scent perfumes the area. I mumble a thank you and turn to press the floor for maternity, keeping my breaths as shallow as possible.

Soon the elevator stops. The woman's heels click as she steps from the carpeted floor of the elevator to the fourth floor oncology wing and with her a wave of familiarity. The monochromatic too-tight pantsuit, the mincing steps, the over-styled, bottle-red hair, and that breathtaking-but-in-a-bad-way perfume — there is no mistake.

I catch the closing doors with a karate chop. "Mrs. Foster," I call to the retreating backside. "It's Taryn."

"Taryn?" Mrs. Foster turns and I can't help noticing the dark circles and the excess cover up across Jen's mother's cheeks.

I let the elevator doors close behind me. "How are you? How's Jen?"

"Oh, you know." Mrs. Foster purses her lips, then waves her hand as if waving away the question.

"Jen told me about your, you know, your . . . I'm so sorry."

"These things happen." She exhales heavily, then begins to play with the strap of her shoulder bag. "I guess I find out my fate today." She smiles, but it's forced.

"Seriously? Is anyone here with you?" Mrs. Foster's fidgeting makes me nervous, but I stay rooted in place.

"You know the kids . . . always busy, and Jen had to watch my baby grandson at the last minute."

"Can I sit with you?"

Mrs. Foster protests, but I follow anyway, taking a seat next to her after she signs in.

"So how's Jen really?" I pick up the question again since I'm not sure what more I can say about a cancer diagnosis.

"Well, I worry about her, but what mother doesn't worry about her daughter, you know?"

I nod. "Yeah," I begin, but I'm interrupted by a voice coming from the elevator.

A short woman in a long, ruffled skirt and low-heeled slip-ons stops in front of us. She leans over to embrace Mrs. Foster. The ends of a colorful scarf covered in geometric patterns falls forward from where it's tied around her bald head.

"Donna, it's so good to see you," Mrs. Foster

says, clearly pleased. "I didn't realize you had an appointment today, too." The woman named Donna takes the empty seat on the opposite side of Mrs. Foster.

"Today's the day when you get your results, isn't it? Of course, I'm going to be here." Mrs. Foster leans over to give the woman another hug, a much longer one this time. When they part, Donna hands her a tissue. "Now don't start that already. Introduce me to your daughter."

"Sorry. Donna —" She stops. "I don't even know your last name." She turns to me. "We met right here in this waiting room. She's my cancer buddy." She forces a laugh. "She's the experienced one, so she picked me up off the floor after the initial shock."

"She's not kidding. No, really, you did just fine. And you'll do fine today." Donna pats Mrs. Foster's arm and then extends a hand toward me. "I'm Donna Weir, breast cancer survivor extraordinaire. So far anyway."

"Taryn and my daughter are best friends," Mrs. Foster adds.

I smile at Mrs. Foster's assumption that the friendship is still intact, or maybe she is just being polite, but inside I'm squirming, itching to ask the obvious question of Mrs. Weir. "Are you by chance from Ideal? You have a daughter my age, don't you?"

"From outside Ideal, actually, but yes, Jackie's my daughter. Do you know her?" Mrs. Weir's mouth forms a straight line.

I plunge forward. "I don't know if you know this, but I've been trying to talk to Jackie and convince her to come back to school."

"Well, funny you should mention that because last night the cute boy from across the way came over and talked to her about the same thing."

"Who, Levi?" I sputter.

"Yes, that Jenks boy." She smiles. "He's so nice to think about Jackie after what he's been through with his brother."

Mrs. Foster grimaces. "The word is his brother's responsible for the fire."

Mrs. Weir wrinkles her nose in response. "It's not possible. Tim Jenks wouldn't, and couldn't, have hurt a fly."

Mrs. Foster smiles and seems to relax more the longer Mrs. Weir stays, but I'm fuming. Here I've been scheming for weeks to get Jackie back to school and Levi waltzes over, flashes a smile, and that's it? Why is he inserting himself into my business? He doesn't even go to Ideal High.

I stand up to leave. "I'm sure my family is

waiting for me." I cross the room and press the elevator button.

Forget about Levi. Concentrate on Jackie coming back. She'll need friends. The Tutor Club will help, right?

The elevator dings. I go in, but hold the door. "Mrs. Weir? When's Jackie coming back?"

"I called the school today, so I expect very soon," Mrs. Weir replies. The elevator closes. Ready or not, Jackie's back.

On the way home to Ideal, Dad pulls into Stan's gas station, as always. Me and Caleb say it with him. "Stan's got a better price than anyone in town."

Dad laughs. "Anyone need anything?"

"I knew you were going to say that." Caleb says.

"Your old dad is that predictable?"

"Apparently, when it comes to getting gas, yes you are." I flash him a grin.

Caleb busts up laughing. "Good one, Taryn."

While my dad pumps gas I flip through pictures of the twins on his phone to show Caleb. "Look at this one. They're so cute."

"Stop saying that word."

"Cute, cute, cute. Get used to it." I flip through

a few more. "This one's my favorite. They're so cute."

Caleb opens the car door. "I'm going into the store. Text me when dad's done."

Two Ideal City police cars pull up to the convenience store, and Mel and another officer enter the building. Could be a planned coffee break. Or something else. I climb out of the car. I don't want Mel to see me, but I'm curious.

I grab Caleb's arm. "Will you do me a favor and see what the police are doing here?"

"You're hiding from the law now?" Caleb jokes.

"I don't want to talk to Mel again, but I'm wondering if he's working on something related to the fire." I admit it. I'm paranoid.

I move behind Caleb when the officers and Stan's son, Johnny, exit the building and walk around to the side of it. Fortunately, it's starting to get dark out, so they probably won't even notice us. I watch as Johnny talks and points and Mel scribbles on a notepad.

"Ready to go?" Dad's done.

"I think I need to go to the bathroom. Caleb, come with me." I drag him along, making sure to keep him between me and Mel. I don't let go until we're inside.

"Are you okay, Taryn?" Caleb rubs his arm where I clung to it.

"Just find something to buy." I grab a pack of gum. "Get this." He takes it, but now he's more confused than ever, I think. We walk up to the counter and present the gum to the cashier who is actually Stan's wife. That's exactly what her nametag says, too. Even after all these years of their family running the gas station, I've never known her first name.

I glance at the entrance before saying anything. "So, what are the police doing here?"

Stan's wife slides a receipt toward me, then leans in, even though there's no one else near the counter but us. "It's interesting that you should ask that. It turns out that our very own Johnny has some information in the fire investigation."

"Really?" I pretend it's no big deal, though inside I'm dying.

"Dad's waiting out front, Taryn." Caleb whispers.

"Tell him I'll be out in a second." Caleb leaves and I'm reminded that time is short. The police might finish their interview outside any second.

"You know, he's so sensitive. I worried about him talking to the police alone, but he said he would be brave." Stan's wife places a hand over her heart.

"I'm sure he's doing great." Johnny's in his forties and has developmental issues. He's been a mainstay at the convenience store for as long as I can remember. "It is really brave of him to talk to police. So, what's he telling them?"

She shakes her head and reaches out to take one of my hands in hers. "I haven't seen you since the fire, dear." She puts a finger to her lips. "Actually, that's not true. Did I see you at the cemetery a few weeks back? It looked like you, but my eyesight's a bit fuzzy these days."

I open my mouth to say I don't think so, but she keeps talking.

"We meet there once a week to express our wishes to the Universe."

The commanding and the doughnuts in the cemetery. I remember.

"It's just something silly we do, it means nothing." Stan's wife squeezes my hand. "But I want you to know that I pray for you and that Manor girl everyday. It's so, so tragic what happened."

My heart's pumping in my throat. Her words reach right in to calm it just a little bit.

But my dad's waiting, and any second Mel and Johnny are coming back into the store. I'll lose my chance to find out anything.

I give Stan's wife my most grateful smile. "I appreciate it, I really do. And I appreciate your son doing what he can to help. Do you mind me asking, exactly what kind of information does Johnny have?"

"He knew that boy. Tim was in here all the time on his way to or from work out at the country club." She places her hand over her heart. "He was so kind to my Johnny. Always asking him about his work at the store and teasing him about girlfriends."

I'm starting to keep time to my heart beat which is now pulsing in my head. Mrs. Stan's wife, please. Answer the question.

"You know what he did that was so nice? Every Friday night on his way home from work he would drop by with a doughnut. We sell doughnuts here, but my Johnny loves Donut King's cinnamon-sugar twists. They were his favorite alright, and Tim knew it."

"Yeah. The cinnamon-sugar twists are a favorite. For a lot of people."

I give up. Our conversation only serves to remind me of the tragedy and Blake and doughnuts.

"Oh, my, they're done." Stan's wife gestures in a panic. She grasps my arm and leans over the counter putting her face inches from mine. I don't dare turn to look at the door. "Johnny saw Tim the night of the fire. He stopped here, but he left with some other kids. Johnny said Tim's car was left parked there on the side for days. Then about a week later, it was gone."

"Hello, Miss Karen. I thought that was your dad parked out front."

"Hi, Mel." I fidget with the gum.

"Mr. Johnny did a great job, Ma'am."

"Oh, good." Stan's wife comes from around the counter to give her son a hug.

Mel glances from me to the other officer and then back to me. I speak before he has a chance to ask for another rerun of the events leading to the fire. "My dad's waiting. Thank you, Stan's wife."

Mel holds the door open for me.

"Don't forget your receipt, dear." Stan's wife picks it up. She leans in to give me a hug, and whispers in my ear. "You see what I'm saying, right? He left his car here before he died, and then someone moved it to Ritter's Crossing. That's when the police found it."

I nod to let her know I got it. I look at Johnny. "My sister and her husband manage the Donut King in town. I'll bring you some doughnuts sometime, okay?"

"Say, thank you, Johnny," his mother prompts.

"Thank you." He shuffles to the candy display

and begins to line up the candy bars in straight rows.

His voice stops me at the door. "You'll bring cinnamon-sugar, right?"

"Yes, Johnny."

"Twists, right?

"Of course. They're the best ones."

I'm suddenly choking on my words, so I make a dash for the car. Dad looks at me, but doesn't say anything. He even silences Caleb when my brother asks what took me so long.

I stare out the window as we drive into Ideal. How long have I known Stan, Stan's wife, and their son? Why didn't I ever take the time to find out that Johnny has a favorite doughnut?

26

I'm sneaking into homeroom late Tuesday morning when my teacher stops me. "There's a message for you, Taryn. You're to report to the office."

I turn around and hike back down the hall and across the courtyard. First thing I notice are police officers. Two huddle with Glenn, the security guard, and a couple more hang out on the steps outside. Once I'm in the office, Phyllis is all formal and directs me to a chair, then goes to her desk and starts typing. She won't even look at me. Something's way off. She never treats me like this.

Am I in trouble? I replay last Friday . . . I told on J.T. That's it, though. Nothing else happened. Wait. Mr. Thomas's class. The catalog, the pop quiz. But that's not grounds for arrest.

Ms. McKinney opens her door and leans out. "Taryn, you can come in now."

The catalog was not my fault. Chelsea gave it to Sam, Sam passed it to me. Sort of. It was never on my desk during the test. A test that, by the way, was handed out before the bell even rang.

I'm ready with my story.

"Please." Ms. McKinney points to a chair before she sits behind her desk.

I drop into it, letting my backpack slide to the floor.

And wait.

She finally begins. "There's no easy way to say this."

The catalog was not my fault. The catalog was not my fault.

"Mr. Myers resigned as principal of Ideal High."

The catalog . . . what?

I erase my thoughts. "He resigned?"

"Yes. I wanted to tell you myself before you heard it somewhere else."

I have no clue what this means. "Is he okay?"

Ms. McKinney exhales sharply. "He tried to keep his head up, make it work, but the tragedy just cut too deep. Losing students at the hand of another student like that. He took it personally."

I'm speechless.

"He always said, 'We're not a Lubbock or a Dallas school,' but the fire, and the issues so far this year were too much. His image of Ideal High was crumbling and he couldn't keep it together."

Poor Mr. Myers. None of this is his fault. The

fire wasn't started by a bullied student out for revenge. I think Johnny proves that. Someone moved his car to the scene of the fire to make it look like Tim stopped there on purpose. Maybe if Mr. Myers knew that he'd be okay. He'd come back.

"We're having an assembly tomorrow, so if you can keep quiet about this, we'll announce it then."

"Sure. But why the police? Is that related?"

"Oh, no. Apparently, there's new evidence about the fire. Nothing to be worried about. They just want to keep an eye on things."

Johnny's report.

Ms. McKinney shows me to the door. As soon as she shuts it behind me, Phyllis jumps up from her desk. "Oh, sweetie, I had to keep my mouth shut. I wanted to say something, but I couldn't. I had to let Ms. McKinney tell you first."

I plant myself in front of her and drop my backpack. "What happened?"

"Mr. Myers went AWOL, that's what happened. Flat out didn't show up Friday. Or yesterday. Missed his meetings. Nobody could reach him. His wife didn't even know where he was."

"I wondered why he wasn't at the game."

"Yep. Missed the football game." She shakes her head. "Sad, so sad."

"Is he still missing?" I'm kind of afraid to ask.

"No, he showed up at home last night, and then his wife drove him to the school superintendent's this morning. It's a done deal. Ms. McKinney's in charge for now."

"Newspaper!" An aide slaps the Lubbock-Avalanche Journal onto the counter. "Do you need anything else right now, Phyllis?"

"No, sweetie. You go on to the library and I'll call over there if I need you."

I should go, too. The bell to start first hour is going to ring soon.

Phyllis waves her hand at me. "Don't you worry about Mr. Myers or nothin'." She moves from around her desk to pick up the newspaper. "You just go have yourself a good day."

"You make it sound like that's an easy thing to do, but thanks."

Phyllis puts one hand on her hip and shakes the newspaper with the other. "I told my boy about you, sweetie. How you stood up for that girl trying out for cheer, how you told the truth about the football players."

Turns out that's why Phyllis was absent from the attendance office. Her son was bullied, but now he's back in school prepared to "stand up like a man," as she puts it.

I want to point out that maybe that's how he got the busted lip in the first place, but I remember her comment about straightening out Ideal High. I shouldn't be giving advice to the elementary-aged set just yet.

A headline from the newspaper catches my attention. "Can I see that?" We spread the paper out on the counter.

"Anti-bullying pledges becoming all the rage." I skim the article. It's about the Lubbock School District raising money for a bullying awareness campaign.

I read out loud, "'Inspired by the Ideal deaths at the hand of a bullied student last summer, they are following the lead of many Dallas-area schools, some of which have raised upwards of $75,000 toward their anti-bullying programs.'" *Ideal deaths.* Don't they proofread this stuff? And they're pushing the same line about Tim.

The price tag hits me wrong, too. "They're going to spend all this money telling kids how to treat each other? Isn't that something our parents teach us from the time we're in diapers?"

"You know they do, sweetie."

"I mean, $75,000." I gesture to the newspaper

like it's at fault. "Just treat each other like human beings. What's so hard about that?"

"I'm right there with ya'. We don't need no bullying in our schools."

The bell rings, but my mind is racing. Yes. Not in my school. Not. In. My. School.

I duck into room 212 after classes and pull desks in a circle for the committee meeting. No one's here yet, and I don't know where Mrs. Ames is, but the quiet is a welcome break from the noise of the day. I open my notebook. I've been scribbling in it all day, every chance I got, trying to get my jumbled thoughts on paper. I've been thinking about $75,000 spent to stop bullying. About Tim taking time to get to know Johnny. I've been thinking about Mrs. Foster and Mrs. Weir, cancer buddies. And about Jackie and making things different so she'll want to come back to school and finish her senior year.

I don't hear Gretchen until she's right next to me. "Can I talk to you, Taryn?"

I brace myself. I never know which way it's going to go with this girl.

"I know it's gotta be hard losing your friends," she says.

Somehow, I know she's talking about a current

event and not friends lost in the Gin Co. fire, but Gretchen isn't done.

"Look, I'm sorry about what I said in the bathroom. You ended up telling the truth, so I gotta give you that. I know you paid for it."

"Yeah." Jen and the football team are still not speaking to me.

Gretchen lingers. "Remember that first time we talked? By your locker?" I look up at her. "I said we didn't need girls like you?" She locks eyes with me. "I was wrong."

I let my gaze wander, unsure of how to respond.

"People should learn to put ourselves out there, like you do."

"It doesn't always turn out for the best, Gretchen."

"It will eventually. Even with Jackie Weir."

"How'd you know about that?"

"I just know stuff."

Our conversation is cut short when the room fills with the other members of the advisory committee. Mrs. Ames bustles in late. "Sorry to keep you waiting. Taryn, why don't you go ahead and get us started." She gives me a knowing look. I need to be careful and not slip up about Mr. Myers' resignation.

I remind the committee of our purpose to advise the student council in promoting activities that will unite our school. Our first order of business is choosing a name for the committee. Advisory Committee is just way too boring, but it doesn't take long for the ideas to get out of hand.

"No, Carlos, we're not calling it The *Increible* Unity of the Ninja Bulldogs."

Chelsea's sitting across from me and she's been absorbed in her phone the whole time. She waves her hand. "How about taking a word from our school motto? I was thinking about pride. We all know what it is, but listen to this part of the definition." She reads from her phone. "'A feeling or deep pleasure or satisfaction derived from one's own achievements, the achievements of those with whom one is closely associated, or from qualities that are widely admired.'"

Great. Pride is probably what causes all the school's problems. No one else says anything, so I'm assuming they're confused, too.

Chelsea shrugs her shoulders at the group. "Don't you get it? We're trying to achieve something that we can all be proud of. Something that we do together. So we'll call the group Ideal Pride, or something like that."

Gretchen nose-dives in and saves Chelsea.

"Wait, wait. I got it." She reads from her own phone. "A pride is also 'a group of lions forming a social unit.' We're not lions, but we could be Bulldog Pride."

I think it's perfect.

I spend the next hour wringing out the very last drop of ideas scribbled in my notebook and the committee devours it all pretty much like a pack of lions. But we're bulldogs.

Bulldog Pride.

I pull out my cell phone when I arrive home from school to call Jen. Somehow Johnny has inspired me with a plan. And it doesn't have anything to do with doughnuts.

"Taryn, I'm glad you called. I have to make this quick, my nephew's fussy. I overheard some girls talking in the bathroom at school today and now I believe the rumors. Homecoming plans bite."

I make a face even though I know she can't see me. "We just barely started planning homecoming, there are no rumors." Maybe she heard that Gretchen was nominated to be the chairman of the planning committee.

"I've been hearing things. Homecoming can be amazing with just a few . . . can I say, tweaks?"

"And you're the one to do the tweaking?" I

don't try to keep the flatness out of my voice.

"Taryn, I know I bailed on you before, and this whole J.T. thing? I'm sorry about that, too. I guess I bailed on you again."

"Ya' think?" I repeat one of Jen's usual comebacks.

After a long pause, she begins again. "My mom said she ran into you at the hospital while she was waiting for her appointment yesterday and you sat with her. She was so nervous and I couldn't be there to hold her hand because I had to babysit." Jen's tone softens noticeably. "She said you stayed with her till her friend came. You didn't have to, but you did."

About that friend. Does Jen know her mom is cancer buddies with Jackie Weir's mom? "I really am sorry about your mom, Jen. If you need anything, let me know."

"It's what you need, Taryn." Jen is back to business. "You need me. You know I chaired Junior Prom."

"Yes, but —"

I hear a baby in the background. "I gotta go, Taryn. So why'd you call?"

"Oh, yeah." I think for a second. "Actually, helping with homecoming is perfect. I'll introduce you to the committee chairman and you can offer to help. How about getting a shake later?"

"Who's the committee chair?"

I put her off. "You'll meet her tonight."

"Fine, but Taryn? You know I was kidding when I said only a few tweaks, right?" Jen is gone before I can utter a word in response.

I rummage through my backpack for my new school directory to send Gretchen a text. "Can you meet at Burger Heaven tonight?"

Day and Night are going to be introduced.

27

I'm on my way to Burger Heaven when I get a call.

"Taryn?" a girl's voice says. "So you're the student body president?"

"Jackie." I state it more than ask it.

"Yeah, this is Jackie."

"I'm sorry. I'm just surprised. Um —" I verbally stumble.

I don't have to say anything because Jackie keeps talking. "I have the same question as before, but it's a little bit more specific now. Why is the student body president calling me?"

I exhale into the phone while my thoughts race. Make nice, then ask about Tim again.

"Are you there?"

"I'm here." I put the phone on speaker while rummaging through my brain for what to say. I need both hands on the wheel for support.

"I want to apologize," I say finally. "Whatever made you drop out of school, I'm sorry." I hold my breath while counting the ticks of my blinker as I sit at a light.

"And you're in charge of the apology committee?"

I wince. "That's good. You're very funny."

"So the student body president wants to offer a blanket apology. Now what?"

"I don't know. It's senior year. Don't you want to finish?"

"Those were the days . . . when I got what I wanted," Jackie says.

I shrink a little. She sounds like I've felt for the past four months and counting.

"Besides, I think I've had my fill of hat jokes."

Now I'm cringing. "Isn't there something I can do?" The light turns green.

"I can still graduate by taking classes online. I don't need Ideal High."

"But —"

"I hope you're not going to say something like 'Ideal High needs you.'"

I force a laugh. "No, that would just be lame." But nothing else comes to mind.

"Thanks for thinking of me, but don't waste your time. This is something I have to decide on my own." I hear noise in the background.

"Wait, don't hang up." I'm almost to Burger Heaven, and almost out of time. "Can we switch topics?"

There's a noticeable hesitation.

"Tim?" She speaks his name almost reverently.

"Yeah."

I hear her exhale into the phone. Finally, she speaks. "I guess I'm ready to talk about him now, but can we meet? I get off work at eight o'clock tomorrow night."

"Okay, tell me where."

"Donut King."

I've got Jackie and our conversation on the brain, but I've got to switch gears to Jen and Gretchen. Somehow I have to get them to take time to get to know each other. We order something and sit down with it at a table outside. After introductions consisting of "Jen, Gretchen, Gretchen, Jen," I start right in. "Jen wants to offer her services to the homecoming committee."

"I chaired Junior Prom," Jen pipes up when Gretchen doesn't respond in less than two seconds.

"That's awe-inspiring." Gretchen looks anything but inspired.

"Is that Purple Midnight?" Jen scoops up Gretchen's right hand like a manicurist schmoozing a client. "Where did you get it? It's always out of stock at Coleman's."

"Bangles & Beads in Lubbock." Gretchen's

tone remains wary, and she pulls her hand away.

"No way. Is that at the mall?"

"Downtown. Where those vintage shops are." Gretchen warms to the conversation. Slowly.

I placate myself with French fries while a discussion of nail products ensues. Once they come full-nauseating-circle by determining that Purple Midnight is a must-wear because of the way it shimmers from black to purple in the sun, I have to stop them.

"So do we have a deal? Jen joins the committee, but remembers that she's not in charge." I look pointedly at Jen who's studying her own pale pink nails. "She's only a committee member."

Jen's head pops up. "Duh, deal. I can totally be a committee member. Just watch me."

"Yeah, I'll watch you." I flash her my best eye-rolling look. "Besides, it's mostly all planned anyway. Gretchen?"

"Fine. Deal," she says. "Unfortunately, we could use your experience."

"Exactly. Now here's what I was thinking." Jen faces Gretchen.

Poor Gretchen. I can't stop the eventual ambush, but I can waylay it because this is not going to turn into a homecoming planning meeting.

"Talk later. Right now I have another issue.

Jackie Weir," I talk faster when I see their reaction. "I think she might be coming back to school. I want it to be different for her." I look hard at Jen. "No more Tacky Jackie."

"Are you still on that, Taryn?" Jen returns my look.

"Has your mom said anything about someone named Donna that she met at the hospital?"

"Yeah, Donna's her 'Cancer buddy.'"

"That's the one. Her name is Donna Weir." I slurp my chocolate shake and let the information sink in before spelling it out. "Jackie's mom."

Jen goes quiet.

"What kind of help are we talking here?" Gretchen inserts herself back into the conversation. "Is this a help-the-not-so-perfect-and-perky-fit-in project?"

"I'm ignoring that, Gretchen. All I want is for her to feel like she made the right choice coming back."

"You just want a miracle." Jen sips her Diet Cherry Coke noisily, quick to bounce back and take control again.

Gretchen shrugs. "Sorry, but I have to agree. How are you going to make that happen?"

"A miracle makeover." Jen sits up straighter, obviously pleased with herself. "We get together, fix her makeup, get her some cute clothes, and do her hair. Maybe some serious extensions. We could take her to my mom's salon. I've seen some amazing before and afters."

"Not gonna fly," Gretchen inserts.

I try to picture Jackie with a full head of hair and makeup covering her pale complexion. "That's a possibility."

"Not gonna fly." Again from Gretchen.

"What size do you think she wears? She's pretty petite," Jen muses.

"Not gonna fly."

"Why do you keep saying that? What's not gonna fly?" I can see Jen's finally allowed Gretchen's repeated comment to get to her.

"The whole makeover idea. It's like a bad teen movie. They want to say 'Don't judge someone by their looks,' and then what do they do every time? A makeover. Then the person's beautiful and they're all popular. It's fake."

"But what about when you look good, you feel good, and you present a better you to the world?" Jen gestures at Gretchen.

"How do I present myself to the world, huh?" Gretchen practically dares Jen to respond.

"Well —"

These two. They can't have a conversation

without a referee. “Look, we’re focusing on Jackie right now. While Jen might be overdosing on talk show theory, she has a point. But I like Gretchen’s point, too. If Jackie can’t be accepted as is, then whose fault is it? It’s not hers.”

“How do you change someone’s perception? It can’t be done overnight,” Jen said.

“‘Perception,’ such a treacherous word, really, but it’s all we have. Perception is reality.” Gretchen chugs the last of her shake.

“What does that even mean?” Jen frowns, then continues. “We can talk to her, sit by her at lunch, whatever, but how can three people change anything? Even when one of them is me?” She adds the last line as if it goes without saying.

Gretchen grimaces and I want to.

Then Gretchen takes over. “Not only that. What about Jackie’s perception. She’s going to be suspicious of anything we try to do.”

“She already is,” I admit. I toss my empty cup across the table to the open trash can, then pull a water bottle from my purse. “I just wish there were a way to convince her, but how do you undo years of torturous school experience? How do you say, ‘Forget about the past, we think you’re okay now?’”

“Good question. Why is she okay now, Taryn? Because you need your project to succeed? I say bag the project and think like a human being, maybe even a friend," Gretchen taps her fingers on the table. "If you were a friend, emphasis on the 'if,' what would a friend do?"

Jen shakes her head, continuing with her own line of thinking. "She's going to come, be the same, look the same . . . the only one with a hat. I mean, she stands out. And, sorry, not in a good way."

I roll the water bottle back and forth across the table in front of me as the comments jell in my brain, the result producing an image from the faraway regions of junior high memory. At our lockers, one Thursday afternoon, Chelsea saying, *Everyone's wearing a dress tomorrow. Want to wear our ruffled skirts?* It went without saying we wanted to be part of Everyone.

I stab the air with my water bottle. "No, no, no!" Jen and Gretchen turn their heads in unison to look at me.

"She will not be the only one wearing a hat!"

Confusion registers on both Jen's and Gretchen's faces.

"We'll wear hats. We'll get everyone we know to wear hats. People will do it. They won't care why."

"Yes!" Jen claps her hands.

"It's perfect," I say.

"Mr. Myers is gonna freak," said Gretchen. I want to say something about Mr. Myers and the fact that he has already freaked, so to speak, but I don't.

Jen claps her hands again, anticipating. "Let's chew gum, too."

"You radical." Gretchen teases.

"And smoke in the bathroom." Jen's eyes widen with her smile.

I laugh at them. "Calm yourself. This is about hats, that's it."

"You're no fun."

We grab purses and toss our garbage. Jen turns to hold the door for Gretchen as we leave Burger Heaven's outdoor seating. "Can I borrow your fingernail polish?"

Ms. McKinney gives me some time during the school assembly Wednesday morning to talk about Homecoming Week and the activities we have planned so far. Things like Hat Day. I also announce that nominations are open for Homecoming Queen. I was hoping to skip that ritual this year, but the committee shot me down. Some traditions run too deep.

I think the announcement of Mr. Myers' resignation has shaken up the student body, because I see some students in tears when I start talking about bullying and how we don't need an expensive program to tell us to be nice to each other.

"Can we just say, 'Not in my school?'" I lean into the podium, channeling Mr. Myers. "We're better than that. We're not Lubbock. We're not Dallas. We're Ideal. We've grown up together. We know each other." I think of Purple Midnight fingernail polish. "If we took the time we'd see that we connect over the dumbest things. We're not that different."

I can't help watching the assembly of police officers along the back wall. I don't like the reminder of why they're here. Finally, I force myself to concentrate on the row of small windows just below the ceiling before I venture further.

"We're not that different from Tim Jenks." From the looks from the audience, I know they don't like the mention of his name. "No, listen. I know the rumors, but we need to withhold judgment until the investigation is finished. No more stupid lists of 'Who deserved to die in the fire.' Tim was a kind person. He loved to draw. He loved learning about space. Sadly, he's no longer with us, just like the seven others that were lost last summer."

I stand up straight and speak right into the microphone. "Ashley, Weston, Kayla, Vaughn, Keisha, Becca, Blake, and Tim, we will never be the same because of what happened to you. We will be better."

Now my legs are like jelly. I didn't plan to say their names. To get so emotional. I stop talking, so I can sit down before I turf it in front of the entire student body.

28

I toss my keys and phone onto the kitchen counter and grab a glass of ice water. The afternoon turned summer-warm and the mile and a half run in P.E. was brutal. I sit on a stool and lay my head on the kitchen counter, wishing Mom was home instead of with Tracy and the babies. My cell phone pings and my first thought is Caleb. I slide it toward me, remembering that Dad plans to pick him up on his way home from work because it's a late practice.

It's a text from Chelsea.

You know when you mention Tim Jenks like that you're just making things worse.

What does that mean?

My cell vibrates. Maybe it's her and I can ask her the question directly.

But it's Jackie.

"I'm really sorry. I can't meet you tonight."

"Okay, when? I can anytime."

She's vague. "I don't know. I'm just not ready."

Jackie, come on. I want to know about Tim.

"Sorry, I have to go. I don't want to be late for work on my first day."

After hanging up, I set the phone down carefully, wishing even more that Mom was home. She's not spending her free time at Donut King anymore — now it's with the twins. She didn't even tell me they hired her replacement.

I notice the blue bowl that belongs to Mrs. Carter sitting on top of the refrigerator. It contained chocolate chip cookies to take home after the barbecue last Friday. Mom hasn't returned it yet. Raising an underarm, I sniff, then grab the bowl and leave the house.

The warm smell of something baking meets me at Carter's door. "Taryn! So good to see you." Mrs. Carter's warmth matches the oven's.

"I'm returning your bowl. Thanks for the cookies."

"I'm glad you're here. I've got something for y'all, but it's not quite ready. Do you mind waiting?" Mrs. Carter leads me back to the kitchen. "I made corn chowder and thought I'd bring over some for dinner since I know your mom is busy helping Tracy." She peeks in the oven. What's chowder without homemade biscuits to go with it?"

"They smell wonderful." But an ache rises in my stomach.

Mrs. Carter wipes her brow. "Now let's dish up some of this creamy goodness." She pulls out a piece of stoneware and a lid.

"The funeral wasn't that long ago," I say it softly, but I'm immediately sorry I brought up Kayla's death. I start again. "We should be doing things for you."

Mrs. Carter shakes her head. "No, no. This is how I cope, believe me. If I can stay busy doing for others, then I'm the better for it." She gathers the pot of chowder with two "Don't Mess with Texas" potholders. "Can you take a hold of the bowl, please, Taryn? I don't want chowder all over the place."

The sight and smell of it as Mrs. Carter pours makes me hungry for an early dinner. No cereal tonight.

Mrs. Carter sets the pot down on the stove and grabs a fresh dishcloth to wipe the edges of the bowl, then applies the lid. She wipes her hands before facing me. "Take Kayla as an example. She was having a really tough time after her grandma and uncle died within months of each other over a year ago, but then she started volunteering as a tutor, and it totally changed her attitude. She was happier. She was able to handle things better."

"She tutored?"

"You know that tiny thing with the skin disease? Kayla was helping her get caught up in her classes. She was so sweet to call me after the funeral asking about Kayla's grave site."

Kayla tutored Jackie Weir. That's news to me.

A large family portrait catches my attention. A smiling Kayla beams from the front row, cute little Hannah on her lap.

"Mrs. Carter?" I force myself to begin before the guilt stops me. "I never told you how sorry I am about Kayla." I close my eyes, not wanting to see pain in Mrs. Carter's face. "I wish I could have done something to help her, to help all of them." I put my face in my hands.

Mrs. Carter places an arm around my shoulder. "Taryn, I hope you've not been carrying this burden. It wasn't your fault. It was no one's fault. That's why it's called an accident. Kayla would not want you to think anything differently. Not for a second."

The buzzer dings, and after the biscuits cool, I leave with chowder, biscuits, and a much better mood.

After dinner and a failed attempt at concentrating on homework, I announce that I'm going out. I can't stay away from Donut King.

Jackie's there and I want to talk to her.

I sit in the parking lot with the window down, acclimating myself to the Donut King air. Breathe in. Breathe out. I can do this.

A face appears at my window. "Taryn? What are you doing here?"

Jackie.

"Please, can we talk? I'll give you a ride home." I'm not above bribery.

She thinks about it at least before shaking her head. "It's too hard. Sorry."

I get an idea. "Do you know Johnny who works at Stan's?"

"Yeah."

"I promised him some doughnuts. Will you drive out there with me to drop them off?" Taking doughnuts, and actually learning Stan's wife's first name — it just seems the right thing to do.

She agrees immediately, and I'm this close to giving her the money and sending her in to place the order, but I stop myself. I need to do it.

"Wait in my car. I'll be right back." I walk up to the store and open the door. The lights blaze. The abnormous logo looms over the counter, and the gold crowns dance along the ceiling when the rush of air from outside hits them. The cartoon drawings of doughnut crowns on photos of celebrities catch my eye, then the quirky signs: "Donuts make the world go round!" and my favorite, or what used to be: "You're the glaze to my doughnut."

I can do this. For the love of cinnamon-sugar doughnut twists, I can do it.

I order a dozen and make small talk about Tracy and the twins with the girl behind the counter.

As I walk out of Donut King with my gold-colored box, I'm proud of myself. But when I reach my car, Jackie is gone.

At lunch the next day, I listen to Jen and Gretchen discuss homecoming plans. I'm impressed how Jen so easily includes Gretchen at our lunch table. Sure, Gretchen, with Persi tagging along, sits at the end, but Jen chats easily between them and Travis, J.T., and the others like it's no big deal. She even talks about Jackie, telling everyone how their moms are cancer buddies and how Bulldog Pride is going to sponsor a fundraiser for cancer research. They're also starting a cancer support group and Jen says we'll be amazed to discover how many Ideal High students are affected in some way by the disease.

"So what do you think, Taryn? You, me, and Gretch go as a group to homecoming?" Jen looks up expectantly from her taco salad. "And Persimmon, I mean Persi, you're totally invited, too."

"You want to go without a date?" Is this the same Jen? Foregoing a date to homecoming?

"We're too busy to be bothered." Jen flips her hair with a wave of her hand. "We've got all the behind-the-scene stuff to worry about."

"Whatever," Gretchen says. "She doesn't think I can get a date."

"That's not true. Now shut up. We're going together." Jen shakes a finger at her.

I frown at them. "I don't know if I have a date or not." Zeke hasn't called.

"Hey, ya'll." Angel plops her lunch tray down in the middle of their table before squeezing in next to Jen. "I've got an idea. To make it up to Jackie Weir let's nominate her for homecoming queen." She smiles a mile wide while drowning her salad in dressing. "She's reenrolling in school. It's perfect."

I shift in my seat. Gretchen makes immediate eye contact and I think I know what her look means.

"I don't know about that, Angel. She's pretty self-conscious," I say.

"Come on. Every girl wants to be queen, don't they? Of course they do."

Gretchen squirms in her seat.

"I'm sorry, what was your name?" Angel leans across Jen to look at Gretchen.

Jen frowns at her. "This is Gretchen, silly. Co-chair of the homecoming committee with me."

"That's an interesting name . . . Gretchen." Angel wrinkles her nose.

"No more interesting than Angel, I guess." Gretchen wrinkles her nose back.

Angel pastes on a smile. "Wouldn't you love to be homecoming queen, Gretchen?"

"I've actually never thought about it, and I doubt Jackie has either. You might want to ask her first before you go off nominating her."

"That would spoil the surprise. We're nominating Chelsea, too. Hilarious, right? It'll be a toss up between the two for the lame-o vote." She laughs. "Hey, Kirstie, it's all set." Angel jumps up when Kirstie approaches and the pair clip-clop out the cafeteria doors.

"Is Angel for real?" Jen wonders out loud.

"I don't know, but I agree with Gretchen." I pull out my phone to send her a text.

I hear you're coming back to Ideal.

She responds quickly.

Apparently my mom really wants to see her oldest daughter walk across the stage to get her diploma. I'll be there Monday.

I text back, Perfect. That's the first day of Homecoming Week. It's Hat Day. Wear a hat.

29

A sea of hat-wearers flooding the parking lot and sidewalks force an anxious smile as I emerge from my car Monday morning. I find Gretchen waiting while Jen leans toward her driver side window adjusting her hot pink baseball cap in its reflection. Gretchen wears a black cap, no surprise, but when they turn toward me I notice both caps sport matching logos.

"Love the hats," I tell them when they get closer. I pull a baseball cap from my backpack and put it on. Across it are the letters N.I.M.S. and Not In My School under it. We're selling them before school and during lunch.

"We got a buy one-get one special last night, thank you very much," Jen replies. "But, don't worry, we're still planning on buying a NIMS hat." She holds out something pink toward Gretchen.

"You and gum." I shake my head. "Did you check her bag for cigarettes, Gretchen?"

"Or worse." Gretchen snorts.

"Ha. Ha." Jen pops a stick of gum in her mouth, then waves the pack in front of my face. Her

Purple Midnight nail polish shimmers.

I ignore her. “I want to find Jackie. I’m starting to feel nervous about this whole thing. What’s she going to think?”

I thought seriously about calling her last night, but wasn’t sure what I’d say. *Just wanted to remind you we’re all going to wear hats tomorrow. We want you to feel like you belong. Now will you love Ideal High and everyone will see we can be one big freakin’ happy student body?*

“It was a good idea when we came up with it. It’s still a good idea. Quit worrying,” Jen begins blowing a bubble.

“But what are we going to do tomorrow? Wearing hats to school everyday is not gonna fly with the administration,” Gretchen offers. “Speaking of which, McKinney’s coming down the sidewalk right now.”

Jen’s bubble pops. She swears then spits her gum into her hand.

“Where can I get one of those?” Ms. McKinney points to my cap.

“We’re selling them in the bookstore.”

“Hat Day. It’s almost like you knew Jackie Weir was returning today. I assume you mean this as a form of inclusion?”

“Of course.”

Once Ms. McKinney leaves us alone I speed-walk to the 200 Building. I don't know if Jackie will show up in my same homeroom or not.

Maybe Phyllis knows. I detour in the direction of the office, but the way is blocked by Kenny, Trek and a couple of their friends. I nod at them, but they don't move.

"Hey, Young." Kenny adjusts the black leather bands tied around his wrists. "We're totally into Hat Day, but what about a Board Day?"

"Board Day?"

"You know, we ride skateboards between classes." Kenny's mouth twists into his version of a smile.

"That would be interesting." I can't help staring at how the sun highlights the white streak down the center of his head of black hair like he has a skunk on his head. "If you're so into Hat Day, you better go buy a hat. They're selling them in the bookstore."

The first bell rings. I will never make it to homeroom on time if I go to the office first.

"Did you hear we challenged the football team?" Trek cocks his head to one side. He seems to be anticipating my reaction, and I can't hide what I'm thinking.

"Challenged them?" I frown.

Trek laughs, and Kenny and the others join him. "To a face-off on skateboards. We're bringing in ramps and it's going to be part of the homecoming pre-game pep rally." He gestures wildly. "Take that."

"You guys are awesome."

"Gretchen said it was your idea."

I shake my head and smile. She would.

It's almost the end of the day and I still haven't seen a sign of Jackie. I think Hat Day's been a waste until Angel Brinton approaches me in the locker room before P.E. She slaps her NIMS hat down on the bench. Apparently, she wants to prove me right.

"Guess who I just saw in the office? Tacky Jackie. We're wearing hats because she's back at school."

"What are you talking about?" I fumble with my locker combination.

"I'm on to you. And I think it's totally rude."

I turn on her. "Why is it rude, Angel?"

Soon others are crowding around listening to Angel. "The hats are Taryn's idea of a joke and I think it's sad. I was so embarrassed walking into the office wearing a hat, and there's Jackie staring at me."

"You don't know what she was thinking."

"Humiliation. That's what." Angel grabs her hat and stuffs it in her backpack.

"Like you gave her anything but that the past two years of high school."

"I never did anything like this, Taryn. This is blatant." Some of the students take Angel's lead and slide their hats off.

"We're not making fun of her. I told her about Hat Day last week."

But now Angel's texting and pretty soon her view of it will be all over the school, even though I know there's no way she suddenly cares about Jackie Weir.

At least Jen and Gretchen are still wearing their hats when I meet them before the homecoming committee meeting after school.

"Sorry. We heard what Angel said," Gretchen tries to console me.

"Should've gone with the makeover." Jen shakes her head. "I tried to tell you, I've seen some great before and afters."

"Hey guys, look." Gretchen cocks her head toward the bank of lockers to our left. Several students are bunched around Jackie.

They're actually talking to her.

“We are so late. C’mon.” Jen pulls on Gretchen’s arm. “The Bulldog Pride is waiting.”

“You guys go ahead. You don’t need me.” I nod my head toward Jackie hoping they’ll get that I want to talk to her.

I wait until she’s alone.

“You need one of these.” I hold out an extra NIMS hat I’ve been carrying around all day.

“Not in my school?”

“You missed the assembly last week. I talked about bullying.”

Jackie studies the hat and nods. “Got it. I have to admit, though, that makes me nervous. You didn’t mention me by name, I hope.”

“Of course, not.” I take my cap off and smooth my hair down. “I talked about Tim, though.”

“Really?”

“I said he was kind and he liked to draw. That he wasn’t that different from the rest of us.” I stuff the hat into my backpack.

Jackie doesn’t say anything, but I see something building in her eyes.

“You don’t know him,” she accuses. “You use him in a campaign against bullying, but you don’t care about him. Not really.”

I exhale. “You’re right, I didn’t know Tim, but there are people at this school just like him, facing the same things he did. I want to change that."

She seems to think about that. "Fair enough." She runs her fingers over the letters on the cap. "All I want to do is get the school year over with so my mom can see me receive my diploma."

That sounds way too familiar. "That's exactly how I felt when senior year started. Without my friends I didn't even want to live, much less have to go to school. But I found a reason to care. I —" One of the reasons is standing in front of me, but at this point I can't very well admit it to her face. "Don't you want more? Don't you have any hopes and dreams for your senior year?"

Jackie's eyes widen. "You can't be serious. You're talking to me, 'Tacky Jackie.'"

"I've never called you that or ever thought of you that way."

"Does it matter? It's not even that I expected you, or someone like you, to come to my defense, but just to have someone once speak a decent word to me. Ask me to be in their study group. Or even just to borrow a stupid pencil without it being the class joke. Sure my hair's falling out and I wear a hat, but everything else about me is completely normal."

It's the most I've heard Jackie speak. Ever.

"I'm sorry."

"You already said that on the phone last week. But how can you be sorry for an entire junior high and high school student body that decided it was okay to treat me like a non-person? Your blanket apology counts or something?"

Acid tears sting just like the words stabbing at my insides. "You're right. I can only apologize for myself." The words choke in my throat, but I fight to get them out. "Believe me, Jackie, I am sorry. For all those times I stood by and watched, and all the times I looked the other way." I battle my emotions. "I'm sorry that I never really looked past the hat to see you."

Jackie sniffles and her chin quivers. I know I'll lose it completely if she starts bawling. I look away, wishing for words to make it all right, and for a Kleenex. Sorry is the best I have.

Jackie reaches down to pick up the NIMS hat that fell out of my backpack. She holds it out to me. "It's not your fault."

"I want to do more than wear a hat."

"I believe you." At least she's smiling a little bit. "I'm supposed to go back to the office. I better get going." She points at my spiral notebook sticking out of the top of my backpack. "I think Hot Cheetos are hot, too."

Kayla's scribble from eons ago.

"And you want to know something about Tim Jenks? He was bullied the night of the fire. He was on his way home from work when they forced him to go to Ritter's Crossing."

"Who forced him? Weston and Vaughn?"

"I'm saying too much. I better go."

Tuesday after school a bunch of students meet in the courtyard to divide up supplies for our homecoming project. We're painting the inside of every bathroom stall door with a "Not In My School" message. We're sticking with school colors, so we've got red, blue, and white to choose from. I lead a group in the 200 building. It feels so good to redo the paint job in the bathroom stall that started it all. No more stupid list. Not in my school.

We barely make a dent in the project, but we'll be painting again tomorrow and the next day if we have to.

I'm exhausted by the time I head to the door to go home.

"Taryn." Chelsea grabs my arm. "Levi's waiting by my car. Will you get rid of him?"

"Why should I?" I shake her hand off. "You warn me about Zeke and then I see you out with him. What's that about?"

"I was not out with him. He followed me." She

doesn't look at me, but stands watching the parking lot. "You're friends with Levi, aren't you? Make him go away."

"Are you going to homecoming with Zeke?" All I know is he hasn't called me about it when he said he would.

I'm startled by the look on her face. "I'm not going out with Zeke, Taryn. I don't know why you can't understand that."

"The Grapevine? A week ago Saturday?"

Chelsea drops her backpack along the wall and sits down next to it with her long legs sprawled out in front of her. "If you won't talk to Levi, I guess I'll just wait till he leaves."

"I don't like talking to him about the fire either, you know. He actually asked me to go to Ritter's Crossing."

Alarm crosses Chelsea's face. "Are you going?"

"No. Never again."

"Me, either. And I told my parents I'm not going to the country club. Ever."

I drop my backpack, too, and peer out the glass-front doors at Levi. He's pacing the sidewalk in front of Chelsea's Lexus.

I glance at her. She's leaning her head back, eyes closed. "He's pacing."

No answer. I shake my head and face her head on. "How about we both go out there and talk to him for the last time and be done with it. Maybe if we do it together, he'll get the message."

She doesn't move or even open her eyes.

"Chelsea?"

"Do you not get that I can't talk about it?" She scrunches up her face like she's going to cry.

Heat shoots up my neck. "Do you not get that I don't have to be having this conversation? I'll talk to Levi, but only because I have something to say to him."

Chelsea opens her eyes.

"And it doesn't have anything to do with you or the fire." I snatch up my backpack.

Her eyes begin to water.

I look out at Levi again. Now he's leaning against his truck. I turn back to Chelsea with a feeling of resignation. "Okay, what is it?"

"What is what?" She mumbles without looking up.

"What's going on? You keep talking about getting stories straight, people causing accidents, but it makes no sense."

Chelsea locks eyes with me and the look sends a shudder across my shoulders. "You know I didn't ride with everyone else that night, Taryn. I should've, but I didn't." She pauses.

"You mean with Kayla and Becca? I saw you all leave the party together."

"Don't tell anyone. We stopped at Stan's, then Weston drove."

"Weston? So —" I want to see if she'll continue where Jackie left off.

"I promised my parents I would be the only one driving the Hummer. It's just better if everyone believes I was." Chelsea stands up and pulls out her cell phone. "I'm texting my mom and telling her to pick me up over by the gym."

But I want more. "Who cares who was driving? Tell me what happened, Chelsea. Were you guys harassing Tim Jenks that night?"

"How do you know about that?"

"You lied to Levi. His brother didn't start the fire, did he?"

"I have to text my mom." Her finger lingers over her phone.

I lean against the glass door. Any conversation with Chelsea is useless. "Don't. I'll deal with Levi. Just, please, tell me this. If Weston was driving the Hummer, where were you? How did you get to Ritter's Crossing? How did Tim get there?"

"You really don't know anything, do you?"

"Just tell me the truth."

Chelsea eyes bore into me. "I should have died with everyone else, Taryn. Try that truth." She hoists her backpack and shuffles away from me into the school's foyer.

The more she reveals about the tragedy, the less it makes sense.

I watch Levi for a minute, then push my way out the door and down the sidewalk. He looks good in his gray jeans and white, long-sleeved T-shirt, but I remember why I'm mad at him. "Why don't you stay out of other people's business?"

He jumps up when he sees me, but my words stop him. "What are you referring to exactly?"

"Oh, sorry. I forgot. You make it a habit to butt in where you aren't invited."

"Again, what are you referring to?"

"I could mention any number of examples, but I'll stick to recent history. Jackie Weir. You knew I was trying to get her to come back to school. And then you go right over there and just do it yourself."

"I'm confused. You wanted her to come back. And you're not happy . . . why?" Levi takes his baseball cap off and runs his fingers through his hair.

"I called her and called her and even went out to her house and, well, wouldn't it bug you if someone just came along and accomplished what you had been trying to do all along?"

"Maybe it's like a jar lid. You loosened her up and then she was ready."

"Or you smiled at her and, you know."

Levi laughs, and I do my best to ignore it. When he does it shows off his smile and the corners of his eyes crinkle. *Increible*. Carlos's Spanish word comes to mind. Because Levi's smile really is incredible.

"Wait. I know what it is." The smile and eye crinkles disappear. "You want credit, don't you? This was your project and only you were supposed to do it."

"No —"

"I think yes." Any traces of smile turn cold, even around his eyes. He walks straight to his truck and opens the door. "Don't worry, now I'm starting to see who you are."

"Levi, it's not like that," I insist, but he climbs in and shuts the door anyway. I tap on his window. "Levi —"

He rolls it down. "Take credit for Jackie. I don't care."

On the seat next to him I see a phone. The case has a black and red design with the words "BE THE CHANGE" across it in white block letters in a spray-painted-look font.

I grip the edge of the car door. "Where did you get that phone?"

His jaw tightens. "Do you recognize it?"

"Tell me! Where did it come from?" It's all I can do not to barrel through the window's opening to get to it.

"If I tell you, will you help me?"

"Anything."

"I found it at Ritter's Crossing under a bush."

I cover my mouth with my hands. "It's Blake's."

"I've been able to charge it, but it's locked. It needs a pass code." He picks up the phone and turns it on. The same photo I have from Junior Prom pops up as Blake's wallpaper. "How well did you know this Blake?"

"I will hate you forever if you don't give me that phone right now." I lunge for it, but he holds it at arm's length.

"Do you know the code?"

"Give it to me! You have no right to it." I'm beyond fuming.

He still holds it away from me. "Taryn, I have to unlock it."

I slam my hands down on his car door. "Stay away from me, Levi Jenks. I don't want to see you, I don't want to talk to you." I twist away from his truck and march to my car. I'm done.

Soon Levi revs his engine and is gone.

When Chelsea emerges from the school, I shut myself into my front seat and turn on the radio. A love song's playing. Once upon a time I was falling in like with Levi, and now I don't care if I ever see his face again. The familiar heartache of missing Blake and the way things were before the tragedy washes over me.

I'm startled back to reality by a pound on my window.

"Taryn. Open up."

"Um . . . Zeke?" I roll down my window.

"Are you okay?"

"Been better."

"Wanna go for a ride?"

"Sorry, not really in the mood."

"I thought we could talk about homecoming. You know, if we're going to go together."

Blake is gone forever, and Levi, too. And just maybe I want to talk to Zeke. Ask him what's going on between him and Chelsea, why he's her personal bodyguard all of a sudden.

He opens his passenger door and I climb in.

30

I burrow into Zeke's chest, allowing him to shield me from the bitter wind that's howling tonight.

"I should let you go," I say again. "I've still got homework."

"Tell your mom thanks for dinner. What was that again?"

"You mean the lasagna?"

"I know that, but what was in it?"

"The eggplant?"

"Yeah, interesting."

"Let me guess. You're stopping for a burger on your way out of town."

"Maybe."

"Well, you're the one who accepted my dad's invitation to dinner, so don't blame me."

He laughs, playfully pulling me closer. He lifts my chin to his with a free hand.

He's not going to kiss me, is he?

"Uh, Zeke?" I mumble, stepping back to put space between us. "It's been fine hanging out with you today, and my dad loves that you came over to talk football, but, I can't. I'm not ready to —" I take a breath. I don't add that my mom is just glad I'm not talking to "that boy Levi" anymore.

Zeke pulls me back to his chest. "What? I'm just here for you. A friend, okay? And I meant to ask you. That Jenks guy isn't bugging you anymore, is he?"

"When did I ever say he was bugging me?" Which is stranger — Zeke bringing up Levi in the middle of our goodbye or the fact that Levi crosses my mind while almost being kissed by Zeke?

"I'm just saying. I'll take care of him and he knows it."

"He's not going to be talking to me anymore. I think he finally gets that I'm not going to Ritter's Crossing with him."

"He wants you to go out there?" Zeke pushes me to arm's length, so he can look me in the face. "That's just wrong. Forget him."

"I know. He's crazy. I'm never going there again in my life. I mean I understand how he feels. He's trying to figure out what happened to his brother, but —" I think about Blake's phone and shudder. If Levi's not giving it to me, I don't care about him or his brother.

Zeke's wraps me back in a hug. "I said forget him, Taryn."

"Don't worry." I relax into Zeke's hold. "He wasn't there that night. He doesn't know how horrible it was. I'd have nightmares within my nightmares if I went there again."

"Well, you weren't really in it. I mean you got out of the building before the fire got going, right?"

"That doesn't matter, Zeke. I heard it. I smelled it. I saw the empty Hummer. I saw Blake . . . and Kayla . . . and Chelsea . . . and . . . sorry, we are not talking about this." I move back, but Zeke presses.

"Hey, no, you're right. I'm sorry." He strokes my hair as I force even breaths.

He's too close. I want to ask about Chelsea, but I'm feeling a little claustrophobic. "It's cold. I better go in."

"Maybe I'll see you at the homecoming game Friday night, and then I'll try to get to the dance Saturday if I can."

I'm in the house and shutting the door before he can say anything else.

31

The gym is packed with students. Apparently geeks and losers, as Chelsea once called them, are a loyal group. They turned out in record numbers for the pre-game party last night and again this morning for the humanitarian project. We put together hygiene kits, wrote letters, and packed cookie boxes, all for servicemen.

I smile at the red, white, and blue decor — Ideal High's colors, and perfect for the homecoming theme, The Spirit of Ideal. Jen's idea. Who knew her father was killed while serving overseas when Jen was small. I really need to get to know people better. Whether it's Jackie's hats that hide embarrassment and hair loss, Gretchen's Goth-themed attire, or Jen's designer jeans and makeup, none of it tells the true story of who they are.

I laugh at Gretchen, who looks uniquely-eye-catching in a lace top, full tulle skirt and leggings. She's all-black except for red lace gloves that reach her elbows and looking pretty awkward as she tries to two-step with an elderly gentleman. They both wear black boots.

I played it safe and wear navy blue, but with silver-jeweled accents there's nothing boring about the style. I should do my duty and find an elderly guest to dance with, too. Only another twenty minutes and the older guests will be escorted home or back to the veterans' nursing home.

I glance at the main double doors of the gym, wondering again if my-possible-date, Zeke, will show up. He didn't exactly commit, and even tonight hasn't answered my texts. I thought he'd be thrilled to come to Ideal's Homecoming as the big college football hero, especially after his interception in the game against Central Arkansas. Everyone's talking about it. My dad especially, and he was so disappointed when Zeke didn't pick me up at the house to pose for pictures before the dance.

I scope out a wrinkled prospective dance partner wearing a pale blue tux complete with ruffled-front shirt and a cummerbund, but Kenny Grimes stops me. He's wearing the opposite of his usual black. His white tails wave like a flag, matching the strip down his head.

"Wanna dance?" he asks.

"Of course."

He leads me to the dance floor where we pretend to dance like old people. I tower over him in my heels. "Your pregame show was awesome yesterday, by the way. I don't think I've seen anything so funny as some of those football players trying to copy your moves."

Kenny smiles his crooked smile. "Some of them actually had some skateboarding skills, but did you see the coach? He was about to bust a nerve."

"Totally. He was not happy when the team insisted on doing it."

The Veterans' Dance portion of the night comes to a close and wheelchairs and walkers mass-exit the gym. Next we'll get the homecoming queen announcement over with, and then begin dancing for real. I'm heading to the makeshift stage when I notice Chelsea come through the gym door with her mom. I guess Mrs. Manor doesn't want to miss seeing if Chelsea's photo will be going up on Ideal High's Wall of Fame and Perpetual Beauty.

Chelsea's formal, while stunning in its design, hangs loosely on her shoulders. Its royal blue color overpowers her sallow skin, highlighting dark circles under her eyes that even the most expensive make up can't hide. Maybe Chelsea really has been sick all those days she missed school.

Mrs. Ames takes the microphone as the students gather around the stage at the south end of the basketball-court-turned dance floor for the announcement of Homecoming Queen. After the drama over nominations and the withdrawal of Jackie's name, no new nominations were accepted, though the committee allowed a write-in vote. My own name was on the list, mostly an honorary thing, I figure, since I'm president. Or maybe it was for the "lame-o" vote Angel talked about. Jen's, Angel's, and Kirstie's names are also on the list. No surprises.

Mrs. Ames reads our names, pausing after each as we get positioned in front of the group. I straighten my dress and stand like a statue on the end next to Jen, willing the spectacle to be over.

Knowing the entire room waits, Mrs. Ames pauses even longer for effect. "Our fifth nominee for Ideal High School's Homecoming Queen is Chelsea Manor," she says finally.

I make a face at Angel who's at the opposite end of our line-up. I'm not a Chelsea-fan, but I don't like the idea of nominating someone as a joke. Chelsea seems reluctant, but after prodding from her mother, she laughs her annoying laugh and moves forward, taking a place next to Angel.

"We have a sixth nominee this year," Mrs. Ames announces. "Jackie Weir."

I elbow Jen. "What?"

Jen shrugs her answer.

"Will Jackie please come to the stage and join the rest of the nominees?" Mrs. Ames shields her eyes from the glare of the spotlight as she scans the room.

Someone yells Jackie's name from the dance floor and several others take up the chant. "Ja-ckie! Ja-ckie!" It sounds so much better without the "Tacky." If only Jackie were here to appreciate it.

"She isn't here, Mrs. Ames." I whisper loudly.

"She's coming, though," Jen adds.

"She told me no," I insist.

"Well, she is." Jen fiddles with the diamond pennant at her throat and flashes a smile. "You don't know everything, Taryn. You have your projects and I have mine."

"Jackie earned enough write-in votes to be considered for queen." Mrs. Ames looks around the room one last time. "No Jackie? I'll have to go ahead and announce the winner then." She doesn't waste any time now. "Your Homecoming Queen is Chelsea Manor."

Pasting on a smile, I accept a sash and a rose, then step to the side with the rest of the Queen's Loser Court, as it's traditionally called by the student body. Chelsea's frozen smile looks almost painful as she leans down to be crowned and receive her bouquet of red roses. She does not look well and I wonder if it's somehow not a joke, but just a pity vote. The fire, the lawsuit, her strange behavior. Maybe the student body feels sorry for her.

I don't. I survived the fire, too, but I'm getting up every morning. I'm putting one foot in front of the other and moving forward.

I look toward the door again for Zeke. If I'm going to salvage the night at all, having a good looking, popular football hero for a date will help. If he doesn't show can the student body president ditch homecoming?

"Congrats, 'Loser Court' Pal." Jen hugs me. "After we're done with photos, let's go find Gretchen and get a picture taken."

Angel and Kirstie stand, already posed and beaming at Chelsea's right. A student photographer pushes me and Jen into place and begins snapping photos. "Say 'Chelsea's queen,'" she calls out. It sounds more like "Cheesy's queen" through our broad smiles, and I think it's appropriate.

"There's Gretchen, go." Jen propels me that direction when the photographer finally calls it good. And just in time. I don't think I can fake-smile another second.

"Those red lace gloves are a nice touch, Gretch," Jen says.

"You know you should have gone with the red dress you picked out first, don't you? I tried to tell you. It's a power color."

Jen strikes a pose. "I figured not too many girls would be brave enough to wear white and I was right."

"As always." Gretchen makes a face.

"Obviously, you forgot we were supposed to wear red, white, or blue," Jen says. Gretchen wiggles her red-gloved fingers, but Jen waves them away. "The gloves don't count. Look around. The only ones wearing black are the boys."

"You stand out in white, I can stand out in black."

"Will you two shut up? Smile for the camera," I tease them.

"Let me wear those gloves for the picture," Jen demands.

After the photo Jen and Gretchen leave to avert a crisis in the refreshment department and I slip into the bathroom to stash my rose and sash in my purse. There's no tradition that says I have to wear it all night. Jackie Weir stands at the far sink adjusting a new head of hair.

"Jackie, you came. And your hair. You look great."

"It's borrowed. Jen's mom found it for me.

You don't think it's too much, do you?"

"No. It's so pretty." I reach out to touch the soft white-blonde curls. "It looks like your real color. I didn't know she was doing this. It's not like Jen not to announce her good deeds to everyone."

Jackie laughs. "She gave my mom a wig, too." Jackie beams, then gets emotional. "You'll have to see it. She said she's always wanted to be a redhead."

"Sweet. Now stop. You'll mess up your makeup." I hand her a paper towel. "Did you come with a hot date or do you want to hang with a date-less loser like me."

"Like you have ever in your life been a loser, Taryn."

"Actually, I need to tell you something."

"I made Loser Court?" Jackie says.

"Who told you?"

"Probably ten different people on my way from the door to the bathroom."

"I promise it was not my fault. I had them take your name off the nominations, but you were a write-in."

"It's so embarrassing." Jackie tosses the paper towel in the trash.

"Why?"

"I can't believe they wouldn't ask if I wanted to

be nominated in the first place. Can you imagine how awful it would be to have to get up in front of everyone knowing I was nominated as a joke or even out of pity?"

"You look great. You wouldn't have been embarrassed up there," I insist. "I love your dress, by the way. That's a really pretty blue."

"Jen borrowed it from her cousin. Hey, I heard you made Loser Court, too. I'm glad, 'cause you deserve it. Well, you know what I mean. You could have totally been queen."

I make a face at her.

Jackie turns away from the mirror. "So who's your date really?"

"Actually, I'm still wondering if he'll show up."

"Me, too. I'm supposed to meet mine up front since I have the tickets. Oh, and I have something for you, but I left it in my car." Jackie heads toward the bathroom door, but I stop her.

"Hey, did you know a couple of years ago there was a girl with Alopecia Areata who won Miss Delaware. She even took off her wig on TV." The story came up when I Googled Alopecia.

"It's okay, Taryn. I don't have to be crowned queen. There's some middle ground, you know. How do people treat you?"

"Over the last couple of months? You don't want to know."

"Well, I just want to be treated like any other student at Ideal High. I don't have to have all the friends in the world, but normal school stuff would be okay. Actually, it felt kind of nice to have people talk to me when I came into the dance tonight. And last night was my first Ideal High football game. I got a matching red T-shirt and sat with the Senior Spirits."

"So just normal stuff, right? Why don't you come eat at our lunch table?"

"Because I joined the Paw Pals Club and we help the special needs kids get lunch. Your table is not that special, sorry."

"Point taken."

Jackie doesn't say anything, but I can tell she wants to.

"Taryn, you're done with me, aren't you?"

"What?" I protest.

"I mean as a project."

"Please don't remind me that I looked at you that way."

"But you are, right?"

"Okay, make me say it. Yes, I'm done."

"I've got a new one for you. How about you eat with me and my tutor sometime next week? She has problems. I think you're the only one that can help her."

"What can I do?"

"Promise me you'll do it?"

"Who is it?"

"Promise?" Jackie isn't giving in.

"Okay. Whatever."

"It's Chelsea Manor." With that revelation Jackie pushes her way out the bathroom door.

I'm not sure which feels worse, the fact that Chelsea beat me to the tutoring punch or that I just made a promise to Jackie that I can't keep.

32

I enter the gym and watch Jackie navigate the mass of mostly red and blue formals that dot the dance floor. Many are paired with guys in black tuxes, but some just congregate in groups and it's hard to tell who is dancing and who's just talking. I find a shadowed corner to sit and slip out of my heels when a wash of white catches my attention. Kenny and Trek with their skater friends all dressed in white tuxes crowd around the punch table. Some football players join them and they start talking and laughing.

I spot Jackie again waiting by the gym doors. One of them opens and in walks her date. It has to be because she links her arm in his.

It's Levi Jenks.

It was nice of him to come with her. I'll give him that.

I slide into my shoes and peel myself off the folding chair I'm glued to. I don't care a bit about Levi, but I don't want him to see me sitting alone at homecoming. The gym door opens again and Zeke walks in right behind Levi and Jackie. Perfect. I cut a path across the dance floor to the gym entrance.

"Yo, Miller! Zeke!" Several call out his name. Eyes turn toward the football star as I glide to his side. Yes, he's my date, ladies.

"You made it." I pull him toward the middle of the dance floor, realizing it'll be awkward having Zeke and Levi face to face. Levi isn't a Zeke-fan. He made that clear. And vice-versa.

"Is that Tacky Jackie with new hair?" Zeke says.

"Shh." I tug on his arm. I'm just glad he showed up. Now I can dance and forget about everything else.

Immediately a bunch of jocks crowd around, and I end up on the edge of high school's version of Sports Center. Angel and Kirstie cling to Travis and J.T., their prized jock-dates, and seem as eager as the guys to get close to Zeke, even if it means that dancing literally comes to a standstill.

"What are you doing with him, Taryn? Didn't I warn you?" Levi's hoarse whisper too close to my ear breaks into my thoughts.

Heat flashes across my cheeks. "Warned me? I choose my own dates, thank you," I snap back.

"He's a genuine jerk. You know how he treated my brother."

"Zeke's different now."

"What proof do you have of that?"

I scan the crowd looking for Jackie. "I don't even have to be having this conversation with you." Travis and J.T. are grinning and patting Zeke on the back. Zeke says something I can't hear and everyone laughs. "He's just different, okay? But what about you, Levi?"

He shakes his head. "What?"

"I know two things about you."

His face registers confusion.

"One, you're a liar, and two —" I point at the cowboy boots he wears with his tux. "You don't know how to choose appropriate footwear for a formal dance."

I make a move back to the jocks-and-their-dates circle.

"That's not fair." His hand touches my arm, but he quickly drops it when I give him a death-stare. His look softens. "Why do you say I'm a liar?"

"You said you would never set foot on Ideal High property again. And yet." I gesture dramatically at his feet like I did that morning in the parking lot eons ago.

"I did it for a friend. Only 'cause Jackie asked me," he replies. "Plus it's dark. No one will notice me." He flashes a smile.

"Jackie's a good reason," I answer quietly,

ignoring his attempt to lighten the mood. “But that doesn’t explain the footwear.” I turn away, not giving Levi a chance to reply.

I push my way to Zeke and hang on his arm, but he pulls away. “I’ll be right back.”

He disappears into the crowd with J.T. following him. Some date he is. I steal a glance behind me to make sure Levi’s gone, too. Hopefully, he went back to Jackie where he belongs. That’s his one redeeming quality. At least he treats Jackie like a human being.

For a few minutes I watch Jen and Paco dance. Jen knows how gorgeous she looks in her princessy ball gown as she dips and turns to his lead. Gretchen dances nearby with Trek Lyons who’s at least two heads shorter. No fancy moves for them, but they are laughing about something, and then Jen and Paco are laughing with them. At least someone is having a successful homecoming.

I retrieve my purse, then slide out a side door, seeking some fresh air and quiet. Immediately, strained voices accost me from around the corner of the building.

“Not here, Zeke.” It’s Chelsea.

Zeke left me to talk to her? Jerk.

“I said don’t touch me.” Chelsea’s voice rises. “How many times do I have to tell you?”

"You okay out here?" Levi's voice. I hear his boots as they hit the sidewalk.

"Leave us alone. We're fine." It's J.T.

"Chelsea?" Jackie's with Levi.

"I'm coming in now," Chelsea answers and then I hear her muffled, "Thank you." The sounds of two pairs of high heels are followed by the boots back the way they came.

Obviously, Zeke has his own agenda, but I have my car here, and there's nothing keeping me at the dance. I palm my keys, contemplating the necessity of saying goodbye to Jen and Gretchen. No, I'll just text them.

Zeke, and his tagalong, J.T., stand between me and the parking lot. I pull off my heels and round the corner, moving past them to the parking lot without looking back.

"Taryn, where are you going?" Zeke calls.

"Home."

"What's wrong?" He drapes his arms around me when he gets closer, but I shrug him off.

"You'd rather hang with the guys than me, plus there's something going on with you and Chelsea and I'd like to stay about a mile away from whatever it is."

"Taryn." He puts an arm back around me.

"My dad will hate me in the morning, but Zeke,

I'm done." I slip out from under him.

"Can't you take an apology? C'mon. It's your homecoming. We haven't even danced."

"Exactly my point. Goodnight, Zeke."

He holds onto my arm. "I said I want to dance." I tremble more at his tone than his grip.

"Hey!" Levi pounds the pavement between the gym doors and the parking lot. "Is that all you know how to do, Miller? Harass people?" he yells.

I twist away, now worrying about Levi and how badly he'll regret accusing Zeke of anything. Where did J.T. disappear to?

"Following me, Jenks? I could drop you so fast. Just like I did your brother," Zeke snarls.

"Don't you ever talk about my brother." Levi's voice sounds strained, unnatural. "And if you're going to threaten me, smart to do it on school property. Of course, that's never stopped you before, has it?"

I look down the sidewalk at my car. Escape sits parked only a few yards away, but I drop my keys into my purse. Better to get these two separated and back to the dance where they'll be surrounded by people. Witnesses.

I take Zeke's arm. "Let's go back inside."

"Whatever." Zeke pushes past me to the gym door, muttering under his breath. The volume of a popular dance tune rises and falls as the door opens, then bangs shut behind him.

An image of Blake in a tux placing a delicate rosebud corsage onto my wrist settles in my memory. Junior Prom seems forever ago. What I would give to dance with him again, but he's gone. Just a balloon dot floating forever out of reach.

"Are you okay?" Levi watches me.

"Do I have a choice?" I can't be that free-floating pink balloon sailing along beside Blake's. As always, the only choice is to keep moving, keep pretending I'm making progress, keep lying to myself that I'll be over the tragedy someday.

But that doesn't mean I have to follow Zeke back into the dance.

"You better go find your date, Levi." I head toward my Corolla. Once inside I wilt into the front seat and close my eyes, hoping he'll go away. Hoping it all will somehow go away.

I hear a knock on the window, but it's Jackie peering at me from the other side, her eyes wide with panic.

"Taryn, hurry. I'm scared." Her hand suppresses a sob. "It's Chelsea."

Jackie practically drags me from the car into the gym where she pushes me into the girls' bathroom. She doesn't follow.

The area in front of the sink is empty, but one stall door is shut.

"Chelsea?" No answer.

"Are you okay?"

More quiet, then finally a reply. "Why is everyone always asking me if I'm okay? I'm sick to death of it."

"Maybe 'cause they're worried about you?" I offer.

"They should stop."

I remember the promise made to Jackie less than an hour ago. "I'm worried about you, too."

The silence stretches again.

"Chelsea?"

The stall door opens slowly to reveal Chelsea's gaunt figure, her crown hanging at an odd angle. She holds a prescription bottle in her hand.

I stare at it, alarm surging through me. "You didn't take any of these pills, did you?"

"I wanted to."

"I'm so sorry, Chelsea." And for the first time in forever, sympathy for her feels real.

"For what?"

"That you wanted to," I reply

She shuffles out of the stall to busy herself at the mirror, leaning heavily on the sink with one arm as she fluffs up her hair. I move next to her.

"Are you really?" She twists and falls against me. I bring her down to the floor till we're sitting, a mass of shimmering shades of blue. I pluck the bottle easily from her fingers, wondering about the bruises along her wrist.

"Chelsea, did you take these pills? Tell me the truth."

"I did."

"You did take them?" Panic grows from the knot in my stomach.

"No, I mean I told you the truth. I didn't."

I breathe for what seems like the first time since being pushed into the bathroom by Jackie. "Chelsea, let me help you."

33

"Help me?" Chelsea pulls herself back up to the mirror and adjusts her gown. "Since when have you wanted anything to do with me, Taryn?"

I stand up, too, making sure to tuck the pill bottle into my purse before she notices. "I'm talking about right now." I can't keep the sudden defensiveness out of my voice. "Can I see if your date will take you home?"

She laughs. "I came alone, Taryn. Does that make you happy? The homecoming queen came alone." Chelsea drags the crown from her head and drops it in the sink. "Who wants to go to the dance with the psycho queen? Why did anyone even vote for me?"

"Did your Mom drive you? Do you need a ride?" I'm all business, wanting to get her away before the whole school finds out that Head Cheerleader-Homecoming Queen Chelsea Manor has been sitting on a toilet in Ideal High's bathroom contemplating swallowing a bottle of her mom's prescription pills.

"But better to come alone than with Zeke,

Taryn. He's just using you. Just like he uses everyone."

"Chelsea, stop."

"No, Taryn. I know you hate me, but that doesn't mean I want to see you hurt."

"Let me take you home."

"Don't deny it. You hate me. You've tried to avoid me every single day of school here at Ideal High. I've been like Jackie Weir to you. Invisible. Or you wish I was."

"What? When we got to high school you started hanging out with Becca all the time." My throat tightens. I feel bad bringing her name up.

"Because you quit talking to me! What am I supposed to do when my best friend ignores me? And it started back in ninth grade, before I even met Becca. I didn't know her until we were sophomores."

"I started feeling like you and Kayla didn't want me to hang out with you anymore. I'd see you going to her house all the time, but you wouldn't invite me."

"That was only when we were studying for the American History Bowl. We were supposed to practice with our teams, remember?" Suddenly, Chelsea's hands ball into fists. "No!"

I brace myself.

"It all started because of the A.H. Bowl?" Her mouth hangs open in an unsightly gash.

I know my silence confirms the ridiculous truth, but my mind's numb. Any sort of redeeming explanation fails me.

"No!" She says again. "I had nothing to do with that."

"What are you talking about?" I shoot back. "You chose your team, and I wasn't on it. Kayla was, but I had to be with Harrison and the Fletcher twins. We lost in the first round. It was sickening."

Chelsea slams her clenched fists onto the bathroom counter, her beautiful formal swishing and swaying with her every movement. "Mr. Whidden made me, Taryn. I chose you, but he made me and Harrison even out our teams. He didn't want the top two students together."

"It wasn't even. Your team took first."

She gestures wildly. "We practiced almost everyday to win that stupid competition." Now she doesn't stop the tears which flow in streaks of mascara. "Do you know what it's been like? Going to all the parties, hanging out with the same friends, being in the same classes, but you ignore me?" Chelsea slides to the floor in a royal blue silk puddle and drops her face to her knees.

"Do you know what it feels like to lose my best

friend and not know why?" Now her voice cracks and slows as she fights to speak through tears. "Seven of my friends got trapped in a burning building and I couldn't help them. I wanted to . . . I really wanted to." She curls into a ball, her shoulders shaking. "I needed you, Taryn. I needed a best friend." She speaks in a hoarse whisper to her pulled-up knees.

I'm too stunned to move. "I don't . . . I can't." Words are meaningless. The realization cuts too deep — I haven't had a best friend since Chelsea. And I've needed one, too.

But it's way too late.

I hug the bathroom door, my exit from the mess I created, but have been denying for years. I press against it, but it won't budge.

Then it opens and Jackie peeks her head in. "Is she okay?"

"No one's okay." I move past her out of the bathroom. "Will you stay with her?"

I take a deep breath and head for the exit. Even when confused looks from Jen and Gretchen jump out at me from the dance floor and Zeke calls my name from the refreshment table, I keep walking out the door and down the sidewalk to my car.

Who would have predicted that losing my friends, and becoming president, and helping Jackie would force Chelsea back into my life? I could have gone my entire senior year ignoring her just fine and then after graduation I'd never have to see her again.

I'm behind the wheel again, my eyes transfixed on the banner that hangs above the gym doors: *Ideal High School Homecoming! The Spirit of Ideal!*

A story starts playing in my head. A sort of flashback to my campaign speech, but with a new spin.

It's about a girl. She wanted to make things better at Ideal High and she thought she knew how. Then she learned people aren't projects. They don't want to be forced into someone else's view of what they should be or what they should want.

I picture Chelsea with the bottle of pills and her queen crown, and how everyone was oblivious. If it wasn't for Jackie.

She learned people matter. Not awards or titles.

The knots in my throat dissolve one by one.

If those who died were able to speak one last time, wouldn't they say, take care of each other because we're all going through hard things — whether it's the fire or personal situations no one at school even knows about.

This time the story is about me. How I needed to open my eyes and see what I haven't been seeing.

To treat others the way they want to be treated, and deserve to be treated.

How I was stupid enough to think that I could take Blake's place.

I toss my shoes into the back seat and start the engine. Levi appears at the door under the banner, and promptly starts down the sidewalk waving at me to stop. I jolt the car into reverse.

At the first light I turn left. Soon I'm on Wellman Boulevard and turning onto Winslow. The cemetery parking lot is empty, the gates shut and locked. I pull into a spot at the front and cut the engine.

I've climbed the low wall nearest the gate once before, but, of course, not in a formal. The rocks of the graveled lot dig into my feet, and I step lightly until I reach the sidewalk. I refuse to put my heels back on.

I'm losing my sanity. I just left my senior year homecoming dance alone, and now I'm sizing up my best approach to scaling the cemetery wall as if it's perfectly normal behavior. Truth is, my formal is way too nice, so if possible, I am going to have to be graceful about the whole thing.

One thing I know for sure. I want to be with Blake on homecoming night.

Is that why I'm here? Or am I just avoiding the

mess I left at school? I ignore the question and hike my dress to my knees with one hand. I grab the lamp post that sticks out from the top of the wall with the other, and plant a bare foot onto a rail of the heavy cemetery gate. I swing the other leg onto the brick wall. The hard part done, I tuck my dress into both hands and brace myself. I'm not going to slide down like last times. Not in the dress.

I make a perfect leap onto the grass below. After landing on my feet, I beat a straight line to Blake's grave. Pumping adrenaline is making me sweat despite the cool temperature.

I fall to my knees in front of his gravestone to run my finger across each letter of his name like I've done before. I stop at *Beloved* and ball my hands into fists.

I hate you, Blake Montgomery. It's homecoming. Why aren't you here to dance with me?

I lean back and wrap my arms around my knees.

"Remember senior year and everything it was supposed to be?" I speak the question out loud, but it's lost in the wailing of the wind through the trees. Its scent promises rain.

I've been mourning Blake's death all this time, but, really, I'm not sure what our relationship meant. Maybe I've been mourning the loss of what might have been.

Finally, a new question emerges. "If you can't be here, can I, please, just have a sign? Something, anything, so I'll know I'm going to be okay."

The wailing becomes louder. I feel a smattering of raindrops, but nothing more.

I don't know how much time passes, but, finally, I stand and smooth my dress. I reach out to touch Blake's headstone again. "I'm going to have to do it without you, aren't I?"

I trace his name one more time. "Blake David Montgomery. Beloved . . ."

My fingers flutter over the word, lingering, before I reach down to pluck a leaf that has blown up next to the metal vase in the stone's foundation.

A folded square of paper falls forward. The quote from Kayla's funeral: *Sorrows, disappointments, and even tragedies are events in life, they are not life itself.* I snatch it up like it's my last hope and close it tight into my fist without opening it.

Lifting my skirt with one hand, I retrace my steps to the cemetery gate and repeat my climb-and-leap over the wall. The moment my feet hit the ground I see my car. The autumn-colored Corolla is covered in Flamin' Hot Cheetos.

34

The porch light reflects off the white pickup parked in front of my house when I pull into the driveway. Levi, still in his tux, climbs out of the front seat and meets me at my car.

"Who told you about Hot Cheetos?" I demand.

"What Hot Cheetos?" he smiles, wide open as the Panhandle.

I narrow my eyes at him. He's not even trying to pretend he's innocent.

Levi picks at some that are stuck around the windshield wipers. "I can't believe Hot Cheetos are even visible on a car this orange."

"You of the lime-green buggy, emphasis on the "bug," should not be commenting on the color of other people's vehicles." I slam my car door. "You followed me."

"Okay, that's my work truck only, and, technically, me and Jackie followed you. She was worried."

So this was Jackie's doing. "Where is she?"

"I took her home, but she convinced me I should make sure you made it home okay. You didn't answer her texts."

"She convinced you," I repeat.

"She practically threatened me with bodily harm if I didn't."

"Yeah, and she's pretty big and scary."

Levi pauses for a long few seconds, then his voice softens when he speaks. "Truth is she could tell I wanted to."

"Why? So I could make fun of your boots some more?" A nervous giggle escapes. I can handle the verbal sparring, but I'm not sure about this new, gentler tone.

"I have to say you're wrong about the boots, Taryn."

Back to the sparring. That's a relief.

"Check these out. They're my best pair." He pulls at a pant leg and I love him in that moment. Boots and all.

I wrinkle my nose, testing him. "Do you wear big shiny belt buckles, too?" Or maybe testing myself. Do all the cowboy trappings matter that much if underneath beats a tender heart? If I've learned anything so far this school year, I know not to judge people by their "covers."

"Sometimes."

"Do you listen to country music?"

"Always."

I bite my lip. So different than Blake, but so perfect in all the ways that matter.

"Okay. What if we were in your truck and I changed the radio from your favorite country station to —"

"My radio only plays country."

"No, really, I want to know. What if I said don't wear cowboy boots anymore?"

"Let's talk about how we're in my truck together. Who cares what's on the radio or on my feet." Levi shortens the gap between us and the silence wraps around, tying us together with anticipation.

"Look, Taryn." He picks at his bow tie till it comes loose, his words low and musky when he finally speaks. "I need to say my piece and then if you want me to get lost I will."

I hope he isn't going anywhere.

"I've had kind of a one-track mind lately. Somehow I've done the opposite of what I wanted to do."

"Opposite?" The sound of my voice surprises me. I'm caught up in the sea-glass shine of his eyes.

"I wanted to be with you. Figure you out, so that you would want to be with me. I should have thought about what you were going through."

"I should have been more sensitive to your

feelings about your brother."

"No, it's my fault. I tried, but always messed everything up."

Did he try looking at me with those eyes, because . . . yeah.

I don't see his eyes anymore because he closes them and leans in.

Suddenly, I can't breathe, can't think, as time slows.

He hesitates, possibly trying to guess my reaction, or only to prolong the moment. The moment it will take to move mere inches. Finally, Levi closes the space between us, but turns his lips to my ear. "Taryn, remember when I said 'you were part of my problem'?"

I nod, electricity strobing from my earlobe.

"You're the kind of problem I want to have."

Suddenly, his mouth brushes mine, then it's gone. When he pulls back he reaches for more Cheetos from off the windshield and showers them over my head.

"Feel better?" He raises his eyebrows.

Now my own voice goes soft. "Yeah. I kinda do."

"Hot Cheetos really do the trick. That's what Jackie says."

"Hot Cheetos. Totally."

His hand catches mine and I don't let go. I gaze at the pools of blue in his eyes, squaring this Levi with the one standing at the mic announcing his brother's name to the memorial assembly. I think of earlier tonight when he explained why he was at the dance, "I did it for a friend."

I squeeze his hand slightly, tentatively. "I think you do the trick, Levi Jenks."

He laughs at that, his eyes crinkling at the corners. Jumbo-size raindrops begin to fall, but we don't move.

"Should you be getting your tux wet?" I pat his lapel with my free hand.

He frowns. "Probably not."

"I'll let you walk me to the door. I may not have danced a single dance at homecoming, but having a guy in a tux to tell me goodnight makes it worth it."

"You didn't dance? Not once?"

"Nope."

"Meet me on the porch." Levi runs to his truck, the rain coming harder now.

When he reaches me at the door he sticks one bud in my ear and the other in his. He adjusts his phone till the twangy simplicity of an unfamiliar but sweet country love song streams straight into my heart.

Levi draws me close and we dance under the porchlit night. My first, last, and best dance of senior year homecoming.

35

"So what happened last night?" I snuggle into my comforter, keeping my cell phone close.

"You mean the best dance of my life?" Levi's honey voice feels warm in my ear.

I beam into the phone. "I mean after I left Chelsea sitting on the bathroom floor."

"We took her home."

"Really? Second of all, that was nice of you, but first of all — she let you? I thought she never wanted to see your face again."

"Jackie didn't give her a choice."

"You were busy last night, Levi. Dropping people off, shopping for Hot Cheetos, showing up at my house —" I roll onto my side, coming face to face with the Junior Prom photo. I can barely make out Blake's face in the light coming from under my bedroom door.

"Jackie already had the Cheetos. She was going to give them to you at some point. Some kind of thank you gift, I guess."

I open the drawer of my nightstand and stare at what's stashed there. "I still have Chelsea's mom's pills. How am I going to get them back to her?"

"Hand them to her and say Chelsea needs help. It's the truth."

"You're right." I slide the drawer shut. "I guess I'll go over there tomorrow. I kind of owe her an apology."

"Chelsea or her mom?"

"Both." I sigh deeply into the phone. "Sorry I couldn't see you today. My mom had this whole family thing planned for the twins' homecoming from the hospital. I would've invited you, but —"

"But your parents only think of me as the guy that interrupted the memorial."

"Kind of. Sort of. But I'll clear that up, don't worry." I face the alarm clock away from me. I don't want to know how late it's getting.

"Well, I'm sorry, too."

"For what, Levi?"

"That I didn't get to see you today."

I hug my pillow.

"I'm going to hang up, Taryn, but I left something for you on your doorstep. Get it before you go to bed, okay."

"What is it?" I throw back my covers and scramble for my bathrobe with my free hand.

"It's something you should have, so just go. But hang up first."

"Are you sure?"

"Yeah, goodnight."

On the porch I find a brown paper bag with the top neatly folded down. It says Taryn on the front in block letters.

Inside, a snack-size bag of Hot Cheetos.

And Blake's phone.

I fall asleep with them next to my pillow.

36

I wake up before my alarm and lay in bed cradling Blake's phone in my hands. We're there onscreen with our smiles and prom king and queen crowns. It's a little blackened and the screen is chipped and broken across the bottom pretty badly, except not over my left side. Where my heart is.

I wonder if his mother knows the pass code to unlock it. It's weird, but I've only talked to Mrs. Montgomery once since Blake died and that was when she called to tell me about his gravestone. Even at the funeral all I did was nod at her. There were no words.

It would be pretty awkward to call and ask for his code, and, really, the phone should be hers, not mine.

But not yet. Maybe tomorrow.

I just want to hold it for one day.

Unfortunately, I have to go to school. I jump in the shower and ten minutes later I'm out and dressed, drying my hair.

There's a text from Levi.

So you're not going to hate me forever?

I laugh out loud. That's what I told him last week when I first saw him with Blake's phone. I text back.

No. Because that would just be exhausting.

We text back and forth until I insist we stop so I can finish getting ready for school.

In the kitchen, mom's pulsing green drink in the blender.

"Mom, I'm so glad you don't have to sell doughnuts in the morning anymore. It must have been brutal."

"You just miss my noisy blender, don't you?"

"Yeah. Now where's Dad's juice?" I pour myself a glass.

The whirring stops. "Taryn, did you see this in yesterday's paper?" She points to the open Lubbock Avalanche-Journal. "It says, 'Levi Jenks, brother of Timothy Jenks, one of eight victims of the Ideal fire last June, has been banned from the site of the tragedy. Witnesses report seeing Jenks at the scene last Tuesday roaming the area. Ideal City police remind residents that the site is not safe. The remains of the old Ideal Gin Co. building will be bulldozed beginning Monday.'"

Levi neglected to tell me that part of the story.

Mom folds the newspaper carefully and drops it in the recycle bin. "Now do you see why I don't want you around that boy?"

"Because he cares what happened to his brother?"

"His behavior is erratic. Who knows what he'll do next?"

"Wait until you get to know him, Mom. You'll see."

"Now why would I —?"

"Bye, Mom." I'm out the door.

When I get to school, Zeke's sitting on the IHS bench that's out near the sidewalk. I feel his eyes on me as I park and get out of my car. Maybe he's waiting for someone else and he's not going to say anything. Of course, I'm kidding myself.

He cocks his head toward me. "Hey, you left me Saturday night."

Jerk. What part of "I'm done" is so hard for him to understand? "And you totally called to make sure I got home alright . . . no. And you called yesterday to see how I was doing . . . no. I meant it when I said I was done, Zeke."

"So you don't want to go out with me, but can't a guy be a friend? Offer a shoulder?"

"You, offer a shoulder?"

"Stab me in the heart, why don't you, Taryn? C'mon, let me make it up to you. Let's go to Donut

King for breakfast."

He thinks he's flirting with me, but that's not what it feels like. And the students coming onto campus can't help staring.

"What are you really doing here, Zeke?"

He paws at my backpack's side pocket and finds the bag of Hot Cheetos. The one from Levi. I jerk my bag away. I don't want him finding Blake's phone.

"Give me the chips back. I have to get to class." I hold out my hand, but he stands up, keeping it out of reach.

"C'mon, share." He rips open the bag and stuffs a few in his mouth. Immediately, he makes a face and spits in the grass. "These Cheetos bite."

"You're a wimp." I snatch the bag and walk away. Too many eyes are watching us and I'm done making a scene.

Zeke falls in beside me and takes a hold of my arm. "So you're hanging out with Tacky Jackie now? Who put you up to that?"

I yank my elbow out of his grasp. "Don't call her that. If you started noticing anyone besides yourself, you might see that people are pretty okay, even the ones that don't worship the football field you walk on."

"You've been talking to Chelsea, too? And I

thought I told you that Levi dude was bad news."

"Why do you care who I talk to?" I keep my voice low, hoping the students we're passing will ignore us.

"Taryn, we need to talk. But not here." He takes my arm again, gripping too hard this time, and it spikes a warning across my shoulder blades.

What's his problem?

Across the courtyard, J.T., Paco, and some of their football buddies hang out near the gym doors.

"Look, Zeke. Your fans." I wave. "Hey, J.T. Hi, Paco." They'll be all over Zeke in seconds.

My cell phone buzzes in my pocket. "Later, Zeke." Really, I hope not.

I check my phone as I hurry to the 200 building. It's Levi.

Sorry. One more text. Just wondering if you've unlocked Blake's phone yet. No pressure, but I'm curious.

That's why Levi's so interested in the phone. He thinks there might be something on it. An incriminating text or phone message.

The phone is evidence.

I cover my mouth with my hand. I held onto the phone all night thinking it was just a last desperate connection to Blake, but maybe he left clues. Who texted him that night? Who called him?

In homeroom I pull the phone out of my backpack and slide it next to some textbooks I place on my desk. I sit at the end of the last row, so I should be safe. Our faces pop up when I turn it on. So does a number grid, the screen for inputting the pass code. I play around with it, dragging my finger in different number combinations.

I try Blake's birth date. Then my birth date. Just in case.

I try the date of junior prom, of elections last May, the last day of school. All incorrect.

I have no idea what his pass code is.

"Now, students" — homeroom announcements are winding down — "just a reminder that despite the continued presence of the Ideal City Police Department on campus, you should all go about your normal day. They're only here to keep us safe." Ms. McKinney pauses before adding the usual epigram, "Remember pride, unity, and self-respect. Have a good day."

A twist. A change from respect to self-respect. Ms. McKinney mentioned something about that in her assembly speech — how if we disrespect others, we're really disrespecting ourselves. She's sounding more and more like a principal. In a good way.

I hide Blake's phone back in its spot in my backpack and shuffle to English.

Chelsea's absent which doesn't surprise me after everything that happened at homecoming. Another memorable Saturday night dance at good old Ideal High. That's one thing about my senior year — it's anything but boring. By lunch time I'm just grateful that no one, reportedly, has written names on a bathroom stall, smacked anyone with a skateboard, or elected someone by a "lame-o" vote.

I approach our lunch table cautiously. I never officially apologized to J.T. for telling on him. Not that I'm sorry for telling the truth, but I hope he gets that as president of the student body I had to do it. Everyone that sits at our table joined in on all the Homecoming Week activities, so I think things are okay between us.

'Taryn, sit! We need details." Angel and Kirstie lean in when I set my tray down across from them.

"Details?" My first thought is of Blake's phone. There's no way they know I have it.

"Are you kidding me? Zeke. Homecoming." Angel's mouth hangs open in disbelief. "Are you hearing this Kirstie?"

"We're just wondering if you're together now." Kirstie fills in the blank.

"No. Homecoming with him was a big mistake." Where are Jen and Gretchen? And J.T. and Travis? Angel and Kirstie are always the last to arrive at the table.

“But he came and met you before school today. We thought that was sweet.” Kirstie clearly can’t believe she’s hearing this.

I stir my salad with a fork. “I don’t know what you thought you saw, but I did not leave the dance with him Saturday night, and I wasn’t happy about seeing him on campus this morning.”

That shuts them up. They dig into their salads and we eat in silence.

“Chelsea wasn’t happy about seeing him either.”

She says it so softly I’m not sure I hear her right. “What did you say, Kirstie?”

“Nothing. Just that Zeke was talking to Chelsea this morning, but she wasn’t happy about it either.”

“Chelsea’s here today?”

“We saw her before school.” Angel chimes in.

Jen plops down next to us with her tray. “Hey!” She smiles at the table. “Where are the guys?”

“No one knows.” Angel murmurs.

“How are you, Taryn?” She gives me a look. She knows what happened with Zeke at the dance. We talked on the phone yesterday, but I didn’t tell her everything. Not about Levi, anyway. I’ll wait until the time is right.

A few of the football players trickle in to fill

the seats next to us, but they don't say much. I spot Jackie in her blue and red Paw Pals vest. She's balancing two lunch trays while a girl in a wheelchair rolls alongside her.

She sets a tray down on our table. "Sorry, I was afraid I was going to drop it. Can I introduce you all to Olivia? She just moved to Ideal."

"No, it's okay. Sit with us." I scoot over to make room on the end. "It's nice to meet you, Olivia."

Jen points at Jackie. "I need one of those vests. Where do I sign up?" She gestures to everyone at the table. "Did you know teachers let you do whatever you want if you're wearing one of those?"

"Taryn, I think Gretchen Smith wants you." Kirstie points to the entrance of the cafeteria where Gretchen is waving her arm.

I meet her there and we start walking down the hall. She keeps her voice low. "The cops are talking to J.T., Paco, and Travis out in front of the school. I wouldn't think anything of it except that Phyllis said Mel gave her a list of students to call to the office as soon as fifth hour starts. Your name's on it. Plus Jen, Angel, Kirstie, and Chelsea.

"It sounds like they're talking to everyone who was invited to play night games after the end-of-school-year party."

"That's what I thought."

I stop in the middle of the hall. "Thanks for telling me, Gretchen. I'll catch up with you later, okay? I need to go do something."

I walk out the door and through the courtyard. I'm almost to the Science building when I realize my backpack's locked inside Anatomy class. I'm not going to be able to get to it until lunch is over.

I park myself outside the classroom, and when my teacher arrives I'm the first one to get my stuff. I start moving across campus, not sure where I can be alone. I go in circles, trying to avoid anyone and everyone.

Finally, I end up in the bathroom in the 200 building, and lock myself in the last stall. It feels good to see the NIMS sign on the back of the door, but thinking of the phone and what it might contain gets my blood pumping. I pull it out and turn it on.

My cell phone vibrates at the same time. It's Jen. "Are you okay?"

"Yeah, sort of." I wonder if Gretchen told her we're getting called to the office.

"Well, we're talking at the table about Winter Formal. Do you remember the date for that?"

Both hands are holding a phone, so I stick Blake's in my pocket. "Hold on. I can look it up." I find my purple notebook with the "Hot Cheetos are hot" doodled on the front and start turning pages. "It's December sixth."

I put my phone away, then flip to the back of the notebook to me and Blake's To-Do list for our senior year. I run my finger down the page, searching for clues.

Nothing jumps out at me. I pull out his phone and gaze again at the number grid.

I'm kidding myself. I don't know Blake Montgomery. I knew his favorite doughnut and that he wanted to change the world. At least at Ideal High, anyway. But I don't know him well enough to know what four numbers he would choose for a pass code.

The bell rings. Any minute Phyllis will be buzzing Mr. Thomas asking him to send me and Chelsea to the office. If Chelsea's in class.

I guess I'm not in class either.

I unlock the bathroom door and carry my stuff to the sink. I pull my notebook off the counter too late — water has already seeped into it.

I'm pulling the pages apart when Blake's handwriting jumps out at me. It's a quote written in the middle of my notebook. I don't remember him writing in it.

"There is a law that man should love his neighbor as himself. In a few hundred years it

should be as natural to mankind as breathing or the upright gait; but if he does not learn it, he must perish."

I read the quote a second time. It's attributed to Alfred Adler (1870-1937).

I've been thinking about numbers all morning, so the 1870 jumps out at me.

I drag it across the grid on the cracked screen and a lock-shaped icon changes from closed to open.

I'm in.

My own phone buzzes. Jen, again, but it's a text this time.

Didn't you get called to the office, too?

My phone goes back into the pocket of my jeans.

I find Blake's inbox. The text at the top is from his mom. It hasn't been read.

Do I dare?

There's no time for wondering if I should or shouldn't. I click on it.

It's late. Are you on your way home from the party? Getting a little worried. Call me.

That hurts in a place so deep I might never find the bottom to make it whole again.

Poor Mrs. Montgomery.

But I need to hurry. I'll talk to police if I have

to, but I want to know what's in the phone before I do.

The next several texts are from Chelsea. Blake read these.

I open the first one.

Hurry! They won't stop.

37

Deep breath, then I tap the screen again.

They pushed Tim into the Gin Co. building and they're lighting fireworks.

I read the next one.

J.T. and Zeke are being massive jerks. Almost here?

I slide to the floor as if I've been punched in the gut, but in agonizing slow-motion. I read all the text messages from that night. All Chelsea's pleas to Blake for help. They're a deadly timeline that started in the parking lot at Stan's gas station. Now what happened the night of the fire all makes horrific, horrific sense.

I pull my knees up to my chin, craving my bed like I've never craved anything before in my life. Paisley comforter, come swallow me whole.

But no more hiding. No more hiding for anyone.

I jam my notebook into my backpack and slide Blake's phone into the side pocket. I'm halfway to the office when I get a call.

It's Mrs. Manor. "Taryn? I'm worried about

Chelsea. Have you seen her at school today?"

"I haven't, but Angel and Kirstie said they did, why?" A knot in my stomach breaks free and begins its way up to my chest. I slump down on a bench, grateful the courtyard is empty.

"She just sent me an odd text. She said, 'I'm sorry, can't do it anymore.'"

Immediately, tears burn my eyelids as I picture Chelsea sitting on the bathroom floor at homecoming. Weak, needy. Unable to stand up to J.T. and Zeke any longer.

I take a quick breath. How do you tell a mother that her daughter had her pills? I just have to say it. "I have some pills that belong to you. Chelsea didn't swallow them, but she wanted to."

"Is she with you?"

"No. I'm talking about Saturday night at the dance. I took them away from her, but I'll bring them to you. I promise. Plus, I need to tell you why Chelsea —"

I flinch when a beefy hand clamps onto my wrist. It reminds me of sitting on the floor at homecoming observing the neat little row of bruises that dotted the inside of Chelsea's wrist like a chunky bracelet.

"It was your blue truck there that night, wasn't it?" I say slowly. "Chelsea rode with you to Ritter's

Crossing. You and Zeke were the ones that left after the fire started."

I wrench my wrist free and claw J.T. in the face, too angry to care what he can do to me. "You've been threatening Chelsea to keep her quiet. She almost killed herself because of you, do you know that?"

"Take it easy." He paws his face checking for blood. "No one saw me there. You don't know what you're talking about."

"Don't I, J.T.? I've read the play by play."

"Play by play? I'm not stupid, Taryn. You didn't show up till after . . . after —"

"After what? After you talked a poor, defenseless kid into coming with you to Ritter's Crossing? After you dragged him into the Gin Co. building and scared him half to death by lighting fireworks?"

"You better not be saying this stuff to police. Do you want to get me in trouble again?"

"Or do you mean after the old gin exploded and seven of —" I can't finish the sentence.

"I thought we were friends, Taryn."

Chelsea's been grieving and the whole time scared that the secret of how the fire started will come out. "Friends don't bully their friends to keep them quiet."

"We were only playing around. Things got out of hand." J.T. grabs my arm again and wrenches me to his chest in one motion. "It was an accident, Taryn. And you're the student body president who's helping the school get past it, remember?"

His words burn hot in my face. I turn my head, so I don't have to look at him, but he jerks me tighter.

"You better keep quiet, Taryn."

Now I look him straight in the eye. "No, J.T."

Desperation flares in his eyes. "You don't understand. I just want to get on with my life."

Adrenaline kicks in and I twist out of his hold, then pummel his chest with my fists. "And I just want mine back."

He pushes me to arm's length. "You and Chelsea need to let it go, or else —"

"Or else what, Mr. Webb?"

Mel appears from around a low wall of the courtyard.

I've never been happier to see him.

After I give Blake's phone to Mel, and receive a proper "thank you, Karen," I spend the rest of the school day in the office. Phyllis is freaking out and can't seem to stay still. My eyes follow her from one side of the attendance counter to the other while

I talk to the police. I'm grateful for the distraction.

Apparently, Ms. McKinney called my parents because Mom calls and it takes a good thirty minutes to explain everything all over again. Kleenex is involved. Not too long after I hang up from her, Dad texts to say they're coming down. I have to tell the story again when Mrs. Ames comes into the office.

She gives me a long hug which is exactly what I need.

Just after the bell rings ending last hour, Mel announces that they've picked up Zeke, but they're still looking for Chelsea.

Chelsea.

I was telling Mrs. Manor about Chelsea having her pills. I totally forgot about our interrupted conversation.

Just then, Jen and Gretchen find me in the office. It's still police grand central, so they pull me out to the foyer. When Travis, Paco, Angel, and Kirstie show up we all huddle together. Paco, especially, is taking it really hard. J.T. never told him a thing.

We're still group-hugging when Jackie appears. I wave to get her attention, then mouth the words, *Where's Chelsea?* But Jackie shakes her head.

"Can't do it anymore." That was Chelsea's text

message to her mom.

She wouldn't. Would she?

I slip away from the group and call Levi.

"Taryn, I was just calling you. Doesn't Chelsea have a red Lexus?"

"Yes, why?"

"She's here. At Ritter's Crossing."

"What are you doing out there?" I think about the news article.

"Tim's body might be here somewhere. I can't let them bulldoze it."

"I think they'll know soon enough, Levi." I hesitate, not sure if I should tell him everything over the phone.

No.

Not now.

"Can you find her, Levi? I'm coming." I pull Jackie with me out the front door. "Call Chelsea's parents and tell them to go to Ritter's Crossing. I don't want it announced to the whole school, though. I'm sure she doesn't want an audience."

I put Levi on speaker when I get in the car. All I hear is him calling her name as I leave the parking lot and head to Wellman Boulevard, then the freeway.

My heart pounds out every second that ticks by as I race down 27. I take the exit near Stan's gas station and within five minutes I'm passing the yellow warning sign to slow down. My call to Levi is dropped, so I can only hope that means he found her.

It's growing dark, and the trees make it even more so. The eerie shell of the burned-out Ideal Gin Co. building casts a jagged shadow across Chelsea's blood-red Lexus when I pull up next to it.

My heart breaks when I discover her shivering in a thin sweater on the gray-green grass, staring at the ruins of the old cotton gin with her elbows propped on her knees. Levi stands a distance away, watching her.

"Taryn, you're okay? Zeke didn't hurt you?" Chelsea peers at me through glazed eyes when I kneel down next to her. She makes a fist around something in her sweater pocket. "Why are you here?"

More pills? My stomach flip-flops.

"Give me your keys, Chelsea. I'll drive you home."

"I'm not going anywhere. Don't you get it?"

"Don't you?" I speak close to her ear. "J.T. and Zeke can't hurt you anymore."

She gestures out in front of her. "I was meant to be with my friends in that fire."

"What is your problem with being saved? Let's

go back to Ideal," I plead.

"I was saved last time and it was a mistake." Chelsea shudders noticeably.

My stomach twists into double knots as I force myself up. It's freezing out here. I give Levi a helpless look. Are we going to have to drag her to her car?

Levi moves in beside me. "I told you, it's over, Chelsea."

I turn to look at him. I don't know how he knows.

He takes off his baseball cap and runs his hand through his hair. "A crew from the city was here with a bulldozer, but they got a call saying the project was put on hold. Then they told me why."

He read my mind.

"It's not over." Chelsea looks up at us like we're the ones confused. "They said if I told anyone what really happened then I would get in trouble, too. They would make sure of it."

"You were being sued." Levi grits his teeth. "Those jerks are cowards. They let you and Tim take the blame for everything." He stands and I can tell his adrenaline is racing.

"But I ruined everyone's lives. If J.T. hadn't followed Tim from the country club after the party that night. If Zeke wouldn't have been at Stan's. If they hadn't started messing around with Tim when he stopped there."

I drop down beside her again. "See, that's a lot of 'ifs' that you had nothing to do with, Chelsea."

"I was in the truck with them. I'm responsible. I begged J.T. to take Tim back to his car, but Zeke kept egging him on. He said Tim got him suspended and almost made him lose his scholarship. Can you believe that?" She drops her face to her knees. "They wouldn't stop setting off fireworks in the building either. Why wouldn't they stop?"

I watch Levi as he paces a few yards away. This has to be killing him to hear what his brother went through.

"I didn't see the Hummer till it was too late." Chelsea's bottom lip begins to quiver. "I didn't know they were there yet, that they were in the building looking for us. They just came to play night games. They didn't know what J.T. and Zeke were doing."

"I know."

"I tried to go in after them, but my ankle . . . I fell . . . I couldn't save them." She begins to cry silent tears.

I look at Levi, but he won't make eye contact, so I just pull myself tighter, trying to keep out the chill. Maybe he somehow blames me. It was my friends that decided to stop at the Gin Co. building at Ritter's Crossing. It was my friends that dragged his brother along. I was there. Couldn't I have done something to stop it?

I rest my chin on my pulled-up knees, a copycat of Chelsea. "Maybe I was meant to be in that fire, too."

The wind rattles through what's left of the walls of the Gin Co. building, and then my bones. Soon I feel Chelsea shift beside me.

"You said you would never come to Ritter's Crossing again. You really came here to save me?" she says softly. "Why?"

I know why.

I need my best friend back. I haven't had one for a really long time.

I rock forward until I'm kneeling in front of her. I press a hand on each side of her face and force her to look at me. "A horrible thing happened here, Chelsea. It happened to us, but it's not who we are. Please, no more balloon dots."

I let go and fall back to sit on my heels. The squeal of tires and sirens announce the arrival of Mr. and Mrs. Manor, the police, and the Ideal City Fire Department. Chelsea makes an awkward attempt to stand up, so I rise, too, to steady her, and Levi wraps his arms around us both.

The Universe that has been spinning off course since the end of last May finally comes to a stop in the middle of Ritter's Crossing, just shy of Ideal City limits. The bitter wind whips and whirls around us. Here where nightmares were born, but healing gets wings.

Fast Forward...

"Better late than never," Jen calls from the far end of the bathroom counter where she's curling Persi's pink-streaked hair. I side-step closer to them to make room for the next wave of girls coming in while concentrating on applying one last layer of mascara. I don't think we can squeeze one more body into this bathroom.

Jen stops. "Gretch, you're wearing red to Senior Prom?"

I laugh at Jen's reflection in the mirror. She looks a little like the Statue of Liberty holding up a curling iron.

"Power color," Gretchen sing-songs back to her.

Chelsea gives Jackie a side hug. "You look beautiful."

"Jen's mom did my makeup. So, Taryn, how's the 'person I admire most' today?" Jackie teases.

"Chelsea, you told her?" I point my mascara wand.

"Sorry, I couldn't help it. It's so cute." She defends herself.

"What's she talking about?" Jen's done with the curling iron and turns to focus on me. She yanks on the wide ribbon hanging at my hip and begins re-tying it.

"Nothing. Phyllis just told me yesterday that her son wrote an essay for school. It was about the person he admires most."

"And it's Taryn," Chelsea interjects. "He got an A+."

"That's so sweet, I think I'm going to be sick." Gretchen holds her stomach and everyone laughs.

Chelsea rolls her eyes. "But seriously, Taryn deserves it after what she's done as student body president." Everyone gets quiet. I wonder if they're thinking about how the year started. I am.

Jackie dabs at her eyes. "Don't start that. My makeup's done."

I wave Jen away and focus on straightening the bow. "It was all of us."

Kirstie quietly zigzags her way up to the mirror next to me. "But you started it, Taryn." Her words are soft and kind.

I give her reflection a sincere smile. "Where's Angel?"

"She's picking up Olivia because the Brittons have that van that can carry a wheelchair. They should be here any second."

Chelsea tugs on my arm and nods toward the door. I follow her out, leaving our friends to more space at the mirror.

"I wrote those letters like the grief counselor suggested." Chelsea's mouth presses into a thin line before she continues. "I laid into J.T. and Zeke, telling them every single horrible way they hurt me and my friends."

"Good for you. I haven't written mine yet."

"Then I threw them away." Chelsea's eyes glisten. "I tore them into tiny pieces and burned them in our backyard fire pit. Then I wrote new letters. I told them I hope they find peace like I have. That's the one I'm going to mail."

I pull her into a hug. "You're my new favorite hero, Chelsea."

"No. I'm your best friend." It feels good to hear her say it.

She slips back into the bathroom, so I steal a moment to glance around at the glitz and glitter of the prom decor and consider how far we've come

"Excuse me." Levi wraps an arm around me from behind, the other holds out a bouquet of pink roses. "Taryn Young, will you not be my date to Senior Prom?"

"There's nothing I'd rather do than not be your date, Levi Jenks." We all agreed we'd go as a group to the dance. No dates. Still, I have a feeling this is going to be the best school dance ever.

"First, though. Do you approve of my footwear?" He twists around me to model polished black and white wing tips.

"I don't know. Do you approve of mine?" I lift the pink poofy layers of my formal to reveal gleaming white cowboy boots.

Levi's grin shows all his teeth and his eyes crinkle at the edges. "People are going to wonder why I'm dancing so much with a hick-from-the-sticks wearing boots to a formal dance."

I slip my arm around his waist. "Just tell them you're trying to make me feel like I fit in."

Before prom ends, Levi leads me out of the gym to the football field where stars light up the night like tiny rays of sun spotlighting our every movement. He doesn't say a word, just takes me through the end zone and past each ten-yard marker until we reach the fifty-yard line.

"Guess what?" He catches both my hands and pulls me to him. "Ms. McKinney called me yesterday. They're going to include Tim's name on the memorial they're unveiling at graduation for those who died in the fire."

"I know. She told me. I'm so happy, Levi." A distant snapshot of a guy in boots and jeans on stage at the memorial service flashes in my memory. I can't suppress a laugh.

"What's funny?" Levi says.

"You're not going to storm the stage at graduation, are you? You'll contain yourself?"

"That's funny, Taryn, but I'll already be on stage. I'm going to read a tribute to Tim."

"Perfect," I squeeze his hands. "Speaking of 'speaking.' Your alma mater in Lubbock called and wants me to come talk to their student council about bullying. Mr. Myers can hardly stand it."

Levi whistles. "I thought I caught him smiling tonight."

"He's all, 'We're not a Lubbock or a Dallas school. We're Ideal. We'll show them how it's done.' Sounds crazy, but I think I'm glad he got his old job back after all." I move my hands up Levi's arms to his biceps. He's been lifting heavy bug-spraying equipment since last fall and even in his suit jacket it shows. "And guess what Phyllis told me? They've hired someone to redo the patch in the wall outside Mr. Myers' office."

"Yeah, so?"

"It's a sign. Finally, Ideal High is getting things right."

"Because of you, Taryn." Levi pulls back and reaches into his jacket. "I know it's a little early for graduation, but I want to give you this." He hands me a present topped with a shimmering pink bow. "My mom wrapped it."

"It even matches my dress." I hug it to my chest like a valued treasure. My first gift from Levi. Unless you count saving my life.

"Open it."

I slip off the bow and carefully tear open the paper. "Um, thanks?" I pull the rest of the wrapping back to reveal a thick paperback book.

"Is that a question?" Levi says.

"No, sorry. I get it. It's for college. And look it's *The American* Complete *Dictionary*. Thoughtful." I tease him.

A grin that has been playing at the edge of Levi's lips spreads into a lop-sided smile.

"What?" I narrow my eyes at him.

"What nothing," Levi replies. Still that smile.

But it doesn't matter. Me, Levi, a dictionary. Alone together on Ideal High School's field of a thousand dreams. I grab him into a hug. I'll survive senior year after all. We'll all survive, even without Blake, and Kayla, and Keisha. Life goes on after tragedy.

Levi pulls me closer, his lips brushing my ear. "I know you're off to bigger and better things in the fall, but can you give me just one ideal summer?"

I whip open the dictionary between us. "I, i…id…ideal. 'A measure of perfection or excellence; a person or thing considered to exemplify or conform to such a measure, and taken as a model for imitation —'" I recite.

"Are you done?"

"No. 'Considered as comprising a standard of perfection or excellence; viewed as perfect of its kind.'" Then I notice the yellow sticky note on the left side of the page with its hand-drawn smiley face with short pony-tails and "TARYN" scrawled under it in all caps. Finally, I look at Levi.

"I can sum it up in one word. You're the definition of 'ideal,' Taryn." His sea-blue eyes fill with sincerity.

I thumb through the dictionary. It's a rainbow of sticky notes and smiley faces and "TARYN" in capital letters.

"And the definition of beautiful, smart, friendly, fair, amazing —" He leans in to kiss me, his breath grazing my cheek. "And a whole lot of other things, too," he adds.

I close the book and clutch it to my chest again. "How about 'cowboy-lover?'" I run my free hand through his hair.

"Hey, I think you're the one wearing the boots." He teases, then his look turns serious. "But I'm the lucky one if you let that define you."

His words land on my heart and I melt into his embrace. "I plan on it, Tex."

Chelsea and Jackie appear at the end zone. "Hey, you guys, it's time to go. You're still coming to my house for the after-party, aren't you?" Chelsea calls.

"We'll be there," I yell back.

"And you have the doughnuts?" Jackie's non-cheerleader voice is harder to make out, but I hear the important word, *doughnuts.*

"We have to stop at Donut King, but Perry the Prince said he'll have them ready for us."

"Okay, hurry!"

"Yeah, we'll hurry." Levi's words are soft and warm in my ear. Meant just for me. And I know we're not going anywhere until we're done savoring the last precious minutes of this important night.

"We missed the last dance of my senior prom." I keep the disappointment from my voice, so nothing blurs the feel of the moment.

Levi slips his phone out of his pocket and taps the screen. He hands me an ear bud. "I don't think so."

Acknowledgments

I wrote this book in the whirlwind. I didn't go away to a secluded cabin in the mountains for six months, nor did I shut and lock my office door. I wrote while taking care of home and family, and my church responsibilities, and, for good measure, I started back to school to finish my Bachelor's Degree.

So first, I thank my husband, Lance, who is my biggest supporter and cheerleader through everything mentioned in the previous paragraph, and my awesome family. Couldn't do it without you and wouldn't want to.

Also, couldn't have done it without Tamara Passey and Peggy Urry for much needed book therapy and "working" lunches over the years. You are the definition of *synergy*.

Huge thanks to Susan Haws and Julie Wallace, who have been fans of my story from the start, plus the other members of the current Skyline Scribblers writing group: Jennifer Williams, Georgia Fritz, Anika Arrington, plus Tamara and Peggy, and former member, Raejean Roberts.

Thanks also to Betsy Love, Tina Scott, Krista Fox, Patti Hulet, and Joyce DiPastena, plus past members of the Scribblers. Thank you all for your kind encouragement and honest critiques. Thanks to Marsha Ward, founder of the American Night Writers, for being awesome, and a mentor to so many.

Thank you to Joan Sowards, the first one to read my first chapter, and to Kerry Blair who was a quick second. Thanks for saying it was good, Joan, and, Kerry, for giving me goose bumps when you talked about it — the experience carried me through many a rough draft.

Thanks to those who read various versions all the way through: Peggy Urry, Julie Wallace, Susan Jensen, Leilani Jones, Tamara Passey, Mauri Crist, Stacy Costello, and Jennifer Shaw Wolf, and editor, Nancy Campbell Allen.

Thanks to my dad for reading it and saying, "Every teenager in America needs to read this," and that's when it was a rough draft, and to my mom who was the real writer in the family.

Thanks, Niles Giberson, for a cool cover.

Thanks, Jennifer Shaw Wolf, for the endorsement.

In small part I dedicate this book that is set in the Texas Panhandle to Amarillo, one of my home towns. When people say they've driven through on I-40, and there's nothing there, I say, "No, there is — it's the people."

And to anyone and everyone who was interested, impressed, surprised, or excited when they heard I was writing a novel, to anyone nice enough to ask me about it and how it's going, I have one thing to say: *IT'S DONE.*

ABOUT THE AUTHOR

Valerie Ipson has had a lot of teenagers living in her home over the years, and was one herself in Amarillo, Texas. This may or may not qualify her to write YA Fiction. Currently, she lives in Mesa, Arizona. Ideal High is her debut novel.

She blogs at ValerieIpson.blogspot.com
& FivePagesofSomething.blogspot.com

If you enjoyed reading IDEAL HIGH,
I invite you to review it on Amazon
& elsewhere

Thanks, Readers! ~***Valerie***